CAPTIVE BRIDE

M JAMES

Copyright © 2021 by M. James.

All rights reserved.

No part of this book may be reproduced in any form or by any electronic or mechanical means, including information storage and retrieval systems, without written permission from the author, except for the use of brief quotations in a book review.

This is a work of fiction. Names, characters, businesses, places, events and incidents are either the products of the author's imagination or used in a fictitious manner. Any resemblance to actual persons, living or dead, or actual events is purely coincidental.

CATERINA

*E*very mafia bride knows that there may be a day when she has to dress for her husband's funeral.

This is a dangerous life we all lead, after all, especially the men. This is a world of blood and violence, riches and excess paid for with short, fast lives that burn hot and bright and flame out just as quickly. I've always thought that was probably one of the reasons why love so rarely factors into mafia marriages.

It's easier to see a black dress hanging side by side in your closet with your wedding gown if the marriage is made for convenience and not love.

I hadn't loved Franco. Not in the way that most people think of love. There was nothing of romance novels in our relationship, very little in the way of passion. The roses and jewelry and grand gestures were because they were expected, not because he was madly in love with me. I was—am—a mafia princess, after all. Courting me meant pulling out all the stops, even if the eventual decision about my marriage hadn't really been in my hands at all.

It had been in my father's hands, and I had always known that was how things would be.

My father.

It's my late husband's fault that my father is dead. That my mother is dead. That I'm standing here in front of the full-length mirror in my childhood room, my knee-length black dress still unzipped, the tulle of the half-veil I'm expected to wear to the funeral crushed in my hands. This is the third funeral I will have gone to in nearly as many months. The third funeral of someone close to me, no less.

How much is one person supposed to take before she breaks?

Gingerly, I touch my forearm. My dress is long-sleeved, not because of the weather but because of the yellowing bruises running up and down my arms like grotesque bracelets. Franco left his hands off of my neck and face, at least, although not all the other parts of my body were so lucky. And it's less than he did to poor Anastasia, at least. He knew at least enough to keep the evidence from the one other man left who would have been furious to learn that Franco had laid hands on me.

Luca Romano. My father's heir. My late husband's supposed best friend. The don of the Northeast chapter of the American mafia.

And now, my only possible protector. I am a woman without a close living male relative, without a husband. In the world I live in, that's a dangerous, vulnerable position to be in. Even my status as a mafia princess, the only daughter of the late former don, won't save me from any number of possible unfortunate fates if I don't have someone to look out for me. If anything, it makes my position even more tenuous. I'm a valuable hostage, an excellent bargaining chip, a coveted bride despite being newly widowed.

But I hope that Luca will protect me from all of that. I'll be able to come back here, to the home I grew up in, that now belongs to me, and grieve in peace. Not for Franco—I can't feel much grief for him after what he did—to my family, Luca, Sofia, and Ana. But I'm still grieving for my parents, and now I'm mourning something else.

The life I'd thought I would have.

Slowly, I cross the room to the closet, ostensibly to get my shoes—sensible black pumps with a pointed toe and short heel, nothing too provocative. But next to my shoes is a long flat box, and I know what's inside of it.

My wedding dress.

I know there's no point in looking backward. But I can't stop myself from cracking the lid anyway, reaching inside to touch the cool satin. Sofia Romano, Luca's wife, helped me pick that dress out only a few days after my mother died. She was a good friend to me when I needed one most, when I was jolted out of my grief into a hastier wedding than expected to keep me safe from Viktor Andreyev, the leader of the Bratva here in Manhattan. And Franco tried to kill her. He tried to kill *Luca*.

So no, I won't grieve for him.

But what I *am* grieving for is the man I thought he was. The carefree, laughing, red-headed, boyish man who my father chose for me. I'd known him already, of course. He'd been Luca's closest friend since childhood, and Luca's father had been close to mine. We'd all grown up together. I'd thought he was handsome, if reckless and a little childish. More boy than man, always. I'd never imagined he would be my husband. But I hadn't been upset that he'd been chosen for me, either. It could have been much worse—or so I'd thought at the time, anyway.

I'd always been aware that my eventual marriage would be to someone who benefited my father. I'd come to terms with that long before my engagement. It was why I'd never really dated, even though it wasn't expressly forbidden. There was no point, in my mind. Why date when I knew I would have no choice in my future husband? Why put temptation in my way when I knew that my virginity was a precious commodity and not my own to give away as I pleased?

The most sensible thing to do was not torture myself with crushes and flings that could never be anything more.

And I've always been nothing if not sensible.

But what that meant was that Franco was my first kiss. My first everything. I'd thrown myself headlong into the relationship after our engagement, wanting to please him. I'd expected him to stray—I knew very well that almost all mafia husbands did. But I'd wanted to delay his eventual unfaithfulness as long as I could. *I went down on him in a limo just after he proposed to me, for fuck's sake.*

The bitterness of the thought startles me. I hadn't expected close emotional intimacy between us, or faithfulness, or even real love. I'd thought that I'd been as practical as I possibly could about what our marriage would be. But I *had* expected some things.

I'd been thrilled that my father had chosen someone my own age. Someone fun and full of life. Someone who didn't take things quite as seriously as so many of the other men around me. I'd seen Franco as, if not a devoted partner, an adventure. Someone that could maybe help me cut loose a little, lighten up. Someone that I could have fun with, laugh with, enjoy being with. Someone who would be an adventurous lover, someone who I could unashamedly explore all the things I'd always been curious about in bed with. A friend, maybe.

Very, very briefly, I'd thought that I'd had that. Our first nights together had been good, even if he'd seemed slightly frustrated by my inexperience. My virginity hadn't seemed so much a turn-on to him as an annoyance, but I'd told myself that was good. At least he wasn't the type of man to fetishize virginity. We hadn't gotten a honeymoon, but we'd gotten a few days to hide away in my family home. I'd done my best to be a happy new bride, even at a time when I was also a grieving daughter.

But Franco had had no patience for that. And our relationship had devolved quickly. I'd seen his irritation, his impatience, his lack of caring for me almost immediately. I'd realized very soon that I was a stepping stone for him, nothing more. That he hadn't had any hopes for our marriage other than to hope that I wouldn't be too much trouble.

That hurt. But everything that followed hurt so much more. And the revelations that came with his death?

Those nearly broke me.

I pull my hand back from the box, pushing the lid shut as I grab my shoes and stand up, slipping them on quickly. Sofia told me to take as much time as I needed, but I know I'll need to emerge sooner rather than later. It wouldn't do for the widow to be late to her own husband's funeral.

There's a knock at the door, and I lick my dry lips, my mouth feeling cottony. "Come in," I call out, my voice cracking slightly as I turn to get my mother's pearls from my jewelry box. Next to them, my extravagant engagement ring glitters in the light, and I snatch the pearls up, shutting the box before I succumb to the urge to grab it and throw it across the room. I wish I could take off all the evidence that I was ever married to him at all, but it would be absolutely scandalous to show up without so much as a wedding band on. Leaving my ostentatious ring off will seem like a show of modesty, but a bare hand would be whispered about for months.

Sofia told me that Luca's done his best to keep the extent of what Franco and Franco's father—his *real* father—did quiet, containing it to the upper levels of the mafia, Bratva, and Irish hierarchies. It's better for it to not spread too widely. It's too insidious, too great of a lie, and too large of a betrayal to let the lesser men know about. It might give others ideas if they knew how long Franco and his father managed to hide it all, how close they came to bringing down an entire family and their heirs.

"Caterina?" Sofia Romano, my closest friend now—especially after everything that's happened—steps into the room. She's wearing a simple black dress, high-necked and knee-length, with elbow-length sleeves and her dark hair pulled back into a smooth bun. It's very similar to the one I have on. Still, there's one very noticeable difference between our silhouettes—Sofia's stomach is faintly rounded, the slightest hint of her pregnancy starting to show. It's just barely there. If I hadn't known, I might just have thought she'd had a large breakfast. But I know—I was the one who encouraged her to tell her husband.

Sofia and I have had each other's backs for some time now. And I don't expect that to change anytime soon.

It's a relief to have one person that I feel I can lean on. Two really, if I count Luca, but I'm not certain that I can yet. I haven't spoken to him since Franco's death or since he came back from the hospital. I think Sofia would have warned me if Luca blamed me in any way, or if he intended to hold me responsible for my husband's crimes as well. However, I still can't help but be afraid. Luca has never been as cruel, harsh, or commanding as most mafia men are—men like my late father. But the title of don, the responsibility of it, changes men. My mother told me that. And Luca has never been a particularly warm man, either. He's always been kind to me, but I don't yet know if he'll put the mafia first or my happiness and safety.

I hope it's the latter.

For the first time since my parents' deaths, I simply want to be left alone to grieve. I intend to square things with Luca today, after the funeral. Then, hopefully, I'll be allowed to retreat into my own private sanctuary, a convent of one. I have no desire to remarry or even really take part in this life anymore.

If I could disappear altogether, I think I would.

This life has taken far too much from me already.

"Are you alright?" Sofia looks at me sympathetically. "I know, that's a loaded question. Here, let me do up your zipper for you." She comes to stand behind me, gently tugging up the zipper and smoothing her hands down the back of my dress so that the crisp fabric lays correctly. I look painfully thin, far more than I ever been, although I've always been slender. My cheekbones look as if they're pushing at my chin, my jawline sharp, my eyes tired. Even a generous helping of mascara and concealer couldn't hide the fact that I haven't slept in what feels like months. Once a man lays hands on you, it's difficult to sleep well next to him any longer. But sleeping in another bedroom was never an option for me. Neither was telling Franco no when he required my attention in bed. He'd wanted me to produce an heir for him as quickly as possible, to solidify that hopeful son's eventual rise to the seat that my father, and now Luca, occupied.

I touch my stomach surreptitiously, letting out a sigh of relief for the thousandth time that I didn't get pregnant throughout our short marriage. Sofia is glowing with her pregnancy, and in the brief time that I'd had some happiness with Franco, I'd imagined myself the same way—radiant and happy to be having his child.

Now I can't imagine it. Not just Franco's, but anyone. I've always loved children, but the life of a mafia wife and mother feels light years away now, as if a different woman tried to live it.

I'm done with men. I never expected love, but the thought of marriage, of being a trophy on someone's arm, of sex, makes me feel sick now.

If I have my way, I'll never be married again.

"You don't have to do anything," Sofia tells me gently, resting a hand on my elbow. "Everyone expects you to be grieving. Just you being there is all you need to do." She reaches for my hand, taking the crumpled half-veil out of it and reaching up to pin it into my hair, smoothing it back into a carefully pinned twist.

"Won't I need to say something? A eulogy for my husband?" I lick my lips nervously, looking at my reflection. I *look* as if I'm carrying the heavy weight of grief, because I am, even if not for Franco. But I don't know how I'll get up behind a podium and look out across the gathered mourners, most of whom aren't even aware of Franco's betrayal, and give a eulogy appropriate for a grieving widow for a man that I now hate.

A man that, if I really look into the deepest, darkest corners of my soul, I'm glad is dead.

"I've already told Luca to take point on that," Sofia says firmly, clipping the other corner of the veil into my hair. The black tulle covers my eyes down to the pointed tip of my nose, giving me an appropriately elegant air, and most importantly, hiding how truly awful I look these days. I'm far from my homecoming queen days, from being the most beautiful girl, not just among the mafia daughters, but maybe even in greater Manhattan. I'd always been aware of how pretty I was, perhaps even a little vain about it. I'm sure it will return in time, though I'm no longer interested in what I can buy with that currency. But today, at least, I look much older than my twenty-two years.

"So I don't have to speak at all?" I glance sideways at her. "Won't everyone think that's strange?"

"When he asks you to come up, just start to go and then break down crying. Fake it if you need to," Sofia says encouragingly. "And he'll say something about how heartbroken you are, and Father Donahue will move things along."

I let out a breath that I hadn't known I was holding. "Thank you," I whisper, turning to face her and grasping her hands in mine. I can feel tears gathering at the corners of my eyes. "Thank you for being here for me, through all of this. I know it hasn't been easy for you."

"It hasn't," Sofia admits. "But it's better now—for me, for Luca. We're better. We're finding our way through all of this. And you will too, Caterina, I promise. Things will get better."

She reaches up underneath my veil, brushing a tear off of my cheek with her thumb. "Franco is dead. He can't hurt you, or anyone, anymore. You'll heal from all of this. You just need time. Just get through today, and then you'll have all the time you need to grieve, and heal, and find out who you want to be. Just a few more hours, and by tonight, it will all be over."

I cling to that as I pick up my purse and rosary and follow Sofia out of the bedroom, out to the waiting car.

By tonight, it will all be over.

I can put all of this behind me and start fresh, as my own woman.

Caterina Rossi, a free woman.

It has a nice ring to it.

CATERINA

I keep repeating that over and over, like a prayer or a mantra, all the way down the aisle of the cathedral to my seat in the front pew. I force myself not to think of how, not that long ago, I walked down this same aisle all in white, with Franco waiting at the altar for me. How hopeful I'd been that day! I'd managed my expectations, but I'd still had hope for some happiness. For a good marriage, by mafia standards.

Now I'm walking to my seat all in black, the gold band on my left ring finger burning into my skin like a brand, one that I can't wait to take off. It'll be the first thing I do once everyone is gone tonight and I'm alone again.

Everyone wants to comfort me, tell me how sorry they are, to share how shocked and heartbroken they are at Franco's death. It's all I can do to nod and force myself through it when all I want to do is scream that he wasn't the man that they—or I—thought he was. That he was a traitor, a murderer, that he deserved worse than he got. I picture the horrified looks on their faces if I told them the truth—if I told them about the way he tortured Ana, ruining her dancer's feet forever, or the way he'd punched me in the stomach the first time I got my period after our wedding or rolled up my sleeve to show the bruises from only a few days ago. If I told them how he'd held me down, ordering me to shut up when I told him that I hadn't been in the mood for sex one night, not more than a month after we'd been married.

When you give me a son, you can claim you have a headache all you want. Until then, spread your legs and shut up, princess. That's all you were ever good for, anyway.

Do your duty. I'd heard my mother's voice in my head that night. She would have told me to get it over with, that the sooner I was pregnant, the sooner he'd leave me alone. *Men don't like sleeping with their pregnant wives,* she'd have told me. *They'll find someone else to keep them company, and you'll be happy about it.*

My mother had been very good at managing my expectations when it came to my future husband. But there's no way she could have prepared me for what Franco turned out to be.

Finally, I make my way to my seat, clenching my hands together in my lap, forcing myself to look down at them as I wait for Father Donahue to make his way to the podium to start the service. I don't look at the gleaming casket, surrounded by flowers, or the photos of Franco, smiling boyishly out from the frames. I especially don't look at the one of us on our wedding day, the same hands that are wrapped together in my lap right now clasped in his. I know what photo it is. In it, I'm looking up at him, and he's looking at me. When I first saw it, I thought the possessive look in his eyes was romantic. Now, I know that it's psychotic.

It's the look of a man who sees the path to power and influence in front of him. Not a wife, not a lover. A ladder.

"Brothers and sisters, we are gathered here today to mourn the passing of one of our own, Franco Bianchi." Father Donahue's voice, thick and rich with an Irish brogue, pulls me out of my thoughts. Sofia's hand finds its way to mine, covering them, and I look up, startled. I hadn't even realized she'd sat down next to me, Luca on the other side.

Carefully, I loosen my hands, letting her slip hers between them. It feels good to have a friend holding my hand. Comforting. It makes me think, just for a moment, that perhaps she was right. If I can just get through this, the funeral, and the reception afterward, everything will be okay. I can grieve on my own, alone, in my own way. I can put all of this behind me and start anew. I can decide, for the first time in my life, who Caterina Rossi ought to be.

I hardly hear the rest of the service. I don't really hear Father Donahue give the floor to Luca. I'm barely aware of what Luca says, some manufactured speech about how Franco was like a brother to him, how unexpected his death was, how tragic. Those closest to Luca know the truth, of course but the rest of the sea of mourners in the cathedral will simply be nodding along, dabbing away tears with handkerchiefs, touched by Luca's entirely fabricated eulogy.

I almost miss Luca calling me up to give my own. Sofia's hand on my back helps me to stand, but I have a sudden rush of memory—standing up to speak at my mother's funeral not all that long ago, and then my father's just after that, and the grief that rises up to choke me and make itself known in a splutter of sobs isn't fake at all. It's real, and I clap my hand over my mouth, sinking back into the pew as Sofia's arm goes around my shoulders, supporting me.

Distantly, I hear Luca making apologies for me, the grief-stricken widow. There's a hum of sympathy, and Father Donahue moves things along just as Sofia and I had planned. I'm crying in earnest now, mascara tears running down my cheeks.

I manage to pull myself together as we head out to the cemetery. I feel a tight knot in my stomach as Franco's casket is lowered down next to his mother's. At least the gravesite reserved for him wasn't next to the father whose name he shouldn't have had, the father who wasn't his at all. It was next to his mother instead, whose mistake with his real father started all of this without her ever knowing the consequences it would have.

I can't help but glance across the cemetery towards the grave I know is somewhere over there, where the Irish are buried. *Colin Macgregor.* The man whose last name Franco should have had.

Would things have been different? If his mother had come clean? She'd have been killed, probably, Franco given to some other family in a part of the country far from the offending Irish. It might have started a war, depending on how furious the cuckolded Bianchi husband was. But probably not. My father wouldn't have allowed that, I don't think. It would have been a humiliation, but one that was taken care of quietly.

Instead, it had been allowed to spin out of control. All because of one woman's lie.

It's hard for me to blame her as much as I might once have, though. I know what it's like now to lay next to a man that you not only don't love, but outright hate. I never met Franco's father, but I know it's possible that he was a cruel man too, that Franco's mother had been so desperate for affection, for love, for pleasure, that she'd made a mistake that could have cost her life. She'd been desperate enough to cover it up, too.

You can't change any of it. I watch as they lower the casket down, my hands clasped in front of me. *It does no good to look back. Only forward.* I repeat it as I toss in the required handful of dirt, the white rose. I tell myself over and over again as I get back into the car to go home, a home that will shortly be full of people I'd rather not talk to, all expressing their sympathies for something that I'm grateful is over.

Just get through it. It's almost done. By tonight, I'll be free of it.

I've always been strong. My mother said I had a backbone of steel, but it's been sorely tested lately. Soon, very soon, I'll be able to let go.

What would my life look like without the expectations of men?

I can't wait to find out.

* * *

THE LINE of mourners wanting to speak with me and commiserate with me all over again is as endless as it was at the cathedral. But at some point between the *I'm so sorrys* and the offers of cookies and tuna casserole, I manage to corner Luca in the living room by the fireplace, a little ways away from the clustered groups of guests.

"How are you holding up, Caterina?" He looks at me with those intense green eyes of his, peering at me as if he can see the absolute truth of what I'm feeling. Maybe he can. Luca knows me well—better than Franco did, even. He was close to my father, after all. He helped arrange my betrothal. At one point, I'd wondered if I was going to marry *him*. I'd even asked my father about it before I knew that he'd been promised to someone else, someone he'd never expected to ever marry.

Sofia, of course.

I'm glad that Luca isn't my husband. We wouldn't have been well-suited for one another, even less so than Franco and I were. But now he's in a different position altogether—one of power over me, as the don. And I'm more than a little afraid of what that might mean for me.

"As well as can be expected, I think," I say diplomatically, looking around the room. "I'm ready for some peace and quiet."

"Well, I'll get them out of your hair as soon as I can do so without creating a scandal," Luca says kindly. "My position does come with some perks, you know." He looks at me carefully. "I want to make sure that you're alright here alone, Caterina. That you—"

"I'll be fine," I say quickly. "I'm not fragile. I'm grieving, but I'll heal."

"No, you've never been fragile," he says, his voice thoughtful. "But you look as if there's something on your mind."

I pause, taking a breath. "We haven't spoken since—" I swallow hard, trying to think of the right way to say what needs to be said. "I want to apologize, Luca," I say formally, drawing my shoulders back as I look him squarely in the eye. "I had no knowledge of what my husband was doing or what he had planned, but I was his wife nonetheless. I know that you might hold me somewhat responsible for all that happened. And I want you to know how very sorry I am for all of it and that I wasn't able to stop it. That I was blind to my husband's betrayal of you."

Luca's eyes widen in shock, and he steps forward, gingerly putting his hands on my upper arms. I hate that I flinch at his touch—at any man's—but Sofia must have told him about the bruises because his touch is exceedingly gentle. "Caterina," he says quietly, almost disapprovingly. "I don't blame you at all. How could you think that? Of course none of this was your fault. The fault was entirely Franco's, and he's paid for it. You were his wife, but I had no reason to think that you were his confidant."

It's hard for me to entirely grasp the weight of what he's saying—I'm too overwhelmed by the events of the day still—but I feel relieved, nonetheless. I nod, blinking slowly as I grope for a nearby chair and sink into it, feeling as if I can breathe again. I hadn't realized just how worried I'd been until Luca said, aloud, that he didn't blame me in some way.

"But Caterina," he continues, his voice low and serious. It sounds far away, and I know that I've pushed past the point of what I can take for one day. I'm more tired than I've ever been, on the verge of passing out from emotion and sheer exhaustion, and I dimly see Sofia walking into the room, making her way quickly towards me.

"I do need something from you," Luca continues as Sofia walks to my side, gently helping me up. "For the good of the family, Caterina."

For the good of the family. How many times have I heard that over the course of my life? I nod automatically, leaning into Sofia's arm as she wraps it around my waist. "Of course," I say numbly. "Whatever you need."

VIKTOR

On my way back from my last meeting, cocooned in the cool leather interior of my car, I can still hear the echoes of my previous conversation with Luca Romano in my head.

I told him I'd give him a few days to break the news to my bride-to-be. A few days to put her dead husband in the ground, perform the appropriate ceremonies, let her have a night or two to grieve.

But I'm under no illusions that the late Franco Bianchi was loved by his wife.

And I'm not a patient man.

"Franco Bianchi is dead. Colin Macgregor is dead. Are you agreeable that it's enough?"

Luca's voice still rings in my ears, tight and angry. Angry at the loss of his best friend, even after everything that bastard had done. Admirable loyalty. But too much emotion for a man who leads other men. For a man who, to keep his seat, will have to do violent things. Ruthless things.

Things that might break lesser men.

I have a sort of grudging respect for Luca Romano. In marrying Sofia Ferretti, he kept a promise that he could have broken. The men who had made that promise for him were, by then, long in the grave.

I should know—it was my men who put them there.

He navigated the conflict between our two organizations admirably. He showed loyalty to the man who gave him his position, but didn't flinch at removing him when that same man threatened his new bride. He held his own at the conclave, and he saw to it that Colin Macgregor was delivered and paid for his sins.

All in all, Luca has earned his place at the head of the mafia table. But I still require my own pound of flesh, as it were, to pay me back for all that I've lost in the conflict. Good men. Good soldiers, loyal to their *Ussuri*.

I am in need of a wife. And since Luca Romano took the one that I had intended for myself, he's going to give me the one that I've requested in her stead.

Caterina Rossi.

There's a poetry to it that pleases me, that Franco's widow will pay for his recklessness by warming my bed. She'll pay for his betrayal to his Italian family in the same way, by ensuring that the peace between our families remains strong when she spreads her legs for me.

She's not an innocent virgin like Sofia would have been. But in a way, that's better for my needs. I'm not a young man any longer, and I need more than just a blushing bride.

I need a woman who can handle the life I lead. A woman who understands the way things are, the things that must be done. Who doesn't flinch at the things this life requires of us.

A mafia princess, the daughter of one of the most brutal mafia leaders ever to run the North American side, is just the thing. In fact, I'm grateful now that it will be her and not Sofia. Sofia's half-Russian lineage and innocence had made her a tempting prospect. Still, she would have flinched away from the brutality of the Bratva, would have had to be coddled through every fucking thing.

Caterina will have a backbone, at least.

Of course, a woman with a backbone can be difficult to manage.

But if it does, reminding her of her place will be a pleasure in and of itself.

I shift in my seat, feeling my cock swell at the thought of

punishing Caterina Rossi, of teaching her what it means to be a submissive Bratva wife. *Soon, very soon.* I almost hope that there's some fire to her, that she's not broken when Luca delivers her to me. The prospect of subduing her is intensely erotic, and it's been some time since I've been with a woman who was truly deserving of my—talents.

Leaning back in my seat, I close my eyes and let out a long sigh. *It's a good day.* Soon my new bride will be delivered to me, and my meeting went well. Despite the recent unrest, the latest order for the girls that my men are tasked with kidnapping and preparing for sale overseas was larger than usual. It will clear out my warehouse of stock, as it were. The sale of the girls, particularly two virgin daughters of brigadiers who recently found themselves on the wrong side of Bratva law, will be a lucrative payout.

Now, after the exhausting process of the conclave, dealing with the Macgregors, and today's meeting, I finally get to return to my own home and my children.

I see them the instant that the car pulls into the circular driveway in front of my estate, jumping up and down eagerly as one of the maids tries to keep them from running towards the car. The minute the driver comes around to open the door, they wrench free of her hold, screaming with all the glee of nine and seven-year-old children.

"Papa, papa!" Both girls shout as they run directly into my arms. Though I know it's undignified in front of the staff, I can't stop myself from crouching down, the gravel flying out from underneath their tiny shoes as they throw themselves into my embrace, both of them squeezing my neck at once.

My chest clenches at the feeling of them in my arms, their blond curls cascading over my face as they both squeal out how much they missed me. "I've missed you too, *dochen'ka*," I murmur, hugging them both. And I have. I miss them intensely whenever I'm gone.

My two girls are all I have left of her. Of my Vera, my first wife.

"Anika! Yelena!" Olga, the head of my staff and my interim nanny since my wife died, claps her hands. "Let your father breathe."

"It's alright," I tell her, scooping both girls up with ease and setting one on each hip as I stride towards the house. Olga clucks her tongue, shaking her head.

"A man of your position shouldn't be carrying children on his hip," she says sternly, narrowing her eyes at me like an old grandmother. I just laugh, smiling easily at her.

"We can make exceptions for today. I've been gone too long. Have you changed your hair? It looks very nice."

Olga, a severe woman who keeps her iron-grey hair pulled tightly back at all times and scoffs at the invention of modern beauty treatments like *sunscreen* and *moisturizer*, actually blushes, her cheekbones turning pink. She narrows her eyes, letting out a small huff as she waits for me to walk past. "Well, I suppose for today, we can make exceptions. But you shouldn't spoil those girls, Viktor."

"Well, I have a surprise for them." I set them down as we walk inside the marble foyer, ruffling their blonde hair.

"A surprise!" Anika cries out, her blue eyes widening. "What is it, papa!"

"I'll tell you over dinner. Dinner *is* almost ready, isn't it? Go with Bianca. She'll help you wash up," I add, seeing the pretty, dark-haired servant who helps Olga with the girls appear in the doorway.

"I hope the surprise is a mother for those poor girls," Olga says with pursed lips as I take off my shoes. "It's been three years, Viktor. It's time."

I straighten, looking down at her. Olga is the only member of my staff I would ever allow to call me by my name, let alone speak to me as bluntly as she does. But with my own parents long dead and my wife gone three years past, Olga is the closest thing my children have to a *babushka*. And grudgingly, I'm fond of her too.

"In fact," I say calmly, "it's exactly that. I will be taking a wife shortly, and she'll be here within a fortnight."

A rare smile spreads across Olga's face, the equivalent for her of a less restrained woman clapping her hands with glee. "A good Russian woman, like your late wife, I hope?"

Something inside of me tightens, a bitterness that, by this point, runs bone-deep in me. "I'm not sure I would call Vera a *good woman*," I say sharply. "And I'm sorry to disappoint, Olga, but no."

Olga frowns, her thick brows drawing together. "Then who is she?"

"Caterina Rossi," I tell her coolly. "The late Don Rossi's daughter and a widow. She will be a welcome addition to this house and a good mother to my daughters. I'm certain of it. She was raised in a mafia family. She's acquainted with our—ways."

Olga looks as if she wants to spit. *"Their* ways," she snaps. "Not ours. An Italian woman, here, in my house? A *Rossi*? Raising those sweet girls? Viktor, how could you--"

I feel my expression harden, my voice going cold. "It's *my* house, Olga, and I'll remind you of that only once. This is the Andreyev house, *my* home, and those girls are *my* daughters." My jaw clenches as I glare down at her. "I allow you a great deal of freedom, for the way you've helped me in these past years. I owe you a great debt of gratitude for that, Olga Volkovna. But I will not hesitate to remind you of your place if need be."

Olga seems to shrink back, her face paling slightly, and I have a moment's guilt at speaking to her so harshly. But my life outside of this place is already full of conflict. I won't have conflict bleeding into my own home.

"You will make Caterina feel at home here," I say sternly. "You will respect her as my wife, as much as you ever did Vera. And you will help her to mother *my* daughters and defer to her in all things. Am I understood?"

Olga straightens, her chin lifted. "Yes, sir," she says stiffly, some of the warmth between us dissolved. I feel certain that it will return when things have calmed down. But for now, I feel a small pang of regret at its loss.

I stride past her, heading towards the dining room, where I can hear Anika and Yelena already chattering over the dinner table. A warmth spreads through me at the sound of their voices, followed by a faint pang of conscience.

I've been a part of the Bratva business since I was old enough to follow my father to meetings. I was always the heir, the one who would take over after him, and I always knew it. The deals we make have always been a part of my life, and I always thought very little of them—until I had my own daughters.

To many Bratva men, daughters are a liability, to be raised out of sight and married off quickly. But I've never felt that about my own girls. My Anika and Yelena are dear to me, and since their birth, I've felt that small, faint pang every time I've gone to broker a deal for the sale of the girls kept in our warehouses.

It doesn't escape me any longer that they have families of their own, fathers who perhaps feel something of the same love for them that I have for my own daughters. I can't help but think of the two daughters of the brigadiers, crouched in their cages, drugged and terrified. *What would I do*, I think, as I take my place at the head of the table, *if someone tried to kidnap and sell my girls?*

The answer to that is simple. I'd kill them in the worst possible way, slowly, so that they died screaming. I would teach them a new meaning of pain before they died, by my own hand, not one of my own brigadiers. Such a thing would never be tolerated.

But my way of life, the way of life that I was born into, consists of a few basic tenets that I have always understood. And one of those is that some are lucky.

Some are not.

The Irish have their guns. The Italians have their party drugs and their arms dealing with the Irish. And I have this. It's not as morally grey as selling guns for rebellions in other countries or as sophisticated as high-end drugs for supermodels. I'm well aware of that. The Bratva traffic in flesh, and however I might try to justify it at times—that some of these girls have been pulled out of the gutter to be sold to sheiks, to live in palaces instead of roach-infested studio apartments, or that the men whose daughters were taken deserved to be punished —I know that there is very little moral high ground when it comes to selling women.

But it's made a life for me, my family and for the men underneath me. It brought us out of the old country, where life and death exist

CAPTIVE BRIDE

on the same thin wire, and brought us here, where anything is possible.

My family has built an empire here, and nothing is going to take it away from me. Not even the pricking of my unstable conscience. I can feel some sympathy for the women who pass through our hands, but at the end of the day, nothing will change.

Some are lucky. Some are not.

I dig into the meal that Helen, the household cook, prepared for us. It's delicious, and Anika and Yelena talk nonstop, chattering through mouthfuls of food. Normally I'd scold them for talking while eating, but tonight, I allow it, not only because I missed them and their bright chatter but also because I'm not entirely able to focus on it. My thoughts are tangled tonight, thinking about the girls at the warehouse tonight, about Colin Macgregor and Franco Bianchi cooling in the ground, about Caterina Rossi and how in less than two weeks, she'll be in my bed.

There's one thing I still need to cement my place here, the empire that my father and his father built here in New York.

I love my daughters dearly, much more than most men, but I need an heir.

And Caterina Rossi is going to provide me with one.

After what the Irish and the Italians tried to do to me, my family, my business, my men, I need a new show of power. Taking Caterina for my own is part of that show, to establish once again that Viktor Andreyev, the *Ussuri*, head of the Bratva, is not a man to be fucked with.

Not a man to be challenged, to be lied to, to be betrayed.

Colin Macgregor is dead. Franco Bianchi is dead. And Caterina will pay for her husband's crimes in my bed, taking my cock until she does what my late, cowardly wife couldn't, until she produces a son for me.

That thought lingers in my head when dinner is finished, when my daughters are bundled off by Olga and Bianca for baths and bedtime, and I retire to my own room with vodka and my jumbled thoughts. It lingers through my hot shower, washing off the stress and exhaustion of the past week. I imagine her standing in the grey-tiled shower with me, her slender body streaked with soap, her slim curves naked to my hands.

My cock swells, and I groan, turning off the hot water and reaching for a fresh towel. I should put her out of my head, set her aside as a task taken care of until our wedding night. But even as I dress for bed, I can't get the image of her pale, veiled face out of my head, the last time I caught a glimpse of her at her father's funeral. She was dressed all in black then, her body hidden under the modest dress she'd worn, but in my head, I'm already stripping it off of her, baring her small breasts to my hands, her narrow waist, her pale thighs.

I grit my teeth, my hand sliding down to wrap around my now-aching cock, bracing myself against my dresser with one hand as I start to stroke, my erection rock-hard and refusing to be ignored. I've hardly been a monk since my wife died. There's plenty of women who would do a great deal for a night in the *Ussuri*'s bed, to be able to say they fucked him. But the thought of Caterina Rossi in my bed, her thighs spread for me, inflames me like nothing has in a very long time.

My hand spasms around my cock, squeezing my length as I stroke faster, grimacing with the pleasure of it as I imagine her head thrown back, her dark hair spreading across my pillow, my hand at her throat as I fuck her hard, claiming her as my bride. *Mine.* My wife, my possession, my payment for all that her family put me and mine through. The final nail in the coffin of the conflict between the Bratva and the mafia, the beginning of a new era.

And Caterina will be the catalyst. *Who knows*, I think, as I imagine running my hand over her as she trembles in my bed or forcing her to her knees, her lips parting for my cock, *she might even like it. Perhaps, deep down, she's looking forward to being fucked by Bratva cock.*

The thought of that, of her getting wet for me, of running my fingers over her pussy and finding her soaked for my cock despite herself, pushes me over the edge. I come with a groan, my palm curling over my pulsing cockhead to catch my release, and I thrust against it, my whole body shuddering with the force that I haven't felt in some time.

If jerking off thinking about her feels that good, what will fucking her be like?

I'm certainly looking forward to finding out.

I'm sure that Caterina is expecting coldness from me, harshness, perhaps even cruelty. The Bratva, and I, have a certain—reputation. But I don't intend to be harsh to my new bride.

If she obeys me as she should, I could even be kind to her.

CATERINA

*M*y heart is in my throat when I hear the knock at the door the next night that tells me Luca has arrived.

I've dressed appropriately for his visit, in long wide-legged black pants, a black silk blouse, low heels, and my mother's pearls, the lady of the house accepting the don for a visit. I'm sure my mother would be very pleased if she could see me now. *But of course, she can't, because she's dead. A victim of the pointless war our family waged with the Bratva.*

"Caterina." Luca nods to me as he walks in, polished and handsome as ever. His face looks a bit more worn these days than it used to, but after what's happened recently, it's hardly a surprise.

"Come in." I close the door behind him, gesturing for him to follow me to the living room, where I've already got drinks poured for us both. The consummate hostess. "You still like whiskey, I hope."

"As long as it's not Irish." Luca grimaces, and I almost laugh. Almost. It's still a little too soon.

"It's scotch," I reassure him, handing him a glass. "Macallan 26."

"Ah well, there's been no trouble with the Scots." Luca takes a sip of it. "So far as I know. Do they even have crime families?"

"I have no idea," I tell him diplomatically, taking my own glass and perching on the edge of the loveseat. It's remarkably uncomfortable,

CAPTIVE BRIDE

like most of the furniture in this house. I make a mental note to start redecorating soon. It's my house now, after all, with no one's tastes but mine to cater to.

Luca is looking around the room, not sitting quite yet. "How do you like living here on your own?" he asks suddenly, turning to look at me. "Is it lonely?"

"A little," I admit. "The house feels a bit like a mausoleum, with so many deaths recently. But it'll start to feel like my own in time, I'm sure. Once I put some personal touches on it, and—" I notice a shadow cross Luca's face and stop short. "Are you alright?"

Luca's mouth tightens, and he lowers the glass of scotch, facing me fully. "I wouldn't start picking out new furniture just yet." He pauses, looking very much as if he doesn't want to say whatever is going to come out of his mouth next. "You're going to be leaving here soon, Caterina."

I stare at him, startled into silence for a moment. *You said you weren't going to punish me,* is my first thought, but I bite it back. After all, he's the don, and if he's decided that taking my family estate is a fair payment for what Franco did, it wouldn't be unusual. It's not the worst price to pay, either. This is my childhood home, but it's not exactly as if I have a great deal of warm and fuzzy memories here. I could get a new place of my own, a loft in the city, maybe. A fresh start.

But Luca is still looking at me with a deeply sad expression on his face as if he's not finished telling me the bad news.

"Why?" I ask simply. "Is it because of Franco? Is that why you're taking the estate?" I want to hear him say it aloud, even if I'm certain that's what's happening here.

Luca looks startled. "What? No, Caterina, I'm not taking the estate. Of course not. I would never take your home. I told you—"

"Then what?" I interrupt him, suddenly not caring if it's rude. My pulse is speeding up, warning bells going off in my head, screaming that whatever this is, it's not what I think. Not anything that I've imagined. "Just tell me what's going on, Luca." I laugh a short and bitter sound. "After everything I've been through lately, I can take it. Whatever it is."

Luca hesitates, and then he slowly sets his glass down on the table, directly on the wood. Somewhere in the back of my mind, I think that he should have put it on the coaster, but I can't bring myself to say something so banal right now. Something terrible is about to happen. I can feel it crackling in the air. Something that I hadn't considered.

"Caterina—" Luca's expression is grim now, dark, his jaw tense. "Viktor named his price for peace between our families at our last meeting. After Colin Macgregor's death."

My heart is pounding so hard now that it hurts. "And?"

"The price that he named was you," Luca says, as gently as he can manage. "Viktor demanded you as his wife."

The room tilts, and I hear a ringing in my ears, my fingers going numb. I barely register the splash of scotch across my skirt as the glass drops, the wetness soaking through the fabric, cold against my thighs.

Before Franco's funeral, I'd thought of what price Luca might exact for his betrayal. What *he* might demand to make up for his best friend's traitorous actions, with only me left to punish for it, and for the things my father did to him and Sofia as well. I'd imagined him demanding my family estate, as I'd thought he was doing at first tonight. I'd thought of him banishing me from Manhattan for what my father and Franco did, ordering me to leave the city and make a home on my own, somewhere else, or demanding that I pay a fine to the Family.

Any of those things would have been well within his rights as don. All of them have been done to others, though deep down, I suspect that Luca disapproves of dons who treat widows and their families in that way. But this?

I'd never expected this, although I suppose somehow I should have.

Viktor had wanted me, after all. Luca had moved up my marriage to Franco for exactly that reason, to get me safely within the bonds of holy matrimony so that Viktor couldn't press his suit or have me kidnapped and forced into marriage. I'd assumed that as a widow, with my innocence long gone, that Viktor would no longer have an interest in me.

Clearly, I was wrong.

My hands are shaking, knotted together in my lap as I think of the implications of this. The Bratva is terrifying and cruel, the boogeymen of my childhood, our enemies for decades. And Viktor is the head of them all.

"I can't," I whisper, my voice trembling. "I can't do it, Luca. Please, there must be something else. I'll do anything else."

"I know that you might have hoped that you could marry for love, Caterina, but—"

"It's not about love!" I swallow hard, forcing back the frightened tears burning behind my eyelids. I can feel the life I'd hoped for, the one I'd been looking forward to at the funeral, slipping away from me. *You just have to get through the day.* What a fucking joke. I should have known better. I'd never be able to get free of all of this.

I can feel all of my hopes for a life free of the Family, free of men, free of expectations and demands, disappearing. Vanishing without a trace.

"I didn't love Franco either," I say, forcing myself to sound calm, to steady the tremor in my voice. "But I can't be married to another cruel and brutal man, Luca. I can't do it."

"Caterina—" Luca runs a hand through his hair, his expression clearly unhappy. "This wasn't my doing. But I've spent more time with Viktor these past weeks than I might have liked, and there is some honor in him, whatever else might be true about him and the rest of the Bratva. I think he might not be as bad as some of the others."

"As bad?" I choke out the words, staring at him in horror. "Luca, think about who you're selling me to!"

"I'm not *selling* you." Luca's jaw tightens. "I wouldn't give you to someone that I thought would truly hurt you, Caterina. But in the end, I don't have a choice. After the betrayal of Franco and the rest of the Irish, there needs to be peace. You know that. You know how this works, Caterina!"

"I do, but—"

"Then you also know that marriages are usually how this sort of peace is brokered." There's a finality to his voice, and it terrifies me more than anything he's said so far.

I feel sick. I look down at my lap, at the wet material sticking to my thighs, and I try to slow the racing of my heart. "What will you do if I say no?" I ask finally, lifting my chin to look at him. "What then?"

Luca returns my gaze sadly, suddenly looking very tired and older than his years. "You don't have a choice, Caterina."

I'm reminded suddenly of standing in Sofia's kitchen, having a very similar conversation with her about her marriage to Luca. I remember, vividly, her saying to me bitterly that she hadn't had a choice. And I remember just as clearly what I'd said to her in return.

There's always a choice.

I square my shoulders, looking Luca directly in the eye, reminding myself of who I am. Of *where* I am, in my own house. "There's always a choice, Luca," I say calmly, my voice steadier now. "And I'll tell you what mine is tomorrow after I've slept on it."

He looks at me, his face still very grim. "Caterina—"

I stand up in one swift motion, gesturing towards the doorway. "I want you to leave, Luca. I'm very tired, and I'm still grieving. I need time."

"Caterina—"

"I am still the daughter of Don Vitto Rossi," I continue as if he hadn't spoken. "And I'm still in mourning, even if my husband was a traitor. So please, leave."

Luca stands up slowly, reluctance clear in every line of his body, but I think he can tell that I'm not backing down. "Alright," he says tiredly, walking towards the doorway. But before he steps out, he turns back towards me, and I can see both sympathy and resoluteness in his eyes. "Caterina—you're right. All of those things are true. And that's why you know what the wisest decision is." He pauses, tapping his fingers against the doorjamb, his gaze fixed on mine. "I'll be looking to hear from you tomorrow."

I manage to stay on my feet until I hear the click of the front door that tells me he's left. I rush out of the living room towards it, turning the locks frantically, my hands pressed against the heavy wood as if at any moment Viktor Andreyev might try to knock it down and scoop me up, carrying me away like a villain in a fairytale. I wish I could barricade it somehow, board it up, but the locks will have to do.

And then, my hand on the cool metal of the lock keeping the outside world away from me for now, I press my forehead against the door.

For the first time since my father's funeral, I start to cry.

* * *

WHAT I'D thought would be my first good night in this house alone since my marriage to Franco turns out to be a sleepless one instead, lying wide-eyed in the dark and trying to imagine a life married to Viktor Andreyeva. *Caterina* Andreyva. It sounds so foreign, even in my thoughts. I can't imagine hearing it said aloud.

I try, speaking the name aloud to the darkness, whispering it to my ceiling. *Caterina* Andreyva. It sounds elegant, rich, like caviar. An acquired taste, maybe.

But one that I can't ever imagine personally acquiring.

I'm no stranger to arranged marriages. As a mafia princess, I'd always known mine would be. But I'd also always known it would be to an *Italian* man, a member of the Family, someone that my father knew and held in good stead. Someone that I could trust that, if he wouldn't love me, he'd respect me and never harm me.

My first marriage didn't turn out like that. He wasn't even more than half-Italian, and that was on his mother's side. And now it looks as if my second won't, either.

I know, deep down, that I don't have much choice. I might have said to Luca that I do, but I know better. I understand a little more now how Sofia felt, and I feel a pang of guilt for how I dismissed her fears about Luca, how I told her so casually that, of course, she had a choice.

But she hadn't, really, not any more than I do right now. Her choice had been to marry Luca, risk my father's wrath, or else allow herself to be caught in the hands of the Bratva. And now—

I don't even entirely know how to picture Viktor. I've never seen him up close, only from a distance on the afternoon of my father's funeral. I know that he's older, but I'm not sure by how much. I don't really know what he looks like, other than newspaper articles with quick photos where it's clear that he's handsome enough and not overweight. But none of that would matter, ordinarily. I would always prefer a handsome husband, of course. Still, I'd come to terms long ago with the idea that if the husband who benefited my father most was ugly and fat, that's who I'd have to marry. And there would be no argument.

It's not Viktor's looks I'm concerned with. It's who he *is*. *Russian. Bratva. Ussuri.* Not just Bratva, but their leader. A man who had a hand in attacking my family. A man who is, by all accounts, my enemy.

It's the fact that I'd told myself I'd be free after Franco. I'd really believed it, for just a moment. *How could I have been so foolish?*

It's how he'll treat me once we're married because the longer I lay there in bed considering it, the less and less I can imagine how I could possibly get out of this without consequences that I can't possibly live with.

He won't hurt you, I tell myself, trying to calm my racing heart and the sick, cold nausea deep in my belly. If my marriage to him is to broker peace between our families, then it wouldn't make sense for him to physically harm me in any way. It's a low bar, to be sure, but after Franco, I'm not sure how much lower the bar could possibly be for a second husband.

I go over the choices in my head, but each one comes up short. I don't want to leave Manhattan—it's my home, and I know it's not wise to, anyway. Anywhere else in the country I might go that I wouldn't hate, and maybe even some places that I would, none of the other underbosses will protect me if I defy Luca. Some of them might even actively seek to find me and return me to him in order to curry favor. I'll only make it worse by running, and even leaving the country isn't really an option. There's no place in Europe that the Family can't find me. And outside of it—there's the Bratva to contend with, the Irish in other areas, the Yakuza in still others, the cartels. No matter where I tried to flee, there would be some crime organization willing and even eager to make a deal with Luca or Viktor or both to return me home.

I was born into this life, and there's no escaping it. I've always known that, and it hasn't changed. I know now, beyond the shadow of a doubt, that it never will.

Slowly, I take stock of every small dream I had for myself after Franco's death. The redecorating of my home, the traveling I'd do alone, the way I'd planned to never marry again. The freedom that I'd tasted so briefly and allowed myself to imagine.

I let them go, one by one, drifting out into the darkness, and I feel my heart sink a little after each one, settling in my chest like a lead weight. I've never felt quite as shackled to my life as I do now, not even once I realized what kind of man Franco really was.

For the first time in a very long time, I watch the sunrise outside my bedroom window. And then, as the greying sky gives way to the streaks of color, I get up, feeling the weight of my resolution settle over me.

I've made my decision, and even though there was never really any other way this was going to go, I'm glad that part is done. Now all I can do is look forward and try to make the best of it.

Telling Luca is the easy part. I can tell that it's an effort for him to stay calm when I arrive at his office. He offers me a seat, but I shake my head.

"This won't take long," I tell him calmly. "I'll marry Viktor Andreyev. Just let me know the details. I'll also be keeping my home," I add. "I'll hire staff to look after it while I'm not there."

Luca leans back in his chair, looking visibly relieved. "I'm glad that's the decision you've come to," he says diplomatically, as if there really was any other decision I could have made. He takes a breath and then leans forward, his green eyes fixed on mine. "This will bring peace, Caterina," he says softly. "I hope that makes it worth it."

"And you trust Viktor to keep his word?" I try to keep the cutting tone out of my voice, but it's hard. *I find it hard to believe that a man with a reputation for being so brutal could be trusted.* Luca has yet to establish that sort of reputation—if anything, he's known for being less inclined to war and bloodshed than my father was. So, where does that leave me?

If Viktor mistreats me, I do believe that Luca cares enough for there to be consequences. If not for my sake, then for the fact that he can't be seen as that weak—that the Bratva leader could take a mafia bride of my position and then abuse her. But what if I don't live to see those consequences carried out? What if Viktor simply wants the pleasure of punishing me for Franco's failure, and he's willing to accept those consequences?

You're letting your imagination get the best of you. I take a deep breath. "I'm guessing the wedding won't take place at St. Patrick's?" In a way, I'm glad about that. I don't want to relive my first wedding day on my second.

"No, it won't," Luca confirms. "Viktor will want to be married at the Orthodox church, I'm sure." He hesitates. "Do you want to meet him before? I can arrange it, if—"

"No." I cut him off sharply, my heart suddenly rising into my throat. If I have to see Viktor beforehand, meet him before there's no turning back, I'm not sure if I'll be able to do it. "I'll see him on our wedding day. That's how arranged marriages are meant to be, aren't they? Bad luck to see the bride before the wedding?"

Luca manages a small smile. "I'm glad to hear that you can find some humor in this, Caterina."

"I wouldn't have survived all of this so far if I couldn't." I pause, taking a deep breath. "I'm trusting you, Luca," I say softly, trying hard not to betray how frightened I truly am. Standing here, in the crisp, masculine office that my father once inhabited and now belongs to Luca, where he and Franco planned and schemed and laughed and were once like brothers, I can feel the walls closing in. I'm trapped, and there's no way out.

All I can do is try to make the best of it.

"I promise you, Caterina, you'll be safe." His face looks drawn again, tired, and I can tell this is taking a lot out of him. I can't find it in myself to feel sorry for him, though. He isn't the one who will have to lie down with a Russian, with the leader of the Bratva.

My stomach twists at the thought. Will he be cold? Cruel? Will he hurt me for his own pleasure? Or will he try to force me to like it, so that he can feel better about himself?

I push the thought out of my head, feeling myself turn pale. I can't think about that right now. I'll face it head-on when the time comes. And if I have any choice in the matter at all—

One night is essential, I know. It will have to be a marriage in every respect, consummated and legal. I'm not a blushing virgin to not understand what's required of me. But if Viktor truly intends not to harm me in *any* way, then it's possible I can ask for my own bed, free of him. He can fuck whoever he wants. I won't care. So long as it keeps him away from me.

He's made his demands already. I fully intend to find out if there's any that I can make in return.

But I don't say any of that to Luca. It won't help for him to know that I'm already scheming how to skirt my marital duties when it comes to Viktor, and there's nothing he could do about it, anyway. I won't have him brokering the terms of my marriage bed. Viktor and I will hash it out after the vows have been said, one way or another.

I'm determined to hold my own in this marriage, however I can. Even if it terrifies me to do so.

I text Sofia on the drive back to my own home. *It's done,* I type, feeling my heart sink seeing it in black and white. *I'm marrying Viktor.*

The reply comes almost immediately. *Oh, Cat. I'm so sorry.*

I touch my phone screen, feeling a flicker of warmth despite the coldness that seems to have wrapped itself around me ever since I left Luca's office. I've never been quite as close to anyone as I've come to be with Sofia. I know she doesn't have many friends either, just Ana, and I know she's looked up to me in the past. Like an older sister, maybe, someone who knows this life better than she once did. I tried to be there for her when she was navigating her relationship with Luca. But now I'm the one in need of comfort. Seeing the familiar nickname calms me, though, makes me feel a tiny bit more grounded. No one else calls me Cat. Just Sofia.

Luca promised me he won't hurt you.

I laugh at that, a small, bitter sound. *He promised me the same.*

If there's anything I know about Luca, he keeps his promises.

I lean back in the seat, closing my eyes. That much is true. Luca moved heaven and earth to keep a promise he didn't even make, one made between his father and Sofia's, arranging their marriage without them even knowing. No one would have blamed him for breaking it. He could even have convinced my father to let him marry me instead, maybe, solidifying his position even more. But he didn't do that.

He kept that promise. And now he and Sofia are happy.

Could Viktor and I be happy? I tell myself not to even think it. I'd hoped for some kind of happiness with Franco and been bitterly disappointed. If I go into this marriage clearheaded and with open eyes, knowing that there's no hope of happiness with my husband, there's no possibility of disappointment. I can forge ahead without worrying about trying to make a shared life, finding common ground.

What common ground could I ever have with a Bratva brute, anyway?

I'll be fine, I text back. *I always knew I'd be in an arranged marriage. So it's with a Bratva man instead of Italian. I'll live.* I pause, then keep typing. *He can't be worse than Franco.*

A pause, and then Sofia's reply. *Famous last words.* And then just as quickly. *I'm joking. Luca wouldn't agree if he didn't think you'd be safe.* Seconds later—*I'm always here for you, Cat. You know that. Anything you need. Just like you were there for me.*

It's almost funny how the tables were turned. Not that long ago, I was the one trying to reassure Sofia, to help her understand how marriage to a man like Luca would work, what it would be like. To understand what her choices really were and how to live with them. Now it's her, comforting me. Trying to ease my fear and worry.

Because I *am* afraid, no matter how desperately I'm trying not to show it. I'm terrified of Viktor.

Any reasonable woman would be.

My chest aches when I step inside my house. I walk through it, drifting from room to room like some kind of Victorian specter, touching furnishings and breathing in the scent of it, the clean rooms and the dustier, less used ones. This house is too big for one person. I would have rattled around inside of it. That's why I'd planned to travel—plans that will have to be put on hold now, possibly for good. I can't imagine Viktor letting his wife travel independently, and I have no desire to go on fucking vacation with my Bratva husband.

As far as I'm concerned, the less time we spend together, the better. And I hope he might feel the same. Men like him aren't usually interested in the company of their wives.

This morning, I'd felt something like grief at the thought of leaving this place behind. But now I feel nothing—just empty. Hollowed out, like a shell left on the beach.

I sink into a chair, closing my eyes. *It's for the best,* I tell myself. It's how I'll get through this.

Empty is good. Hollow is good.

Nothing ever comes from *feeling.*

VIKTOR

"I hope you have good news for me, Luca." I wave him away as he gestures for me to sit, choosing to walk over to the gilded bar cart along the wall instead.

"I should just get rid of the chairs," Luca gripes, narrowing his eyes. "No one takes a seat anymore. Are you—sure, go ahead, I guess. Have a drink."

I smirk, pouring two fingers of good vodka into a glass. "It's polite to offer your guests a drink, Luca. Or did your father not teach you manners?"

Luca narrows his eyes. "My father missed out on teaching me many things after he was murdered by the Bratva."

A beat passes between us as I sip the vodka, letting him wonder whether or not I plan to say anything in response. Not too long ago, I wouldn't have allowed the mafia pup to speak to me in that way—but I have bigger concerns. More pressing matters.

"We have bigger things to discuss than ancient history," I tell him, enjoying the sight of him bristling as I pour myself more vodka. I know he wants to argue, but he can't because the peace between us is tentative, and Luca wants it more than I do. "My bride, for example."

"She's the only way you'll accept peace?" Luca frowns. "There's nothing else you will take? No other conditions?"

"We broker the end of this war with marriage, or not at all," I say flatly, sinking at last into the chair Luca offered me. "That's my only and final offer."

Luca looks exasperated. "Aren't you tired of this, Viktor? This constant battle between families?"

I shrug. "I am tired of the bloodshed, yes. But we Bratva are wolves and bears. A little blood between our teeth is how we do business."

He lets out a short, harsh breath. "Caterina has accepted your *proposal*." Luca spits out the last word as if disgusted by it, anger clearly etched in every line of his face. "And I am forced to accept this bargain as well, but I'm not happy about it, Viktor. I told you, I don't broker with people's lives in this way. Her father left her under my protection. If anything happens to her—if she's harmed in any way, it'll be war. You understand that, right?"

I narrow my eyes at him. "I take offense to that, Romano. I've never hurt a woman. I never would."

Luca laughs, a short, sharp bark of a sound. "You hurt women every day, *Viktor*. Just because you don't lay a hand on them yourself doesn't make your trafficking business any less devastating. What do you think happens to them at the end of the line? Pleasure and comfort?"

"For some of them, yes."

"And others?" Luca looks disgusted. "I know the answer already. Abuse and rape. For many more than you'd like to admit, I think. So don't tell me about how *kind* you are to women. You remember that I rescued Sofia from a hotel room where your men had her tied, right? Treated her roughly?"

"I did not tell them to handle her roughly. Quite the opposite, actually. As for the bondage—" I raise one shoulder and let it fall. "Perhaps Sofia's taken a liking to it since."

"You won't speak about my wife in that way." Luca's face reddens.

"And you shouldn't throw stones when your own house is glass. Isn't that how the American proverb goes?" I glare at him narrowly. "Think of the devastation your own businesses cause, Luca. The addictions, the overdoses. The suffering in war-torn countries, the widows and fatherless children. The women I sell end up in the harems of sheiks, in the service of billionaires, in the palaces of princes. A few wind up back in Russia, certainly, serving less-than-gentle bureaucrats, but more often than not, they spend their days in harem silks or bikinis on tropical beaches."

"Enslaved to men who don't know the meaning of the word 'no.'" Luca's face is dark. "Don't try to dress it up, Viktor."

"Did you listen to Sofia's 'no'?" I smirk at him when I see him flinch. "Ah, so if it's desire, all's fair, but if it's money—*tsk*. But money is how you justify the drugs and the guns, no?"

"Those women don't have a choice. Anyone who takes those drugs, or buys those guns, has made a choice of their own."

I shake my head. "If you really believe that, Luca, then you are not as intelligent as I gave you credit for. And as for the choice of women—was Sofia given a choice?"

Luca meets my stare, his own gaze gone cold. "Was Caterina?"

There are several beats of silence between us. Finally, I clear my throat, standing up. "I'll make arrangements for the wedding, to be held two weeks from now. I'll also arrange for Caterina's wedding gown and other niceties." I pause, looking down at Luca, where he still sits. "I'll be kind to her," I tell him curtly. "So long as she understands her place. And I won't hurt her."

There are contracts to be signed then, business to be done. Luca says very little for the rest of the meeting, which pleases me at least. I'm tempted to pay my bride a visit, but Luca made it very clear that she doesn't wish to see me until the wedding. And although I loathe to let her think that she's in a position to make demands of me, I also can see her reasoning. This is a business deal, a marriage of convenience. There's no reason to make it more difficult by a visit that would certainly be awkward and unwelcome.

Instead, I direct my driver downtown to the jeweler where I used to have pieces made for my first wife, including her engagement ring.

Some might say it's bad luck to have him provide the rings for my second marriage.

But I'm a practical man, not a superstitious one.

Henrik, the small, squat German man behind the counter, looks up cheerfully as I walk in. It's a midweek afternoon, and yet the shop still has quite a few customers browsing, all upper-class women with nothing better to do, I suppose.

"Mr. Andreyev!" He looks surprised. "I haven't seen you in some time. Not since—" he breaks off then, paling a little. "I'm sorry. I didn't mean to mention—"

"It's alright," I tell him curtly. "I'm to be married again. Which means I'll need rings."

"Ah yes! I'd be happy to take your commission. How soon will you need them? Six months? A year?"

"Two weeks."

His eyes go round. "Two weeks? I don't know—Mr. Andreyev, a ring of good quality—"

"I'll pay handsomely, you know that. And besides, it's nothing complicated. Two gold bands. You may even have them in stock, although my bride-to-be may need hers sized."

"No engagement ring?" He looks flustered. "Are you sure? A girl without an engagement ring is sure to be disappointed, and besides, it might look—"

"I don't care how it looks," I tell him curtly. "I'm not interested in appearances. This is my second marriage, and it will be a practical one. The rings will reflect that. Two gold bands will be sufficient."

He swallows hard at my tone, nodding. "I'll be right back, Mr. Andreyev. Just a moment."

I turn to the cases as Henrik disappears into the back, glancing over the sparkling array of jewelry there. I can feel eyes on me as I look, something I'm not unused to. I know I'm a handsome man and a feared one. Whenever I'm in a room, men and women both turn to look. But I don't bother looking back. This isn't an outing for pleasure, and I want to be out of this shop as soon as possible.

Diamonds, diamonds, diamonds. There's every shape and size displayed in the glass cases, refracting the light, clear and joyless. I've never been fond of diamonds, although Vera liked to be draped in them. I never bought her anything else for holidays or anniversaries. When the girls were born, I had Henrik make her an eternity band for each of them, with large, glittering clear stones that encircled her slender finger. I thought that they looked gaudy, on either side of her engagement ring and thin gold wedding band. But she loved them.

I'd chosen a diamond engagement ring for her, of course, drawn up by Henrik and made bespoke just for her. But it's not those that catch my eye this time, as I wait for him to come back with the simple bands. It's the gemstone rings, set at the end of the cases, like an afterthought.

Ruby, emerald, and sapphire, and other stones that I don't know as well. One stands out to me more than others, a large oval-shaped ruby, the rich dark color of freshly-spilled blood. It's set in yellow gold, held by prongs, with a round diamond on either side. It looks almost like an antique. Between the size and the rich color, I can imagine some Russian *tsarina* wearing it, a splash of blood on her finger set with diamonds.

I'd already determined that there was no point in purchasing an engagement ring for Caterina. She likely won't expect one, and while I'm a generous man with those who deserve it, I'm also a frugal one in other respects. I know the privations of others back in the motherland, and I know that money isn't something to be taken lightly.

My marriage to Vera began as one of love. I have no such illusions with Caterina, and pretending at it with jewels and promises that I don't intend to keep would be a ridiculous farce, in my opinion.

I'm sure that she, raised in this life as she was, will appreciate my practicality. I'm sure she has no illusions, either.

And I don't intend to give them to her.

"Mr. Andreyev!" Henrik's voice cuts through my thoughts, distracting me and pulling me away from the ruby ring. "I have several bands here for you to choose from. You can pick the one that fits you, and then your bride—do you know her ring size?"

"She can have it sized after, if need be, so err on the side of larger. She's very slender, though."

"A six, then, for now." Henrik fishes a very thin, delicate band out of the box. "What about this?"

"That will do." I pick a medium-width band out for myself, slipping it onto my finger to determine the fit. "There. That's easy enough, yes? No wait necessary."

"Certainly." It's clear that Henrik is struggling to hide his disappointment. I'm sure that when I walked in, he'd hoped for a more extravagant purchase. But my days of buying expensive jewelry are over.

I head back out to the car with the black velvet boxes in hand, grateful to have that finished and behind me. One less thing to worry about. I'll make arrangements for Caterina to purchase her dress—that, at least, I'll spoil her with. I'm not a complete asshole.

But I don't intend to pretend at romance. This is a matter of convenience—*my* convenience. And the sooner the next two weeks pass, the better.

I let out a long breath. In two weeks, Caterina Bianchi, *nee* Rossi, will be my bride. In my home, and in my bed, a mother to my daughters with the bloody past firmly behind us.

Hers, and mine.

CATERINA

Clearly, no one is wasting any time getting Viktor and me married.

The next morning, I wake up to an email—clearly from some secretary or personal assistant and not Viktor himself—giving me the address of a well-known bridal salon and an appointment time. No niceties, nothing personal, just place and time like any other business meeting.

In a way, it's a relief. There's no pretending here. I remember the turmoil Sofia and Luca went through, the push and pull of how much they wanted each other and how hard they tried to fight it. Yet, Viktor seems to want as much distance from me as I do from him. And that suits me just fine.

I assume I can bring someone with me, but I don't particularly care, even if I'm not really supposed to. I'm not about to go to my appointment to choose a wedding dress alone, especially not under these circumstances. Sofia was there for me when I had to quickly select a dress to marry Franco in, shortly after my mother's death, and I know she'll be there for me now as well. It had been difficult then, and I know this won't be easy either, but it'll be a thousand times more so if I have a friend.

I send her a quick text while I make breakfast. *There's an appointment set up for me this afternoon to pick out a dress. Come with me?*

Ever since my parents' deaths, it's been hard for me to eat, and everything that's happened since has only made it worse. I can't stand anything heavy in the mornings, so I opt for some yogurt and fruit, picking at it while I wait for Sofia to text me back. I've been eating at the breakfast nook in the kitchen these days—the dining room feels too large and empty, like it could swallow me whole. I wonder if Viktor's will feel like that too, if I'll rattle around inside of it with nothing to do all day.

Mafia wives usually have charity events or boards to sit on, dinner parties to arrange, and the social side of their husbands' business to manage. *What do Bratva wives do?* I have no idea what their lives are really like—we're told stories about husbands who abuse them, who demand filthy things of them sexually and punish them if they don't comply, of men who refuse to treat them with respect, expecting them to slave away at housework and raising children without any thanks.

Can it really be that bad? Viktor is the leader of the Bratva and a rich man. Surely he has staff? I've never encountered any of the Bratva, but I've heard they're brutal and crass men, rough and unrefined. That picture makes it hard to imagine them holding dinner parties or their wives sitting on charity boards. And what about children?

I feel a cold knot in my stomach at the thought. I know Viktor was married once before, but I don't know anything about his children, if he has any. I imagine them off at boarding school or in the care of a nanny somewhere, but what if he expects a child from me?

That would certainly throw a wrench in any plan to stay out of his bed after the first night.

I grit my teeth as my phone chimes. *I'll figure it out,* I tell myself, tapping the screen. All I can do is get through it one day at a time and handle each thing as it's thrown at me. I know there's no way out, so now it's just a matter of managing things as they come.

The text is from Sofia, saying she's free for the afternoon, and I let out a sigh of relief. At least I won't be alone.

Can I bring Ana?

I hesitate. I have no idea if I'm even supposed to bring anyone along, but the email didn't say specifically to come alone. When it comes to Viktor and my relationship, I don't intend to start out fearing what he might and might not allow me to do. There's nothing wrong with bringing two of my friends along to my bridal appointment, and I don't see why I should act as if there is.

Sure, I text back. *The more, the merrier.*

Besides, I tell myself as I toss my half-eaten yogurt in the trash and rinse out my bowl in the sink, *it'll be good for Ana to get out for a little while if she's willing to come.*

The guilt over what happened to Sofia's best friend, Anastasia Ivanova, still eats at me constantly, even if it wasn't my fault. I couldn't possibly have known what Franco would do to her when he discovered her trying to uncover a way to get Sofia out by conspiring with the Bratva. However, it still makes me sick every time I think of it. She'd once been a talented ballerina at Juilliard, on her way to achieving a *prima* position with the New York Ballet. Now she's in a wheelchair, fighting through weekly physical therapy, her feet damaged to the point where it's a struggle for her to walk on them again.

She'll certainly never dance again.

Sofia meets me at the house just before it's time to go, and I greet her at the door. "You look nice," Sofia says, glancing at me. "Like you're feeling better since the funeral."

"Well, it's hard not to feel at least a little better with him gone." I brush my hands over my dress, a lightweight black chiffon sleeveless dress with a wide collar and leather belt at the waist. I'm hardly in mourning, but I haven't felt like wearing anything other than black since Luca brought me the news of Viktor's demands. If anything, I'm in mourning for myself.

"Ana is meeting us at the salon," Sofia says. "I sent a driver for her, but it's easier for her to go straight there."

"I'm glad she's coming." I manage a smile, looking at Sofia. "I know it's hard for her. I can't imagine the trauma of what happened is going to go away anytime soon."

Sofia nods, biting her lip. "She's in therapy, physical and otherwise. But it *is* hard. She used to be stared at because she was so beautiful and talented. Now it's because she's crippled. I know she'll heal in time—but I'm not sure if *she* knows that. And it's eating away at her. It'll be good for her to get out for the day, to be with friends." Sofia pauses, taking a deep breath. "It's also not your fault, Caterina. It's Franco's, and only his. I know you know that, but—"

"I still feel guilty." I swallow hard, stepping out into the sunlight as we walk towards the waiting car. "I feel like I should have seen something. Some change in him, something that told me he would do something so horrible."

"You didn't even know what Ana was doing." Sofia touches my elbow. "It's in the past now, Caterina."

"Not for her."

"She doesn't blame you, either." Sofia slips into the cool, dark interior of the car, and I follow. "I promise, Caterina."

My heart is in my throat as we drive towards the salon, even though I try not to show it. I'd thought that I'd never wear another wedding gown, but I'll be picking out one today, and I want desperately to be anywhere else, doing anything else. It's all I can do to force myself out of the car when it pulls up, despite Sofia's comforting hand on my arm. But I keep my chin up, plastering a smile onto my face when I see Ana waiting for us. She's even thinner than she was before—and she was waifish as a ballerina—her face pale and her eyes impossibly large in her face but she looks like she's in good spirits. Her thick hair is piled up on top of her head in a fluffy bun, and she's wearing a tank top and jeans tucked into the soft-soled shoes that she has to wear, two sizes too large to accommodate the bandages. Sofia hasn't told me all the details of what the doctors have had to do to try to heal her feet, but I can imagine, though I don't want to.

"Hey, Caterina," she says softly. "Sofia told me about Viktor. I'm sorry. So sorry."

"If it stops all the fighting, it's worth it," I say firmly, as much for myself as anyone else. "I mean that. I want all this to be over."

"It's not your fault," Ana says, echoing Sofia from earlier. "Really, Caterina, it isn't."

"I know," I say quietly.

Sofia has told me a dozen times that if it's anyone's fault, it's her own. Ana was trying to help her when she was caught. It helps a little, but not enough. Still, I know Ana will want to talk about something else, so I just leave it at that as Sofia opens the door for Ana to wheel herself through.

The manager of the salon is waiting, a peppy blonde named Diane, and she smiles broadly at the three of us as we head inside. "Welcome!" she says brightly. "Which one of you is Ms. Rossi?"

A tiny, reluctant part of me can't help but appreciate that Viktor—or his assistant—made the appointment under my maiden name. However, the more cynical part of me, though, retorts that it's only because he doesn't want to remember that I've been married before, a widow instead of a blushing virgin.

"Caterina." I shake her hand, forcing a smile in return. "I'm here for my appointment?"

"Of course! And these are your friends?"

"Sofia Romano and Anastasia Ivanova."

Diane's face changes when she hears Sofia's last name, her attitude even brighter and more eager than before. "Well, come on in, there's champagne waiting for you. The salon has been rented out for two hours for your appointment, so we're all here for you and no one else. All of the girls are ready to help you with your every need."

She's not kidding, either. When we walk into the main part of the salon, where dressing rooms are flanked by velvet couches and floor-length, three-way mirrors with a round platform in front of them, Veuve Clicquot is chilling in a bucket and five girls in their black work uniforms lined up, apparently waiting to help me. It's honestly a little overwhelming, and I glance over at Sofia pleadingly, who instantly walks forward and claps her hands.

"I have an idea of what Caterina might like," she says briskly. "So how about we give her a minute to settle in, and I'll go with you to pull some dresses for her to start with?"

"Sure!" one of the girls, who has a nametag marked *Lead Sales* and *Marnie*, says, gesturing for Sofia and the others to follow her. I sink onto the velvety pink couch, accepting a glass of champagne from Diane as I steel myself for the two hours to follow—although if I can find a dress sooner than that, I fully intend to.

It quickly becomes obvious, though, that they're not going to let me off that easily. The first dress I try on is nice enough, a long white column silk gown with fluttery cap sleeves that skims over my slim frame without clinging too much. I'm not sure if it's fancy enough for the wedding that Viktor has planned—I haven't been given all that much information about it—but it looks pretty on me. I turn towards the waiting girls and Sofia and Ana, trying to look as excited as possible. "This one is perfect," I tell them, trying to infuse my voice with some enthusiasm, but it's very clear that they aren't buying it.

"You've only tried on this one," Marnie says disapprovingly.

"Your fiancé rented out the salon for two hours." Diane gives me an encouraging smile. "So you might as well use it up! Try on some more styles. Make sure this is what you really love."

I have to grit my teeth not to retort that there's no chance of me loving *any* of the dresses since I don't want to be married again at all. But I bite my tongue, catching a glimpse of Sofia's sympathetic face as Diane hands me another glass of champagne, and I dutifully follow Marnie back into the dressing room.

The next gown I try on is a full-on princess dress, with a ballgown tulle skirt, a sweetheart, strapless bodice, and seed pearls scattered over the entire thing. I have to suppress a laugh at the expression on both Sofia and Ana's faces when I walk out, but the other girls look entranced.

"*That's* more like it," Diane says. "You're getting married at the Orthodox Cathedral I'm told, for goodness sake, not a barn. Your dress should reflect it."

"That's all well and good," I tell her as diplomatically as I can, turning to look at myself in the mirror. "But this is a *bit* much. I'm not really interested in looking like Cinderella on my wedding day." *And this is hardly a fairytale.*

And so begins the parade of dresses. I try on gown after gown, silhouette after silhouette, trying to look interested in each in some way without much success. All the girls helping me are absolutely over the moon, rushing back and forth to find more dresses and accessories to match them, lavishing me with attention. I feel bad that I can't force myself to fake more than an average level of excitement. I hear Sofia murmur to one of them that I "just really don't enjoy shopping," and I feel a pang of guilt that she has to make excuses for me. Most girls would love this, to have a bridal salon rented out entirely for them, any dress in the store paid for no matter how lavish or expensive. But no matter how hard I try, I can't find any joy in it.

At the end of the day, I'm being married against my will to a man I've never met and am rightfully terrified of. I feel mired in misery, aching down to my bones with it. I think with a sweeping rush of despair as I walk into the dressing room again that I'll never know what it's like to be in love and excited about getting married. I'll never feel the thrill of trying on dresses because I *want* to. I would have had some of that with my marriage to Franco—I'd at least been hopeful about that marriage even if not in love—but the events surrounding it had destroyed any chance of excitement or joy. I'd been in mourning when I'd picked out my dress last time, and this time I'm just filled with dread.

You're just going to have to get through it, I tell myself as Marnie buttons and clasps me into yet another dress. *You're going to have to be tough and brave, and accept that this was always going to be your life. Love was never in the cards for you.*

The sooner I manage to accept that again, the way I did before my first marriage, the easier it will be to get through this.

I just wish that my life wasn't always something to *get through*, that for once, I could just be happy. But there's no point in wishing for impossible things.

Sofia found her happiness with Luca, and I'm glad. I wanted that for her, even if it couldn't happen for me. She's found her place in this life, and once upon a time, I thought I had too. But nothing has turned out the way I thought it would.

I've lost everything, and now I'm being traded to the Bratva for peace.

When I step out in the next dress, everyone lets out a gasp. Even Sofia, who's done her best to look entirely neutral throughout this whole thing, lets out a soft *oh* as I walk to the mirrors. And despite how much I don't want to feel anything, there's a gentle flutter in my stomach when I look in the mirror. I have to admit, as unhappy as I am with my own appearance these days, I look beautiful. With some makeup to help my pale, drawn complexion and my hair done, I might even approach *glowing*, though I think I'll fall short of *radiant* no matter what.

It's hard to be radiant when you don't fucking want to be there at all.

"It's lovely," Diane says, coming to stand next to me. "Girls? Find a cathedral-length veil."

I look at the dress in the mirror, trying to decide how I feel about it. It has a full skirt, although not as big as the Cinderella dress I'd tried on earlier, a square neckline and elbow-length sleeves, and the entire dress is covered in delicate, fragile lace. The bodice is lace over silk, the sleeves sheer and fitted, and the skirt is a heavy Mikado satin, with lace applique and small seed pearls in the middle of each delicately embroidered flower.

It couldn't be more different from my first dress, which I like. If there had been anything at all that I'd had an opinion on, it was that I didn't want to look like I had at my first wedding. This is grand enough for any church wedding and a bit more youthful than my first dress, which is good because I personally feel as if I look older from the stress alone. The dress makes me look lighter, happier—which, if I can't actually *feel* that way, is the next best thing, I suppose.

One of the girls comes back with a gorgeous cathedral-length veil, even longer than the train of the dress, edged in delicate eyelash lace. When she pins it into my hair, even I have to admit the effect is stunning.

Sofia comes to stand next to me, smiling wanly as she looks at my reflection in the mirror. "Can we have a minute alone?" she asks, glancing at Diane and the other sales associates, and they quickly back off, trailing away out of earshot as Ana wheels up next to me on the other side, my two friends steadying me as I look in the mirror.

"You look beautiful," Sofia says gently. "I know this is hard. But if you're going to do it, you'll look stunning in this dress."

"You look freaking incredible," Ana adds. "Like a princess."

"You *are* a princess, by the Family's standards," Sofia adds. "Viktor should be reminded of who he's marrying. He didn't demand just any girl from Luca. He's marrying mafia royalty. He shouldn't be allowed to forget that for a second."

I reach for her hand, squeezing it as I look over at her gratefully. "I don't know what I would do without you. Either of you," I add, glancing over at Ana. "It would have been so hard to be here alone today."

"We wouldn't have let you be alone today," Ana assures me. "You've always been there for us."

"Especially me," Sofia adds. "You've always got us, Caterina, whatever happens. Viktor won't be able to take that away. I'll make sure of it. Or Luca will," she says with a laugh.

I take a deep breath, smoothing my hands down the heavy satin skirt, feeling the soft brush of the lace against my palms. "Alright," I say, raising my voice so Diane and Marnie and the other girls can hear. "This is the one. And I'll take the veil, too."

This time, at least, there's no argument about whether or not I've tried on enough dresses. Marnie helps me out of it, taking my measurements to have the dress altered to fit perfectly, and then there's nothing left to do except head home.

"Let's have lunch," Sofia says encouragingly. "I know you don't want to go home just yet."

Part of me does, if only to hide away from everything and pretend that it's not happening. But I know that alone, in my big, empty, lonely house, it'll just crowd in on me anyway. It's better to be with my friends, even if I'm not feeling like particularly good company.

Besides, I want to spend time with them while it's all entirely my own.

"Alright." This time, my smile isn't entirely forced. "You pick the place."

And heading back out into the sunlight, I feel a small burst of happiness, even if only for a moment.

These are the ones I'll need to cling to later.

CATERINA

*S*ofia and Ana did their best to keep my spirits up in the days leading up to my wedding. They even planned a "bachelorette" party for me, even though I've already been married once before. But Sofia firmly said that I needed an evening out, a night with my friends before my time was taken up with my new husband and my new home, and it was as good an excuse as any.

That meant a night out at my favorite spots—an Asian fusion restaurant I love and my favorite wine bar, as well as a slightly more lively bar with bespoke fancy cocktails to wind down the night. And it had worked—no one had mentioned the wedding, and for a little while, it had felt like old times, a night out with my friends with nothing to worry about and nothing to feel sad about. We'd laughed and drank, and when I'd come home, I'd fallen into bed and then woken up with a terrible hangover, which I'd nursed with a day in bed watching Netflix and eating Thai soup.

This morning, of course, reality has come crashing back in.

Ana won't be at the wedding, Perhaps—it's not safe for her to be there, and besides, it would bring up awful memories. But Sofia will be, and she's with me now, helping me get ready before we head to the Orthodox Cathedral and my waiting groom.

CAPTIVE BRIDE

It took everything in me to eat a little bit of breakfast, encouraged by Sofia so that I don't pass out on my way down the aisle. She had mimosas sent up too, and I drink two of those quickly, trying to calm my rattled nerves in between bites of fruit and dry toast. I don't know how I'm going to get through the ceremony, only that I have to, and somehow that will have to be enough.

Sofia helps me into my dress, and I try not to think about what's under it, the pretty white lingerie that showed up on my doorstep in a fancy box from La Perla, a reminder of what will happen later tonight.

I keep reminding myself that I'm not a virgin, that this is nothing new, that I can get through a night with Viktor. But I can't shake the cold ball of ice that's settled in my stomach, sending shivers out over my skin every time I think about it.

Sofia efficiently buttons up the back of the dress, dozens of tiny buttons running from the nape of my neck all the way to the end of the long train. However, she only has to button them down my lower back. The dress is perfectly fitted, the full skirt adding curves that I've lost since I've gotten thinner in the past months, and Sofia turns her attention to my hair next, sweeping it up into an elegant, twisted updo that she secures with my mother's filigree combs, pinning the veil in afterward.

"You look beautiful," she tells me gently, and I force a smile, my hands trembling as I smooth down my skirt. I feel small and shaky, but I square my shoulders, stepping into my heels and taking a deep breath. With my mother's pearls on and my hair and makeup done, there's nothing left to do but get into the car and head to the cathedral.

I'm almost glad my mother isn't here to see this. My father might have appreciated the business aspect of it, a bargain done up neatly and tidily. Although, I'm sure he would have preferred to keep spilling Bratva blood rather than make a deal with Viktor. But my mother would have been horrified to see me handed over to a Russian, to possibly have a future grandchild that was half-Russian, an heir to the Bratva even or destined to marry into it further. More than that, she would have been as terrified for me as I am for myself. She'd pushed me to accept the way of things when it came to a good Italian marriage, but she would have fought this tooth and nail.

It almost makes me wonder if I should have. But I can't stomach the thought of any more war between our families, not if my marrying Viktor can end it. I think of my parents, of all the mafia and Bratva soldiers that have died, the staff in the hotel that was killed in the bombing that never asked for any of this. I think of poor Ana's ruined feet, her destroyed career, and I know I could never live with myself if I refused Viktor and the bloodshed continued.

This is the only choice. And that's what I have to keep telling myself.

The cathedral itself is stunningly beautiful. "St. Nicholas," Sofia tells me as we approach, and I peer out of the limousine, looking at the Baroque architecture and grand, dome-topped towers atop it. It looks foreign to me, like no church I've ever been inside, and I take a deep breath as the limousine pulls up to the curb and the driver comes around to open the door for me.

Luca is waiting outside, and he gives me a tight smile as I walk up, Sofia going to stand next to him. "You look lovely, Caterina," he says.

"Thank you." I swallow hard, lifting my chin.

"Thank *you*. You're doing the Family, and me, a great service today. I know what a sacrifice this is for you, and—" he stops as Sofia lays a hand on his arm. "Thank you, Caterina."

"There wasn't much of a choice," I say stiffly. "But I'm here, and I'm willing."

"If *anything* happens, if you need me—all you have to do is call. I'm not abandoning you to them. I promise. You are Rossi's daughter, just as you said. And whatever kind of man he was at the end, he was still my mentor and like a father to me. I *will* protect you."

"I know." My voice is calmer than I feel. Deep down, I don't know if Luca *can* protect me. I have no doubt he'd avenge me, but once this marriage is done, I'll be in Viktor's house, away from Luca's eyes. There will be plenty of opportunities for Viktor to keep me away from the protection of Luca and the mafia as a whole.

I can only rely on myself, here on out.

"I'll be near the front," Sofia says reassuringly. "Look for me if you need anything."

There's no bridal party, and my father is dead, so I'll be walking down the aisle alone. Sofia hands me my bouquet, white lilies tied with a silk ribbon, and I take a deep breath as I wait for them to go inside and then slowly start my walk up the stairs.

The music that starts to play as the doors open is unfamiliar. But I'm glad for it, in a way, pleased that this is so different from my first wedding. I can't manage to banish it entirely from my thoughts. Still, it would have been so much harder to walk down the aisle with Father Donahue waiting there again, in the familiar church, with the familiar wedding march playing. This feels as if I've entered a different world—even the interior of the church itself, with its heavy wooden walls and the brightly red-draped altar, looks so very different.

And then, as I step foot on the aisle that will lead me down to my groom, I see him clearly for the first time, waiting for me at the end of it.

He's more handsome than I realized. That's my first thought as I catch sight of him, tall and broad-shouldered, dressed elegantly in a fitted suit with his dark hair combed neatly back away from his face. His face is sharp and stern, dangerously handsome. Although he's greying at the temples, it only adds to his almost regal bearing.

Whatever the rest of the Bratva might be, this man is not a brute. He's crisp, composed, a leader. This is a man who commands respect and fear, and I feel a shiver go down my spine as I take step after step towards him, my skin tingling with nerves and—something else?

I hadn't thought he'd be so good-looking. He's almost devastatingly attractive, and when he looks at me, his icy blue eyes meeting mine for the first time as I reach the end of the aisle, I'm grateful for the veil covering my face and my flushed cheeks. The tingle that runs through me this time, when his eyes meet mine, goes straight to my core and has nothing to do with fear.

No. I'm not going to think of him like that. I hate that I feel any attraction to him at all, that I looked at him and my first thought was that he was handsome. But he *is*, strong-jawed and tall, and when he takes my hand in his, that shiver runs through me again. *I'm going to have to sleep with this man tonight.*

I'd prepared myself to be a cold statue of a bride, to lay there and let him do as he wished until the marriage was legal, and then let him know how I felt about warming his bed any further after that. If he truly didn't want to hurt me, then he'd have to acquiesce, and if he tried to force me, I could go to Luca. But as his palm rests against mine, the first hint of roughness about him in the calluses there, warming my skin, I start to wonder for the first time if I'll feel some desire tonight.

I don't want to. I want to remain closed off, cold, inaccessible to him. I want to be somewhere else in my mind when it all happens. But I can feel a pull towards him that feels almost sinful, all things considered. When I think of who he is, what he's done. No good girl, no good *mafia* girl, should want a man like this.

And I've always considered myself a good girl.

The wedding itself is a blur to me. I watch Viktor's face through the veil as he says his vows, his hands holding mine, and I repeat mine without even really hearing what I'm saying. It doesn't matter to me; I don't mean any of it. It's not like Franco, where I at least wanted to *try*. Where I might have known that *love* and *cherishing* weren't on the table, but perhaps *honor* was. I could try to *obey*. But here, I know that obedience isn't optional. And this man has taken me, his captive bride. There's no honor in that.

He was married once before, I remember. I don't know what happened to his first wife. They were in love, I'd heard whispered around; it was a tragedy. I don't remember if she'd left children behind. But looking at this hard-faced man, his jaw set as he listens to the priest speak, his fingers wrapped around my hands in a way that lets me know that he will choose when to let go, I feel the flutter of attraction replaced by fear.

What if he was responsible for what happened to his first wife?

I know nothing about who Viktor is as a person, beyond that he is Bratva and the kind of man who would ask for a woman's hand in marriage as part of a bargain to stop the bloodshed. At least I'd known Franco a little at first. Viktor is a complete stranger to me. A mystery.

And if I have my way, he'll remain so.

Somewhere, distantly, I hear the priest pronouncing us man and wife, and my blood goes cold, my skin tingling. *It's done.* There's no running away now, no escape, not that there ever was. I hear him instructing Viktor to kiss me, and when he lets go of my hands to lift my veil, they feel cold, too.

He's going to kiss me. Somehow, I'd forgotten about this part. I'd forgotten that I'd have to touch him intimately before tonight, in front of all of these people. I know before his lips even touch mine that it will be a chaste kiss. Viktor doesn't look like a man who would make out passionately with his bride in church before a crowd. But it still doesn't prepare me for the touch of his lips on mine, firm and hard and faintly warm, or the way it sends a shudder through my body. A shudder of repulsion, I tell myself, but I'm not entirely sure.

Viktor takes my hand in his again as we turn to walk down the aisle, his fingers locking through mine, and his grip is firm, possessive even. I can feel it pressing the thin gold band of my wedding ring into my flesh, and I wonder if it will leave a mark, branding me as his.

The reception is being held in the Russian Tea Room. It's clear when we walk in, the cheers of the assembled guests that it's been rearranged for the celebration. Other than vast sprays of flowers, there wasn't much that needed to be done in the way of decoration. I've never been here before, but it's a dizzying cacophony of red and gold, with a large star chandelier and gilding everywhere. I catch a glimpse of Luca and Sofia, seated at a table with some other mafia Family members that I recognize. Still, most of the reception is full of strangers. I catch a glimpse of flaming red hair and flinch, missing a step as if I've seen a ghost, but when I catch sight of the lean, handsome face below the hair, I can see clearly that it's not Franco.

Of course it's not, I chastise myself.

He's dead.

The red-haired man is probably Liam Macgregor, now the leader of the Irish crime syndicate since his father's death. Viktor would have invited both of the other major families in the area, since this is an event meant to signify peace. He'll want all of them to see that Luca accepted his offer and that he's followed through and married me. That for now at least, the families can expect no more war from the Bratva.

It should feel good to have been part of brokering something like that, but since it was done with my life and body, all I can feel right now is a rising dread. The distraction of Viktor's surprisingly handsome appearance has faded back into the sick feeling in the pit of my stomach, thinking of what's still to come tonight. It's hard to enjoy any of this, knowing what lies ahead of me.

A cold, loveless, passionless marriage. I've always known better than to hope for much more—but isn't that what everyone does? Hope for something more than the lot they've been given?

I'm in a daze as the reception commences. I can't say what is served for dinner or if it tastes good or bad. Nor, can I remember the names of who I talked to after the fact or what I said. I keep a smile pasted on my face, nodding along, and I'm sure they are all pleased. The beautiful, smiling bride of Viktor Andreyev.

His hand rests on mine for a great deal of the night whenever we're seated together, not a loving caress but a possessive one. When he's not there, I stay put, a silent statue until he finally returns, and I realize as I come out of my daze that it's time for us to dance.

Something else I hadn't thought about.

The music that's playing is slow and soft and sweet, romantic strings swelling and filling the air as Viktor's broad palm slides over my narrow waist, his other hand holding mine. "You make a very beautiful bride," he says quietly as we start to move in time to the music, my feet remembering the years of formal dancing lessons on their own, thankfully. "This dress would not look out of place in a ballroom back home."

"Thank you," I manage, not wanting to raise my eyes to meet his. I keep them demurely lowered instead, my heart racing, realizing that this is the beginning. This is the first thing he's said to me since our vows, and it was a compliment. It suggests that maybe he does intend

CAPTIVE BRIDE

to be a kind husband, or at least not a cruel one. It also reminds me that this is the beginning of the game I will have to play with him, learning to manage him, his moods, how to keep my own sanity and sense of self without putting myself in danger. How to keep myself from simply dissolving into his world, vanishing like tissue in water.

He doesn't say anything else after that, turning me elegantly as we spin around the dance floor. I'm suddenly very aware of the physical presence of him, of the press of his hand on my waist, the heat of it sinking through the fabric of my dress, the nearness of him. He's not a large man in terms of bulk, tall and lean instead. Nevertheless, I find myself suddenly wondering what he'll look like beneath his suit, if he's thin or muscled, if he's hiding a belly, or if he'll get undressed at all.

Maybe he'll just bend me over the bed, flip my skirt up, unzip and get it over with. It would be the quickest path, that's for sure. Maybe the best one. But something about Viktor, about his presence, tells me that he's not a man to cut corners. That if he does a thing, he does it thoroughly and carefully. That sends another flutter through my stomach because the last thing I want from him in bed is *thoroughness*. The only thing that I can think of that could be worse than not enjoying my wedding night with Viktor Andreyev *is* actually enjoying it.

"I haven't planned a honeymoon for us," he says, as the music starts to slow, the end of our song drawing near. "I'm not interested in pretending that our marriage is something that it isn't. I see no point in that. But I have a room reserved for us tonight, in a luxury hotel. So for one night at least, I think we will pretend."

My heart skips a beat in my chest, and this time I find the courage to look up at him. He's looking down at me so that his gaze meets mine, and I see that his eyes are very blue, with a hint of grey. Eyes with the barest beginnings of a storm. I can see the muted desire there, but he looks calm. Measured, even. I wonder if this is a man who gets angry, and if he does, what it's like. My father was cold and vicious in his anger, and Franco raged, hot and passionate and burning. Which one will Viktor be if he's ever angry with me?

I drop my gaze again, hoping that the innocence of it will please him, and he won't push me for my own feelings about it. I hear him breathe in as if he's going to say something else, but then the music changes to something fast and bright, and the entire energy of the room changes too. I almost trip; I'm so startled as Viktor passes me to someone else. I see what almost might be the ghost of a smile on his face before I'm suddenly swept up in an unfamiliar dance involving the entire crowd that sends me spinning from partner to partner. It's a whirl that I barely manage, and once again, the tedious lessons that my mother insisted on are paying off. I certainly never learned any Russian dances, but I can follow the rhythm of the music. As I try to catch my breath, I realize that despite the unfamiliarity of it, I'm actually holding my own. I'm whirling like a dervish as I spin into set of arms after set of arms that I don't recognize, my fingers lacing through unfamiliar hands as the circles change, the men and women separating and then coming back together again. I'm panting by the time it's over, and I realize with surprise that it was almost fun. The closest thing to fun, in fact, that I've had all night.

As I look for my new husband, I have a strange thought, Viktor might actually be proud of me. After all, I'm an Italian mafia girl, raised with our customs and our dances, and I managed to keep up with his despite being thrown into it with no warning. I'm not sure why I would even care—but some small part of me feels a twinge of disappointment when I catch sight of him, and his face is once again stern and impassive, his blue eyes flinty.

"Can I have this dance?"

I hear Luca's voice at my elbow as the music slows again, and I turn towards him as I nod, relieved to see a familiar face. He reaches for my hand, steering me back onto the dance floor, keeping a respectable space between us as we begin to move through the steps of the dance.

"How are you holding up?" he asks quietly, and with that one question, the buoyant feeling left from the dance fades away, and I'm reminded all over again why we're all here. That I'm no longer Caterina Rossi, or even Caterina Bianchi, but Caterina Andreyv. A Bratva wife—something that I don't even understand. A role that I have no idea how to play.

CAPTIVE BRIDE

"Fine, until you asked," I tell him ruefully. "I'd forgotten, just for a second, why we're here."

"You made a fine couple during your dance earlier." Luca looks down at me, his green eyes full of sympathy. "You don't have to be brave with me, you know, Caterina. Me or Sofia, either. I know this is hard. I would never have asked it of you if it weren't absolutely necessary."

Part of me wants to tell him I'm fine, that I've come around to the idea, just out of sheer bravado. But it wouldn't be true. Every time I think of going back to sit next to Viktor, every time I think about what will come later, I feel a cold knot in my stomach, dread running its cold fingers down my spine.

"I'm scared," I admit, keeping my voice very low. "He's the leader of the Bratva. I am not the kind of woman who is kept like a slave. If he tries to treat me the way that I've heard the Bratva treat their women—"

"You're not a Bratva slave. You're a mafia princess and now a Bratva queen," Luca says calmly. "I wouldn't have given you to him if I thought he wouldn't treat you like the royalty you are. Your role should come with respect, both from him and from others. But if it doesn't—" he takes a deep breath, his jaw clenching determinedly. "You can always come to me, Caterina," he says, looking down at me. "If Viktor ever hurts you or even threatens it, you can come to me. Or to Sofia, if you don't feel comfortable, and she'll tell me. You will never have to endure what Franco did to you again."

"Thank you," I say softly. His assurances do help, just a little. But not enough to quell the fear still sending icy shivers through my veins. I think of how quickly things could have gone from bad to worse with Franco, too fast for me to call for help, too fast for me to escape and go to someone. If I hadn't been able to calm him down, if he hadn't reined himself in in time. Things could have been so much worse, and there would have been no one to help me.

But I know Luca means well. So I just smile at him. "I'm sure it will be fine," I say quietly, pushing down the fears. There's nothing to be done about it now, anyway. I'm once again married, the vows taken, the ceremony finished.

"Mind if I cut in?"

Luca and I both glance over mid-step, and I see Liam Macgregor standing there, his flaming red hair standing out in the sea of brunette and blonde. At a distance, I'd felt that jolt of anxiety, remembering Franco. But up close, the two men couldn't be more different. Franco was handsome in a boyish way, charming and silly, never taking anything seriously. I don't know if he's always been this way or if his father's death and his new responsibilities have aged him, but there's very little that's boyish about Liam. His jaw is sharp and strong, his eyes green and serious, and there's a hint of manly stubble at his jaw as if he shaved this morning, but it's already coming back in. The only thing boyish about him is his hair, which is brushed back and held in place with some product, but clearly would be wilder if he'd left it alone.

"Not at all." Luca spins me towards him, offering the hand he's holding in his. "Enjoy the dance. I'm going to go find my own wife."

I know that not dancing with Liam isn't really an option. I've danced with my husband, and then Luca, and now the third head of one of the families, and I know that while Luca must have wanted to get me alone for a moment to check on me, this is all really about showing that the peace between our factions is cemented. I, the bargaining chip, must be seen being squired around the dance floor by Luca and Liam, so that everyone can see that Viktor Andreyev is allowing it. Therefore, the rumored peace must be real.

"Nothing like a wedding to bring everyone together," I mutter as Liam and I start moving in time to the music.

"What was that?" Liam looks down at me, and I can see kindness in his green eyes. *Why couldn't I have been bargained off to him, instead of Viktor, if I had to be married to someone?*

The answer is most likely that Liam wouldn't have asked for a bride as part of the bargain. Or maybe he's just hungry enough for peace, like Luca, that he doesn't need anything else to sweeten the pot.

"I asked how you liked the wedding," I lie smoothly, smiling up at him.

"It's very lavish. Not as raucous as an Irish wedding," Liam says with a grin. "Maybe one of these days I'll find myself a lass to marry, and you and your new husband can see how we Irish like to party."

"The vodka seems to be flowing freely enough." I laugh shortly, glancing around. "But maybe Irish whiskey hits a little differently."

"That it does, lass." Liam eyes me, the smiling corners of his mouth suddenly turning serious. "It's a brave thing you're doing, aye? Marrying Viktor to keep the peace. Don't think we're not all aware of it."

I blink up at him, startled. I'd expected Luca to have my back, to an extent. But I hadn't really expected a show of support from anyone else, not even some of the lower-ranking mafia men. For Liam to say something like that is more than a little surprising.

"If you ever need help," Liam continues, his voice dropping very low and his Irish brogue thickening, "I'll be right there at Luca's side to make sure you're safe. I can't abide a man who would lay even one finger on a woman in violence."

For a moment, I can't speak. "Thank you," I say finally, finding my voice before the silence becomes rude. I can't help but think of Franco as I say it, half-Irish and Liam's half-brother, and how Liam might feel if he knew about what Franco did to me during our marriage.

But Franco is dead and buried, and Liam knows enough of his sins. There's no reason to bring up the rest. Not now, of all nights, when I'm trying my level best *not* to think of my first husband and all the ways my second could mirror him if I'm unlucky.

The reception seems both too long and too short all at once. The pageantry of it all is exhausting, especially considering how little I slept last night and how little I've eaten all day. At the same time, I'm dreading what comes after, the luxury hotel that Viktor mentioned and what will happen there.

But there's no avoiding it. So when the time comes for us to leave, showered in seeds from the guests, I clench my teeth and steel myself as we head towards Viktor's limo. I can be afraid, but I refuse to show it. I don't want to give him that satisfaction.

The hotel he takes us to is gorgeous, deep in downtown Manhattan, one I've never been to but heard of many times. We're taken immediately up to the penthouse suite. When we walk inside and the door shuts behind Viktor, I feel a cold chill run down my spine at the finality of it.

I look around the suite, trying to ground myself, taking in the smooth white linens, the soft carpeting, the fireplace along one wall, the velvet lounge sofas, the expansive bathroom that I can see just beyond one door. There's probably a soaking tub in there, maybe even with jets. At that moment, I wish more than anything that I could make Viktor disappear and simply sink into a tub full of hot water and suds until the world itself disappeared around me, and I could relax.

"I'm going to freshen up," Viktor says stiffly, loosening his tie. "I can help you with your dress when I come back out if you like."

Well, at least he didn't throw me on the bed and ravish me. I'm not sure if it makes this better or worse that he seems to be as uncomfortable as I feel. Maybe not *as* uncomfortable, but he doesn't seem to be enjoying this either. Not as much as I thought I would, after how strongly he demanded Luca hand me over.

Maybe this has nothing to do about a desire for me at all, just power. Perhaps it really is just a means to flex his control, to show that he can and will demand what he wants, even from the don of the northeastern American mafia. It's certainly a possibility.

And it's one that might mean he will be more willing to leave me alone after tonight than I'd originally hoped.

As Viktor disappears behind the bathroom door, I walk towards the balcony, pushing open the French doors and stepping out into the warm night air of very late spring. The city air is far from fresh, but it's familiar, and I breathe it in, trying to steady myself. Trying to remind myself that whatever else happens, I'm still here, still home in New York. I haven't been shipped off to Russia. I haven't been sent away. I'm among familiar things, even if the man in the other room is wholly unfamiliar to me.

I look down over the balcony, at the street so many floors below me. I think about what comes next, after tonight, the years of marriage to my family's enemy, to a man who is cold to me, to whom I'm nothing but a contract. I have a sudden thought that right now, I could throw myself off of it. That could be my choice. Instead of walking back inside and going to bed with Viktor, allowing him to undress me, to be inside of me, I could end this now.

I'd told Luca that there is always a choice, and I now see that I was right. I can choose a life with Viktor, or I can choose to deprive him of his bride. And I know in that instant, looking down at the concrete below, which choice is harder.

But I also know which choice is the right one.

So when I hear Viktor calling my name from inside the bridal suite, I slowly uncurl my fingers from the railing, taking one last longing look at the vast darkness below.

And then I turn and walk back inside.

VIKTOR

I am not a man who is often unsure.

I've always prided myself on being a decisive man, a man who knows what he wants. One who rules strictly and sternly, who doesn't falter. But in this, I am, for the first time, unsure.

My first marriage was one of love—of passion, even. It doesn't often happen in circles like ours. Vera was beautiful, elegant, with a pedigree and a trust fund to match, and highly sought after. It was luck, even fate, I once believed, that had led us to each other. There was no fighting, no tears, no bargaining for her hand, except in terms of what her father wanted for the marriage. She wanted me, and I wanted her, and we barely made it to our wedding night with her still a virgin. As it was, by the time it arrived, she was only a virgin in the strictest sense.

We were crazy for each other, and though that love changed over time, became something darker and more twisted, I still believe it was love—or all I've ever known of it. With Vera, there was no question of how the wedding night would go.

But with Caterina, I'm not entirely certain how to proceed. This marriage is a business transaction, but I can't deny that I want her. I'd already known she was beautiful, but in lace and satin, walking down the aisle towards me, she was a vision. On the dance floor, with her waist in my hands and the scent of her perfume in my nostrils, I felt a desire that I hadn't felt in years.

She's no virgin. She knows what will happen. But what I can't decide is how to go about it. Should it be cold and unfeeling, businesslike? Or should I try to seduce her, to bring her pleasure so that tonight isn't only about the consummation of a contract? I don't want to mislead her, to make her think that this marriage will be anything but one of convenience.

My desire for her, on the other hand, is making it very *inconvenient*. It would be much easier if I could simply order her to the bed, unzip, and quickly consummate our marriage. But I want more. I want to savor my prize. I want to enjoy her.

I plan to enjoy her many more times over the coming weeks and months until she gives me my heir. And if I can make it pleasurable for her, perhaps that will be easier.

I don't want to frighten my new bride. But if there's one lesson I learned at a young age, it's that in this life, emotion means death. Coldness, cruelty, harshness, those are the things that earn you respect, even the fear of others, when respect can't be found. Those are the things that keep you alive. To be soft, in our world, is to die.

Caterina should know that. She was raised in this life, after all. But then again, so was Vera. And she couldn't handle my coldness, what she called my *implacability*, my *emotionlessness*. It drove her over the edge until there was nothing left for her. Her inability to handle the harshness of my—of *our*—life, cost her hers.

I don't want that for Caterina. And as I walk into the bedroom with a drink for each of us and see her standing on the balcony, a cold chill runs down my spine. I imagine her looking down, thinking of throwing herself off, ending this before it begins.

I would like to think that marriage to me isn't a fate worse than death, but I know not everyone would agree.

"Caterina," I call out her name, sternly but not harshly. Loud enough for it to carry but not to sound angry. "Come inside, please."

I see her stiffen, her back straightening as if she's steeling herself for what lies ahead. And then she slowly turns, her chin raised regally as she walks back inside towards me, closing the French doors behind her.

She truly is a vision in her wedding gown, a mafia princess in every sense of the word. Strong, beautiful, brave. She's a match for me in every way.

It's a shame I no longer want a partner. Only a means to an end.

"I made you a drink." I extend the cut crystal glass to her. "Vodka soda and lime. I can make you something else if you like."

"No, this is fine." Her words are cool and clipped, and I can tell that she's holding back. I don't know what, exactly—anger, desire, fear—and I don't intend to ask. She can feel however she likes; the night will proceed. And if it goes well, it will be good for both of us.

If not—

Well, I've done more distasteful things than claiming a beautiful woman on our wedding night, regardless of her feelings on the matter.

I take a deep slug of my drink as she sips hers and then set it aside, motioning for her to turn. "I'll undo your buttons."

"There's a lot of them." She turns obediently, though, and I can see that she's telling the truth. They run from the nape of her neck down to the hem of her gown, and though I only need to unbutton them partway, it's still daunting. Women's clothes have always been a mystery to me.

Gently, I brush the hair away from the nape of her neck, and I feel her tense under my touch. Her hand goes very still, the glass halfway to her lips, and then she takes a sip, swallowing convulsively as I undo the first button.

And then the second. And the third. The fourth.

I slide my finger down her spine, tracing the line of her skin as I slip another loose and another. The time it takes to undress her feels somehow erotic, something I hadn't expected. I've barely touched her, and I can feel my cock starting to stiffen with the anticipation of what comes next, like unwrapping a gift at Christmas. A feeling I haven't had in a long time.

A feeling that could be dangerous if left unchecked.

I have the sudden urge to rip the dress open, to send the buttons flying, tearing the lace down to the small of her back and stripping it off of her. But instead, I keep slipping the buttons loose, tracing my fingers down her back until I've nearly gotten them undone down to the base of her spine.

And then, without thinking, I give in to the sudden urge to lean forward and press my lips to her skin, between her shoulder blades, breathing in the scent of her perfume. She feels soft beneath my lips, and I think of what she'll feel like lower down, the softness of her pussy, the taste of her—

"You said we weren't going to pretend." Caterina's voice is sharp, her back tensing under my touch. "You don't have to pretend to be romantic."

The cutting tone of her voice breaks the spell. I pull back sharply, my hands dropping away from the sides of her dress. "You'd prefer I rip the dress off of you and take you like an animal? Maybe here, against the dresser?" I can hear my voice roughening as I say it, my accent thickening, and my cock throbs as I see her flinch at the sound of it. The idea of Caterina bent over, holding onto the dresser as I rut into her from behind, is one that holds a certain appeal.

"I'd prefer you not touch me at all. But since that's not negotiable, you don't have to pretend to care. Won't this be easier if we don't lie to one another?"

"If you want your time in my bed to be cold and without pleasure, that's up to you." I can feel myself tensing, shutting down, anger coiling in my gut. I could have treated Caterina as roughly as I pleased from the moment we walked in. I could have fucked her already twice over and left her there with my cum leaking out of her while I enjoyed a stiff drink. But I'd wanted to make this something better, perhaps, than what she'd expected.

"I'd hoped to at least make it good for you. To show you that the Bratva are not animals, that we can be gentlemen—"

"That's not what I've heard." Caterina's spine is ramrod straight, stiff as iron. Stiff as my cock, which ought to have softened during our fight, but hasn't. If anything, her lack of fear, her cold defiance, turns me on more. But instead of making me think of ways to pleasure her, it makes me think of ways to break her.

To bend this princess to my will.

"Fine then." I shrug, stepping close to her again, and this time I grab her hips, pulling her backward and pressing mine against her ass so that she can feel just how hard I am. "You want me to behave like a brute? Feel how hard you make me, then. Virgin or not, your lovely body makes me want to fuck you until you're so full of my cum it drips down your thighs. And I will, *printsessa*. Now."

I grab the shoulders of her dress, yanking them down her arms. I feel her flinch, but she doesn't pull away or cry out. She just stands there like a statue as I pull the dress down over her breasts and hips, revealing the white satin corset beneath it, the panties that curve over her heart-shaped ass, sliding into the crack of it. *One day I'll take her there*, I think to myself, sliding my hand over the cheek. It's full and soft, and I have the idea that I could do it tonight, that I could punish her for defying me like this. Caterina Andreyv might not be a virgin bride in the traditional sense. But, I'd be willing to bet the red-haired coward who married her first never fucked her in the ass.

But no. Not tonight. Tonight, I won't force her to her knees to suck my cock, or spread that pretty ass and take that hole for my own. Tonight, I'll consummate our marriage in the most traditional way. I'll take my time with the rest, breaking and punishing my pretty bride until she learns that defiance is no way to find peace in Viktor Andreyev's household.

"Turn around," I tell her sharply, and a moment passes before she slowly obeys, turning to face me with her dark eyes cold and resigned. "Take down your hair."

She doesn't move, and I feel a flare of cold anger.

"Take down your hair, Caterina. Do as your husband says. Or do you not remember that you vowed to *obey*?"

I see a flash of defiance in her eyes, and another beat passes. But then she reaches up, her hands only trembling slightly as she starts to pull the pins out of her hair.

When her thick, dark curls tumble around her shoulders, it's breathtaking. She was beautiful and elegant with her hair up for the wedding, regal even, but with it down, she looks captivating. More gorgeous than I could have hoped. The pale swell of her breasts above the bustline of her corset makes my mouth water, and my hands crave the feeling of her slim hips under my palms again already.

What's more, I can choose to touch her there, or anywhere else, whenever I choose. She's mine, and the sooner she comes to understand that, the better.

All of her belongs to me now. To do with as I please.

"Go." I jerk my head towards the bed. "Lay down for your husband."

Caterina's shoulders stiffen, but she turns away from me, walking towards the bed with a slow, purposeful gait that tells me she's fully aware of what I'm doing and how this will go. I feel a sharp rush of anticipation watching her that I hadn't expected. I hadn't come into our bridal chamber expecting a battle of wills. Nor did I think that I wanted one. But something about Caterina's defiance, however small, arouses me even more than the perfection of her body.

I watch her recline back on the pillows, her dark hair cascading over the white linen. As I toss my tie and jacket aside, beginning to undo the buttons of my shirt, I allow myself to enjoy the sight of her, my gaze slowly raking over every line of her body—her small breasts pushed up in the tight corset, the slope of her slim hips, the slender thighs that I'll soon part. She's a bit thin for my taste, almost waifish, but Olga will change that soon enough. And I'll enjoy her as she is now, and her curves later, when she's been fattened up a bit.

Soon, she'll grow new curves for a different reason—because she's full of my child. My heir, if all goes well. *If not, I'll keep fucking her until she provides one.* It won't be a hardship, that's for sure. My cock is iron-hard, stiffer than I've been in years just looking at her, pale and perfect and waiting for me packaged in white satin.

"Do you know what you represent?" I ask idly as I slide my shirt over my shoulders and toss it to join my jacket on the chair. I see her eyes, despite herself, start to slide down my chest, and I can't help but wonder what she thinks of what she's seeing.

But then she turns her face away, her jaw tensing. "I don't care," she says flatly. "Does it matter?"

I ignore the question. "You represent the power of the Bratva. *My* power. That I can tell even Luca Romano, Don of the American mafia, to hand me over a woman of your standing to be my wife, and he will. In that way, I've won. Even Luca must answer to me if he wishes to keep his streets clean."

Caterina's jaw clenches. "You don't know anything about *clean*," she spits, her gaze turning back to mine and flashing fire now. "I've heard about what you do to your women. I'm not under any illusions, Viktor. I know Luca made a deal with the devil for the sake of peace."

I laugh coldly at that, undoing my belt. "You don't know anything about devils, *printsessa*. I could show you if you like. I'd thought I should be gentle with you tonight. But you test my patience."

There's a flash of fear in Caterina's eyes at that, brief, but there. I can see it, even if she doesn't want me to. I've seen too many frightened women trying to be brave—*ad*, I've seen plenty of fear in faces, both male and female, over the years.

I hadn't wanted to frighten my new wife. But neither am I going to engage in a battle of wills with her every time I come to her bed or demand her in mine. I married Caterina to end a war, not begin a new one.

Slowly, I unzip my trousers, and I see her gaze following my hand, the movement in her throat when she swallows hard. My cock throbs at that, thinking of her throat squeezing around it, of her swallowing convulsively as I come in her mouth.

"So, in the interest of not *pretending*," I continue, pushing my trousers off and stepping out of them, then hooking my thumbs in the elastic of my boxer briefs, "I will tell you, here and now, how things will be between us, *printsessa*."

"Stop calling me that," she whispers, her voice suddenly quiet. "Stop."

"First, I will call you what I like. I am your husband now, your lord and master." I push the elastic over my hips, nearly groaning with relief as my heavy erection finally springs free, throbbing as it strains towards the object of its desire. I see Caterina's eyes flick down and then widen, and I feel a deep satisfaction. From the look on her face, she's never seen a cock this large before.

"I'm not in the habit of forcing women, *printsessa*," I tell her calmly, my voice cool and even as I approach the bed. "There has never been a time when I've needed to. But you are my wife, and I will need from you the one thing that my first wife could not provide for me."

I see the question in her eyes, but she refuses to ask. So I answer it for her.

"You will give me a son. An heir. I will fuck you as often as I please until you do so, until you are pregnant. After you give me a son, you can do what you like, so long as you raise him properly. It won't matter to me. This marriage is for convenience, not for love, and for my pleasure, not for yours." I can hear my voice turning harsh, but I don't make an effort to soften it. I'd tried to be gentle with her, and she'd rebuffed me.

"You will be a good, faithful, and obedient wife. You will serve me as I command in all ways, but *especially* in my bed. And when you have given me what I bought you for, then I will find someone new to warm my bed. But not until then."

I look down at her, my gaze cold. "Do you understand me, *printsessa*?"

CATERINA

My heart is racing so fast that I think surely Viktor must be able to see it, but not from desire. Not even entirely from fear. There's a healthy dose of anger mixed in there too. Though none of that has kept me from being exactly where I knew I'd end up, on my back in the bridal bed, watching as my new husband approaches like a wolf stalking his prey.

Ussuri. That's what his men call him, I've heard. *The Bear.* Bears don't stalk. They attack. They savage, devour, tear apart their food before it's even dead. Nothing about Viktor's demeanor suggests that he plans to ravish me. He looks cold, calculated even, as he begins to undress.

I have to force myself to look away when he takes off his shirt. I don't want to give him the satisfaction of seeing even a flicker of desire in my eyes. Unfortunately, my husband gives the term *handsome* an entirely new dimension.

It's the only word I can think of for him. *Attractive* isn't strong enough. *Gorgeous* or *beautiful* suggests a softness that he doesn't have. No, Viktor is *handsome* in the truest sense of the word. Everything about him is strong and sharp and dangerous, from his cutting cheekbones to his angular jaw, his ice-cold blue eyes down to the corded muscles of his arms and chest. He's dark-haired, not blond as so many of the Russians are, with gray streaking his temples and shining in threads through his hair, catching the light when he turns a certain way. His chest is lightly furred with the same dark hair, not thickly enough to be unattractive. Despite myself, I see it and wonder how it would feel to the touch. Would it feel soft?

Most women want a handsome groom, not one that's ugly, fat, or old. But I almost would have preferred that. I could have handled feelings of disgust or revulsion while my husband labored over me, thrusting his cock into me until he came as quickly as most men who don't care for their wife's pleasure do. But feelings of attraction, of desire even, for a man like Viktor?

That, I don't know how to handle. And I don't want to feel it.

My gaze is still turned away from him as he tells me how things will be in our marriage. And as he does, my heart begins to sink. My intentions to stay out of his bed after tonight, to put distance between us, are disappearing as quickly as my dreams of a life of freedom had after Franco's funeral. My thoughts are racing as I hear his zipper come down, wondering what to do, how to make the best out of a situation that I can feel rapidly spiraling out of my control.

Just get through tonight. My motto lately, it seems. *One day at a time. One night at a time. And if he forces you or hurts you, you can go to Luca.*

I force myself to look back at my husband as he starts to take off the last of his clothing. To see who I've married in his entirety. And as his cock springs free, huge and thick, I feel both a stab of fear and a tremor of desire all at once.

My eyes widen; I can't help it. I've never seen any man so big. Franco certainly wasn't, and he was pretty much the limit of my experience. He'd been long and thin, curved slightly downwards, so that he never looked entirely hard. But Viktor's cock is ramrod straight, so hard that I can see the throbbing vein running down the shaft as he starts to walk towards the bed, the swollen tip red and already pearling with his pre-cum.

He wants me. I can see the evidence of it right there, thick and eager for me, and it terrifies me. This isn't a man who will be satisfied with one quick fuck to make it legal tonight. I don't know how I'd ever thought he could be.

My heart starts to race again as he joins me on the bed, kneeling in front of me as his gaze rakes down my body. I'm still mostly covered—the corset covers me from my breasts to my hips, and my panties are still on, but the way he looks at me makes me feel as if I'm already naked. It sends shivers over my skin, making it prickle, and Viktor laughs softly.

"Cold?" he asks, and if I hadn't been before, the sound of his icy voice would have chilled me to the bone. "I asked you a question, *printsessa*."

How I hate the sound of that nickname already. It sounds mocking, to me, a reminder of my position as Vitto Rossi's daughter and how I belong to Viktor now. How he claimed a mafia princess for his own simply by demanding it. He's proud of himself. I know that now. Satisfied with his prize.

Well, I don't intend to give him any more satisfaction than necessary.

Gritting my teeth, I look up at him defiantly, refusing to answer.

"There's more fire in you than I thought," Viktor says, sounding almost amused. He leans forward, his hands pressing against my thighs, and I feel the calluses on his palms scrape over my soft skin. It feels good—better than it should. Better than I want it to. I clench my teeth, forcing myself not to gasp when he pushes them apart, his thumbs pressing into the soft flesh of my inner thighs as he slides his hands upwards, moving to kneel between my spread legs.

"You look lovely like this," he says decisively. "Spread out for me, like a bounty. Like a feast."

For one brief, terrifying moment, I think he might go down on me. His gaze flicks hungrily down between my legs, and in my mind, I can't stop thinking, *please, please no*. I know how good that can feel, and I don't want to fight my reactions. I want this to be over quickly, for him to stop drawing it out. But Viktor doesn't seem to be in any hurry.

His hands slide all the way up, reaching for the edge of my panties.

His cold blue eyes flick over my breasts, the corset that's pushing them up, and I can see the desire there. He pulls my panties down slowly, over my hips, and down my thighs, and when he tosses them onto the carpet next to the bed, he pushes my thighs open even wider. Baring me, exposing me. I can feel myself flush with the embarrassment of it, even as my body responds to his touch despite myself.

Viktor's hands slide up my inner thighs again. "Let's see that pretty pussy that I've bought for my pleasure." His words make me flush even more.

"You make me sound like a whore, not a wife." I turn my face away, not wanting to look at him as he touches me for the first time. His hand slides higher, his fingers delving between my folds, and he laughs as his fingers graze my entrance.

"Only a whore would be so wet for a man she claims not to want." He thrusts two fingers inside of me roughly, and I bite my lower lip hard to keep from gasping. The sudden intrusion is slightly painful, but it also feels good. His fingers curl inside of me, and I feel a sudden pressure, a burst of pleasure, as he finds a spot that Franco never did in mere seconds of being inside of my body.

Slowly, he rocks his fingers inside of me, curling them against that spot as he rubs his fingertips against my inner walls. "Ah, yes, there it is. You can lie to me, my pretty wife, but your body can't. You open like a flower for me, despite yourself. I can feel how wet you are for this cock." He grips himself with his other hand, and I clench my teeth so hard that they feel like they might crack, trying to hold back any sort of reaction. A gasp, a moan, a squeak of pleasure.

I won't give him the fucking satisfaction.

Viktor thrusts his fingers into me twice more, then pulls them free. My pussy clenches instantly, my traitorous body missing the fullness, the pressure of his hand. *If his fingers felt like that, what will his cock feel like?* I'm terrified to find out.

He reaches out, grabbing my chin and turning my face so that I'm forced to watch him as he raises his fingers to his mouth, his tongue running over them as he licks my arousal off. "You taste sweet, *printsessa*," Viktor says, his voice deepening. His accent is thickening as his desire grows, his words rough and almost foreign, and I feel another shudder of combined arousal and desire.

No one ever told me how fear can feed desire, how adrenaline and arousal can go hand in hand. I'm terrified of the man kneeling naked between my legs. At the same time, I can feel the pulse of my heartbeat in my veins, throbbing with anticipation in the same way that his thick cock is. I can see it, and my heart starts to race as Viktor reaches forward to grab my hips.

"I could have made you come first, *printsessa*," he says, almost mockingly. "I could have eaten that sweet pussy until you screamed. But since you want to fight me, I'll take you now, like this. My cock doesn't want to wait any longer, and neither do I."

When he presses the swollen head against my entrance, I gasp. I can't help myself. I can feel how big he is, too big for me, really. I have the sudden wild desire to beg him to stop, to try to get away, anything to keep that monster from forcing its way into my body.

"Don't fight, *printsessa*," Viktor growls, as if reading my thoughts. His hands tighten on my hips, holding me in place. "It will go easier for you if you relax."

And then he thrusts, and for a second, I think I'm fucking losing my virginity all over again.

The pain is sharp and intense, shooting through me in a way that makes me dizzy for a brief second as his cock slides into me to the hilt. There's no hesitation, no wait for me to adjust. He groans aloud, a guttural sound of pleasure, his face twisting with the sensation of it as his fingers sink into my skin.

For a second, he goes very still. I can feel the shudder that goes through him, his eyes closing for a moment, and I think with a bitter viciousness as my pussy clenches around him despite how raw and painful it feels:

I fucking hate you.

But then he starts to move.

The pain lasts for a second more, and then it turns into something else. He's moving in long, measured thrusts, pulling out almost all the way and then thrusting back in hard, his eyes focused somewhere above my head. His movements are tense, almost businesslike as if he's decided to stop toying with me and simply go about the business of consummating this fucked-up marriage. But my body has different ideas.

As the pain fades, I become suddenly viscerally aware of how *full* I feel, how good his cock feels, stretching me to the limit. With each thrust, he touches every nerve inside of me, the thick head of his cock rubbing over that spot that he found with his fingers, his throbbing shaft impaling me, filling me, making it impossible to think about anything else. He's rock hard, not just his cock but his entire body, rigid with focus, and his hands are still gripping my hips so tightly that I'm certain I'll be bruised tomorrow.

And with every thrust, I feel a rising pleasure that's almost impossible to hide, no matter how hard I grit my teeth or try to remain expressionless, even bored.

Franco never made me come. He thought he did several times, but I always finished myself off afterward. It was trial and error, for a while, to figure out how to touch myself in the right way, how to pleasure my own body to push myself over the edge. But once I did, I'd wished more than anything I could experience it with someone else. By then, all hope of happiness or pleasure in my marriage was gone. But I'd fantasized, occasionally, about some fling where I'd learn what it would feel like to come on a man's cock. I'd never planned to actually find out, of course. Cheating for mafia men is a birthright. For their wives, it's a death sentence.

But now, with Viktor's cock thrusting into me in long, slow strokes that seem to touch every nerve ending in my body, I feel that knot in my stomach unfurling, my heart starting to race, the muscles in my thighs starting to tremble, my breath coming faster despite myself. *I don't want to come,* I think desperately. *Not with him. I won't give him the satisfaction.* But I'm not sure I can stop myself. He feels so big, so good, each powerful thrust sending sensations through my body that I never knew existed, and when he suddenly pulls me harder against him, his hips rocking forward so that his pelvis bumps against my clit, I know I won't be able to stop.

It takes every bit of self-control I have not to cry out, moan, or claw at the sheets. The pleasure bursts over me suddenly, my clit throbbing as waves of it wash through me. I feel my pussy clench around him, spasming as I fight to just go tense and not arch my back, not grind against him the way I so desperately want to.

But I can't fool him. He goes very still suddenly, and when I open my eyes, I see a look of pure lust in his, darkening that ice blue of his gaze until the hunger I see there sends a tremor of fear through me in the wake of my orgasm.

"Ha!" He laughs, his voice thick and deep. "Even the little *printsessa* couldn't resist coming on a Bratva cock." He starts to thrust again, faster this time, and I can see his own rigid control slipping. My orgasm has turned him on even more, making it harder for him to treat this as something to get over and done with, and I feel a small rush of victory at that. If I lost control, then he should too.

"Perhaps I'll make you come many more times," Viktor growls, thrusting harder, faster. "You thought you were too good for the pleasure of my bed, but your body knows better. It knows what it was made for." Faster now, harder, his hands gripping my hips as he slams into me, panting as he nears his own climax. "You were made for me, *printsessa*. Made to come on my fucking cock. *Fuck!*"

He snarls that last as he thrusts into me once more, hard, and I feel his hips jerk in the instant before I feel the first hot rush of his cum. Viktor throws back his head, and I see the cords of his throat tighten as he growls out his pleasure, his cock throbbing as it spasms inside of me, his cum filling me. He looks almost primal, dangerous in a way that makes my heart race and my breath catch in my throat.

It's in that moment, watching Viktor in the throes of his pleasure, I know for certain that I've married a very different man from Franco. And I know, seeing him lose control for that brief span of time, that I need to be very, very careful.

Viktor may have a good reason not to hurt me. But I've married a very dangerous man. Not unhinged and careless, the way Franco was, but calculating and intelligent. And that makes him far more deadly than Franco could have ever been.

One last, violent shudder ripples through his body, and then his hands go lax against my hips, his eyes opening. I see the moment he takes control of himself again, his expression going carefully blank, and then he pulls back, his cock slipping free.

I can feel him on my thighs, warm and sticky. Tonight could be the night I get pregnant with his child—and wouldn't that be better, really? He said he'd fuck me until I was, so the sooner it happens, the better. But the thought makes my stomach knot with a sick dread.

I push myself backward on the bed, scooting away from him as quickly as I can. Viktor gives me space, moving to his side, but I'm already clambering off of it, stepping back. "I'm going to go take a shower," I tell him, refusing to meet his eyes. I don't want to look at him or speak to him more than necessary. I feel humiliated that he made me come, sickened that my first orgasm with a man was with him. Why would I have responded to his—his...*brutality*?

But even as I think it, I know that wasn't really brutality. It was a rough, emotionless fuck, but I've already seen brutal. And I know that if he wanted to, Viktor could far exceed what I experienced of brutality with Franco.

It wasn't even that bad, I tell myself as I spin on my heel and hurry towards the bathroom, slamming the door shut behind me. *You're being dramatic.* But all I want is to burst into tears. The worst thing I'd imagined was for me to actually enjoy going to bed with Viktor, and I did. No matter what else I tell myself, I can't pretend that he didn't feel good.

I won't let it happen again, I think to myself, striding towards the shower and angrily turning on the taps. *I'll figure out some way to keep him from fucking me again. I just need a plan. But I won't do that again. I can't bear it.* If I can't trust myself to lie back and ignore it until he's done fucking me, then I can't stand to go to bed with him at all.

It's all I can do not to burst into tears as I step into the shower. I don't want him to see me with swollen red eyes and know I've been crying. I wanted to be a statue with him, an ice princess, and it makes me feel weak knowing that I failed at that.

I stay under the hot water for as long as I can manage it, hoping that maybe he'll fall asleep and I won't have to face him again until tomorrow. I scrub myself until I'm raw and pink, until I've used up all of the floral-scented soap in the shower, and then when there's nothing left to wash with and the hot water is stinging my skin, I lean against the wall and try to gather myself.

There's nothing I can do to escape being Viktor's wife. All I can do is survive one day at a time, adapt as things come, and do my best. I'd hoped not so long ago that my life wouldn't be this anymore—but it is. I can either force myself to get through it, or I might as well have flung myself off of the balcony earlier and saved myself the humiliation of what happened between us in bed.

When I finally step out of the shower and dry off, wrapping myself in one of the thick, fluffy hotel robes that thankfully cover me from neck to calves, I expect to see Viktor—if he's still awake—waiting for me with smug satisfaction on his face.

But that's not what I find at all. He's awake when I walk back into the room, sitting in one of the armchairs by the fireplace with a drink in his hand, but he doesn't even look up at first when I walk into the room, as if he doesn't hear me. And then, when he finally seems to register that I'm standing there, he looks almost startled. I notice that he's dressed again, changed into black silk pajamas that somehow make him look powerful and elegant instead of ridiculous like most men would look in something like that.

Almost immediately, his face smooths back into careful blankness. Even so, I don't miss the way his gaze trails over me, from my wet hair tangled around my shoulders to the armor of my fluffy robe covering almost every inch of me. His eyes flick down to my feet and painted red toenails—*please God, don't let that be a fetish of his*—and then back up to my face. When he meets my eyes again, there's no triumph there, not even grim satisfaction. Viktor just looks tired.

"I'll sleep in the other room of the suite," he says flatly. "There's a sofa there; I'll be fine. I've slept in more uncomfortable places," he adds before I can protest. Which—I wasn't going to. The idea of having the entire bed to myself, after what just happened, is welcome yet unexpected. The last thing I'd thought Viktor would do is offer, gentlemanly, to let me sleep alone. After his comment about intending to get me pregnant, I'd wondered if he'd planned to keep fucking me all night.

"There are others you'll need to meet tomorrow," he continues, tossing back the rest of his drink and then rubbing his hand over his mouth. He takes a deep breath as he stands, his blue eyes still resting on mine. "My life is more complicated than you realize, Caterina," Viktor says quietly. And then, as he turns away: "We'll talk more tomorrow."

When he disappears into the other room, I let out a breath I hadn't known I was holding. I feel as if all the air goes out of me at once with relief that he's really gone, and I stagger backward, landing on the bed as I close my eyes.

The first few tears fall then, trailing down my cheeks now that there's no chance of him seeing them. I'm alone, finally alone for the first time since very early this morning, and I feel the weight of everything that's happened come crashing down on me all at once.

Still wearing the robe, I crawl under the covers, unable to find the energy to get something to change into out of my bag, and unwilling to sleep naked anywhere near Viktor, even with a closed door between us.

And then, in the silence and darkness of the room, as I flick off the light, I finally allow myself to really, truly cry. The tears run down my face, my eyes pressed tightly shut. I press my mouth into my pillow to muffle my sobs until my entire body is shaking with the effort, clinging to the pillow like a life raft as I cry and cry.

Tomorrow, I'll have to be strong again. I'll have to face all of this, and get through it somehow.

But tonight, at least, I can cry myself to sleep.

So that's exactly what I do.

VIKTOR

When I wake the next morning, I feel as exhausted as if I hadn't slept at all.

Nothing about my night with Caterina went as I'd expected it to. Even thinking about it now, in the cold light of day, makes me angry —with both her and myself. I hadn't expected her to push me in the way that she had, to fight back, to not accept my generosity in trying to at least make our night together pleasurable for her. And I hadn't expected to lose my own self-control, either.

I hadn't thought, after the turn the night had taken, that I'd make her come. I'd expected the sex to be cold and soulless after that— which was for the best, considering the kind of marriage I'd set out to make was exactly that. But when she'd started to shudder around my cock despite her best efforts to remain unmoved, something had broken loose inside of me.

I hadn't meant to say the things I'd said to her, to fuck her the way I had. It had felt fucking incredible—too much so, in fact. I don't want Caterina to become a distraction, something I crave, and I can see all too well how I could start to slip down that path if I'm not careful.

In the future, I'm going to have to proceed with caution. I see that now. I need a son, but I also need to remain detached. I've been in love with my wife before, passionately so, and I've seen where that road leads.

I refuse to put myself and my children through that again. Crime families often make marriages of convenience, and I've come to see why. That's the road I intend to take this time, regardless of how beautiful my new bride is or how good it feels to be inside of her.

I won't allow her to get under my skin.

Caterina is still sleeping when I walk back into the suite's bedroom so that I can wash up and change. I grab my things quietly, careful not to wake her, and retreat into the bathroom to shower. Today is an important day—more important to me, even, than yesterday was.

Today is the day when Caterina will meet my children.

I'd slept on the sofa in the adjoining room for more than one reason last night. I wanted to give Caterina space to process our wedding night, to gather her feelings and get them back under control, but I'd also wanted space for myself. I have no doubt that Caterina is a woman capable of controlling her emotions. It's one of the reasons I asked Luca for her in the first place. She knows what this life requires of her and the strength that it demands. That's a quality that I value now in a wife.

But I didn't trust myself, either. I didn't know if I could sleep beside her and not give in to the urge to wake her in the night and fuck her again, or take her this morning in the early hours, so that I could see her face still soft from sleep, her hair tangled and her body warm and languid. Those are the things that a man in love looks forward to and craves. Those are not things for Caterina and me.

When we come together in the future, I intend for it to be cold and clinical, a fucking intended to get her pregnant with my heir, and nothing more.

I will *not* allow myself to be seduced by her. It doesn't matter how beautiful she is.

A thing that I have a difficult time remembering, when I walk back out of the bathroom dressed and ready to find her sitting up in the bed, her robe sliding towards one shoulder and her dark hair wild and thick around her face, still curling at the ends. She's as beautiful without her makeup as with it, her skin perfect and her wide dark eyes fringed with long lashes, still hazy with sleep.

"Good morning," I say curtly, and she flinches as if she hadn't quite realized I was there.

Quickly, she grabs at the shoulder of her robe, yanking it back up, wrapping her arms around herself as if to add an extra layer of protection. Just seeing her there like that is enough to make me want to join her in the bed, to part those slender thighs again and lose myself in the sweet, tight heat of her pussy. The orgasm I'd had last night was better than any I'd had in years, a pleasure I had forgotten was possible. I could have spent all night fucking her. I could spend *days*. The idea of hiding myself away with Caterina, doing nothing but fucking and sleeping, and occasionally stopping for meals, sounds so singularly good that I can feel myself getting hard just at the thought, my cock rising until I have to grit my teeth and look away from her.

She's too fucking beautiful. But then again, would I have married a woman who wasn't?

"Good morning," she says stiffly. "I suppose we're expected to have breakfast together before we leave?"

"I'll order room service, yes. I'm sure it will be here by the time you're dressed. And then we'll leave together, to go home to my estate. It's just outside of the city. My home is quite beautiful. I think you'll like it there."

Caterina presses her lips together tightly, but she doesn't say anything. She's less combative than she was last night, which I take to heart as a good thing. I don't intend to spend my days fighting with her. If she wants a battle, she'll quickly learn the tactics I don't mind using in order to win.

"Alright," she says finally, swinging her legs out of bed, careful to keep the robe so closely wrapped around herself that I don't catch a glimpse of flesh beyond her ankles. "I won't take long," she adds, grabbing her bag from where it was left by the dresser and disappearing into the bathroom without looking at me again.

There's an awkwardness between us that I'd hoped we could avoid. I'd thought that her upbringing, and her previous arranged marriage, would have made this easier for her to accept. But apparently, the fact that I'm Russian and Bratva, precludes all of that.

It's a bitter pill to swallow, but it's hardly a surprise. I'm used to being treated in this way. Bratva are never welcome at anyone's table. If we're there, it's because we've forced our way in, achieved our place through violence and intimidation far beyond what the Italians or the Irish will lower themselves to commit. We're considered the dogs of the crime world, and it's only by clawing our way up that my Bratva has ceased being called upon to do the bidding of others. Now we rule our own territory, under our own laws.

Caterina is one of us now, my wife. *Andreyv*. The sooner she comes to accept that, the better.

She looks more composed by the time she steps out of the bathroom, wearing dark slim jeans and a fluttery blouse that looks soft to the touch and only serves to highlight how painfully thin she is. She's pulled her hair back in a messy bun, as if she was hoping to downplay her looks, but nothing can hide how astoundingly beautiful she is. Even with her hair messily pulled back, it only shows off her high cheekbones and wide, dark eyes.

Without looking at me, she walks towards the cart holding our breakfast, picking up one of the plates and retreating to the table. When I do the same, I see her flinch as I sit across from her.

"You'll have to get used to sharing meals with me," I say sternly, uncovering my plate. "Except for when I'm away on business, I make an effort to be home and at the dinner table every night."

Caterina doesn't look at me, stabbing her scrambled eggs with her fork instead. "How very domestic of you," she says coolly. "I suppose I'll be expected to make those cozy dinners?"

I laugh shortly. "No. I have a cook and household staff. You're my wife, Caterina, the wife of the *pakhan*. You have not lost status by marrying me."

She sniffs but says nothing, still pushing her food around her plate.

"You need to eat. If you're unhealthy, you won't be able to become pregnant and carry my child."

Caterina's jaw tenses at that, and she slowly sets down her fork. "So," she says carefully. "I'm not just your wife. I'm a broodmare."

A surge of anger rises up in me, but I carefully tamp it down, chewing my food methodically as I count to ten in my head in an effort not to shout at my new wife. I swallow, looking up to meet her defiant gaze.

"You can think whatever you like," I say calmly. "I've married you for a purpose, Caterina. I need a son. You have the ability to give that to me, and you will. Or you will bear the consequences, instead of a child."

Her eyes narrow. "Luca won't let you hurt me—"

"Luca knows the conditions of our marriage. I wouldn't lean too hard on his protection if I were you." And with that, I turn my attention back to my breakfast, ignoring the way her cheeks turn pale, her eyes widening.

I don't actually have any intention of hurting Caterina. But a little fear, at this point, seems as if it might go a long way. I'd hoped to be kind to her, to make our life together as pleasant as possible. But I won't sacrifice my own peace to make that happen.

She will bend, or she will break.

I'm capable of finding pleasure in either option.

She remains silent throughout the rest of breakfast, all the way until we get into the car to head back to my estate. Even then, she looks out of the window as we drive, ignoring the door I hold open for her and remaining stubbornly quiet until the car pulls up in the circular driveway in front of my house, the driver killing the engine and stepping out to open our doors. It's only then, as I see her eyes widen slightly at the sight of my home, that I remember I haven't actually told her about my children.

I open my mouth to tell her as we step out, but true to form, I can see them running towards us before I can even speak, always alert to the sound of their papa coming home. They both tear down the path to the driveway in a flurry of dresses and blonde curls—until they see Caterina standing next to me, and both skid to a halt a few feet away, looking suddenly shocked and shy. Olga is coming down the path behind them, out of breath and glaring.

When I glance over at Caterina, her face has gone pale again. She's staring at my daughters, as shocked as they are, her mouth slightly open.

"Viktor—" she says quietly, swallowing hard, and I reach for her hand. I feel her flinch at the touch, but I don't let go. Instead, I curl my fingers around hers possessively and lead her forward, towards the two girls who have now been corralled by Olga and are looking suspiciously at Caterina.

"Caterina, these are my daughters," I say slowly, looking at them and then back at her. "Anika and Yelena. Girls, this is Caterina. She will be living with us now, and I expect you to be very welcoming to her."

Yelena looks as if she wants to cry, but Anika's eyes narrow as she looks up at Caterina. "Is she going to be our new mother?" she asks accusingly.

I can see from the stubborn look on my daughter's face that she's not going to take this well. *Perhaps I should have introduced them to the idea before I brought her home,* I think tiredly, seeing in hindsight already where I've made mistakes. Olga, no doubt, will outline them thoroughly for me later. I have the sudden urge to kneel down and take my daughter in my arms, to soothe her and promise that Caterina is not a replacement for their mother, but I know that won't help matters. The girls need to accept her if there is to be peace in the household. And I know no other way than to be stern about it.

"We were married yesterday," I tell my daughters firmly. "Caterina is my new wife, and so yes, she will be your new mother. I expect you to respect her as such, listen to her, and not give her trouble. Just like you behave with Olga, I expect you to behave with Caterina."

"We don't *want* a new mother!" Anika says sharply, her small voice rising. She fumbles for her sister's hand, likely looking for solidarity. However, Yelena is still staring at Caterina as if she's not entirely certain she's real. Yelena has always been the quieter of the two, but now with Anika fuming next to her, she speaks up in a tearful voice.

"She doesn't *look* like our mother," she whispers, her blue eyes starting to well up. "Not at *all*."

Yelena is right about that. Caterina looks nothing like Vera. My first wife was curvy and blonde, with large, full hips that she was self-conscious of and breasts that filled my hands to overflowing. She'd been far from plump, with a narrow waist even after our children. Still, she'd spent thousands of dollars and endless hours trying to slim herself far beyond what her natural body was meant to look like, desperate to emulate the waifish, ballerina types that so many of the other Bratva men sought to wed.

I had found her devastatingly beautiful just as she was, but as in so many other things, she never listened. And Caterina, tall and dark and slender, is the opposite of my late wife in so many ways. Only her elegance is the same, but it too is understated, whereas Vera loved glamour and jewels. Sometimes I'd wondered if she loved the trappings of our life and my position more than she'd loved me.

In the end, though, I know the truth of it. She desired those things because they temporarily filled what I could never give her. And I've paid for that many times over since.

"She's not, Yelena," I say as patiently as I can. "But she will be a mother to you now. You and Anika both, and if we're very fortunate, you'll have a little brother soon. Would you like that?"

Yelena appears to be considering it, but Anika shakes her head stubbornly. "We don't *need* a little brother," she says firmly. "We just need you. And Olga," she adds as an afterthought, and I hear the old woman sniff.

"Well, girls," Olga cuts in, kneeling down to their level the way I wish I could. "This woman here is going to live with us now. Your father has married her, so there's no going back. The best you can do is be kind to her. Don't you think that's what your mother in heaven would want?"

Yelena starts to sniffle, and Anika grips her hand tighter, shooting a death glare among the three of us. "Momma in heaven would want to *be* here, with us!" she yells, her voice reaching a high pitch that makes me grit my teeth.

If she wanted to be here, she would be, I want to snap angrily, but I bite the words back. I've been careful never to let my anger with my dead wife bleed into my daughters' memories of their mother. And the last thing I want to do is yell at my children. But yesterday was taxing, last night and this morning more still, and my patience is wearing thin.

"Girls." I inject more sternness than usual into my tone, and I see both girls go quiet, although, Anika is still looking up at me with defiance in her eyes. She got her temper and stubbornness from me, I know. Yelena is more like her mother, prone to going quiet or crying when she's sad, but Anika lashes out. Caterina will have her hands full with them both. "Girls, listen to me. I've chosen Caterina very carefully because I know she'll be good to you."

"Olga is good to us," Anika mutters, and I frown at her.

"Olga has been wonderful since your mother passed, but she can't do everything. She needs help. And so Caterina is here to help her. Does that make sense?"

Anika's expression is guarded, but she doesn't say anything in response, which I take as a good sign.

"She'll be very kind to you. But I expect you to be kind in return. Do you understand me?"

Anika purses her lips. "So she's like a nanny?"

I let out a sigh, looking at Olga helplessly. I don't dare look at Caterina. I can only imagine what she must be thinking right now. Just as I shouldn't have sprung it on the girls, I should have warned Caterina sooner about my children. But goddamn it, I've had enough on my plate over the past days and weeks and even months without worrying about my own domestic matters.

Olga gives me a quick nod, and I relent.

"Something like that, yes." I feel Caterina stiffen next to me, but I'll deal with her later. For now, my primary focus is on mollifying my children so that they'll at least give Caterina a chance.

"Go back inside with Olga now, girls," I say quickly, before Anika can come up with another reason to be upset. "We'll all have lunch together later, but first, I want to get Caterina acquainted with her new home."

Anika nods, still tight-lipped. She glances up at Caterina, her blue eyes narrowed as if she's inspecting her. "The gardens are nice," she says finally, and then turns on her small heel, following Olga back inside with a ramrod-straight spine, her chin lifted defiantly.

"Lord, save me from women," I mutter under my breath. First, Caterina fought with me, and now Anika is determined to test the limits of my patience.

"I don't know why you expected it to go smoothly," Caterina says tightly, pulling her hand out of mine now that they're gone. "I see that you didn't tell them anything more about me than you did me about them."

I fight the urge to pinch the bridge of my nose. I can feel a headache coming on. "I should have prepared everyone better, yes."

Caterina's mouth turns down as she eyes me. "Admitting a mistake. I thought men like you never made mistakes."

"For Christ's sake, woman, can you not give me a moment?" I glare at her. "You want to fight with me now, here, on the steps of your new home?" *I thought you wouldn't be so combative, coming from one arranged marriage already,* I want to say, but I don't. I'm not the one who seems to be spoiling for a fight this morning.

"You should have told me you had children," Caterina says quietly.

"You didn't ask me, either." I can feel the small muscles in my jaw working, leaping with tension.

"I thought you would tell me anything pertinent." Caterina lifts her chin, looking for all the world like Anika did a moment ago, stalking back towards the house.

Very, very slowly, I let out a long breath.

"Let me make this very clear, then, since I was not clear enough before," I say tightly, leveling my gaze at hers. "I need two things from you—the reasons why I married you, beyond brokering peace with Luca. I need a mother for my children, and I need a son to be my heir. I don't need love or a wife to be my partner or pleasure. I've done fine without the first two, and I can find the last wherever I please. What I need is for you to do your duty and do it without disrupting the peace of my household."

"Then I'm just a glorified nanny that you get to fuck." Caterina spits out the words, glaring at me. "You could have told me that sooner."

"If that's how you want to look at it, then that's fine." I glare at her. "But those are the things that I need, and that's how it will be. This is not a negotiation, Caterina. The vows are made, your pussy has been fucked, this marriage is sealed. I am telling you, as your master and your husband, what I require of you."

"No one is my *master*," Caterina hisses. "Least of all, a Bratva dog."

"That's not what I heard of your last husband." I smile cruelly at her. "And if Luca could tell you whose marriage bed to go to, then that's two masters you've had before me."

Caterina looks as if she wants to slap me for that. Her cheeks are burning red, her eyes flaming, but she holds herself back.

"We'll talk more after I show you around about how the house is run and what I expect from you," I tell her coolly, as if she isn't looking at me like she'd prefer to see my head offered to her on a platter. "But for now—"

"I have a stipulation," Caterina hisses, and it's all I can do not to laugh.

"I told you this was not a negotiation." I look at her, half-astounded that she's still fighting me. "There's nothing you can say that—"

"You also told Luca you wouldn't hurt me." Caterina nearly spits. "*That*, I believe, *was* a condition of this marriage."

"Nothing I've said so far involves harming you in any way." I look at her curiously. "What are you implying, exactly?"

Caterina glares at me. "That if you force me to your bed without my permission while I am actively telling you that I do not want you and will not willingly fuck you, then it's rape. And I believe that's the very definition of hurting someone." She smiles coldly at me. "Would you like me to tell Luca that you're raping the woman he entrusted you with?"

It's only through sheer force of will that I manage to keep my jaw from dropping open. I understand at that moment that Caterina is not someone to be toyed with, nor someone to underestimate.

But what she needs to understand is neither am I.

She's not wrong, though. If I force her into my bed and she goes back to Luca crying rape, it could undo the careful peace we've brokered, especially if he takes her side. If her father were still Don, I'd expect him to give her a scolding himself and send her right back to me, with a lesson on how to behave as a proper wife should. But Luca is still a wild card, and he has a soft spot for women in need. How he behaved with his own wife is clear evidence of that. I'm not at all certain that he won't start bloodshed again over her, and while I'm not opposed to war, my men believe we're at peace. Some of them are happy about that, some would prefer to keep smashing heads and prying off fingernails, but there's a good many who would see Caterina running back to Luca and breaking the peace as *my* weakness, *my* inability to keep my wife in line, *my* inability to keep my word. It could undermine everything I've worked so hard for.

Not to mention, I don't have much taste for forcing women. Breaking her to my will, perhaps. But forcing her when she's made it clear that her answer is no makes me feel sick. I might traffic in flesh during the day, but I have no desire to make my wife into my sex slave.

"What, then, do you propose we do? What is this *stipulation* of yours?" I let out a breath, narrowing my eyes. "You're putting me in a bad position here, Caterina. This is bad faith. You married me—what did you expect would happen? That we'd fuck once to make it legal, and then I'd never touch you again?" I see the look that crosses her face before she can stop it, and I laugh aloud. "*Blyad*, that is what you thought. And here I'd thought your previous experiences would have taught you better." I shake my head. "Maybe your Italian gentlemen are willing to suffer a cold bed, but Bratva men expect theirs warm. Although from what I've heard, your first husband didn't, either."

"Stop talking about him," Caterina hisses.

"Stop making a scene," I counter. "The staff can see us, and I guarantee they're watching. This isn't the kind of thing I tolerate here. So if you have something to say to me, say it. Or come inside with me, and I'll show you your new home."

Caterina's mouth tightens. "I understand you *need* a son," she says slowly. "But I don't want to sleep with you again, Viktor. We've made it legal. I knew that much was required. But there are—other ways of conceiving. And I would prefer to explore those."

It takes me a second to realize what she's suggesting. "You want to do IVF." I hadn't expected that. It's a creative solution, to be sure, but also an expensive one, which is my first argument against it.

"You're suggesting you don't have the money?" Caterina smirks. "I don't believe that for a second."

"I'm saying I think these things are better done the old-fashioned way."

She snorts inelegantly. "Of course you would. You're a man. You *want* this." Caterina folds her arms, the expression on her face still stubbornly defiant. "I didn't come into this marriage blind, Viktor. I knew there would be things expected of me. I think you could have done a better job letting me know beforehand what they were—or letting Luca know so that he could tell me. But then again, you probably didn't want me to know everything I was walking into." She lets out a breath, looking almost as tired now as I feel. "I've married you, and there's no going back on that. I have no desire to have come this far and destroy the peace between our families, either. But I will not go to bed night after night with a man I hate."

"So—what? You just get what you want?" I feel a stubborn resentment rising up in me, a memory of similar words coming out of my mouth during a fight with Vera. I don't want my marriage with Caterina to end the same way. But neither do I want to start this off with her feeling she can demand whatever she wants. I rule my household, and I intend for it to remain that way.

"We both get what we want." Caterina sighs. "I'll be a mother to your daughters. I'll care for them, help Olga with them, whatever is necessary. I'll carry your child and be a good mother to him too. If we have a daughter, I'll carry another until I give you a son. I'll be a mother to any and all of your children. But I've already fucked one man who couldn't be a good husband to me and never meant to. I won't do it again. If that means going back on my word and going to Luca, so be it. But I won't willingly come to your bed again."

She means it, I can tell. I can rage and shout and show her just how angry she's made me, but something deep inside of me knows that she won't bend.

Is fucking her worth it? Is winning this fight worth it? If I give in, at least for now, it'll mean letting her win the first real battle between us. A small voice inside my head, however unwelcome, whispers that she's given up something already to marry me for the sake of peace. Perhaps it's my turn.

"Fine," I say angrily, gritting my teeth. "Have it your way. I'll see that the appointment is made. But I won't be wasting time. The sooner you're pregnant, the better."

"Agreed," Caterina says with a tight smile. "Shall we go in?"

CATERINA

My heart is racing as Viktor opens the door for me to walk into my new home. I hadn't expected to win that fight. I hadn't even known what I'd really do if he'd refused to back down, if he'd ordered me to his bed. Would I really have gone to Luca and threatened the fragile peace in order to save myself from sleeping with Viktor again? Could I have lived with myself and all the bloodshed that would have followed if I'd done that?

It doesn't matter now, I tell myself as I walk inside, because Viktor gave in. We'll do IVF, and my life won't be what I'd hoped for after Franco's death, but I won't spend night after night in the bed of a man I despise at least. I love children; I can handle mothering his daughters. I'll enjoy having children of my own, and hopefully, it won't take long for me to become pregnant. With any luck, the first baby will be a boy, and I won't have to tolerate Viktor any longer. Men in any crime family aren't known for being hands-on fathers, and I doubt Viktor will have anything to do with the child until he's old enough to be taught his father's business. For a few precious years, my child will be all mine, and Viktor will likely only be a cursory presence in our lives.

Or so I'm hoping, anyway. He was already much kinder with his daughters than I would have expected. *He seems to take some interest in them,* I think, as he starts to lead me into the main part of the house. *But maybe it's just because their mother is dead.*

I still don't know what happened to Viktor's first wife. I don't even know what her name was. He doesn't strike me as a man who would have killed her, but the entire thing still makes me uneasy. What if she was unfaithful? What if he lost patience with her? Could that be me if I don't tread carefully?

Viktor is terse and curt as he shows me around the house. It's hardly welcoming, and the curious glances I catch from the staff as we pass by don't help either. But the house itself is beautiful. The outside was stone, with an arched doorway and ivy climbing up the grey and white stone, and inside, it has the same sort of old-world, almost rustic feel, but with a kind of elegance. The ceilings have dark wood exposed rafters, and there are expensive rugs everywhere, covering the gleaming hardwood floors. "There's a lot of the house you won't need to bother with for a while," he says shortly, showing me the main living room. "I don't often throw parties or dinners, but I expect now that I have a wife some of that will be expected me—and therefore of you. But you'll manage to explore the whole house on your own in time."

The furniture in the main living room, which is huge and hung with art that all looks expensive, with a massive stone fireplace as the centerpiece, is comfier-looking than I would have thought it would be. It's all elegant and expensive, not exactly child-friendly. The deep green velvet sofa looks like something I'd enjoy curling up on. It's deep and covered in pillows, and I'm absolutely certain from that and the rest of the furnishings that Viktor didn't decorate this place himself.

Which leaves me to wonder, did his dead wife decorate? Am I living in her home, really? And if so, how does that make me feel?

I shouldn't care. This place isn't really ever meant to feel like my home. I'm here because in the end, it was my only real choice. Not for love, not to make a home. But part of me aches at that thought. If I can't have love, shouldn't I at least have a place where I feel good? Where I feel safe?

I push the thought out of my head as Viktor shows me the rest of the house. He takes me on a quick walk through the kitchen, where he introduces me to Helen, the household cook. She's pleasant enough, although she makes it clear she doesn't want to see a great deal of me in the kitchen, "puttering about," as she puts it. He points out his study, which he tells me pointedly not to go into, and where Anika and Yelena's rooms are. There are more guest bedrooms than even in my old home, and a library that I can see from the moment we walk in will be a haven for me. It's a dream, floor-to-ceiling bookshelves, a fireplace, and lounge chairs. My heart sinks when I hear Viktor say that he likes to spend evenings in there. My hope is to stay as far away from Viktor as possible, not pass evenings in the same room with him.

"You'll sleep with me in my room," Viktor says, and before I can open my mouth to protest, he holds up a hand. "If we sleep separately, there will be gossip. I, personally, will have to deal with Olga's disapproval over this hitch in our new marriage, and so will you. And since you'll be spending a considerable amount more time at home here with her than I will, I'll warn you now, Olga's disapproval is not a pleasant thing."

"You sound as if you like her." I laugh when I say it because there is a certain fondness about how he speaks about her. It surprises me because I hadn't really thought Viktor could feel that sort of fondness for anyone, let alone the elderly housekeeper.

"She's been a great help to me with Yelena and Anika since their mother died," Viktor says. "She's worked very hard to see that my daughters were not neglected, in addition to everything else she has to do to keep this house running. Now that you're here, I expect that her workload will decrease a great deal. And that begins with not causing unnecessary gossip among the servants. Do you understand me?"

I want to fight him on it. There's nothing I want more than a room of my own, a place to sleep alone, to not have to fall asleep next to Viktor every night. I want peace and quiet, to be left alone more than anything else in the world. But I know instinctively that this is not a battle I should fight. If I do, I risk losing the battle I've already won, the one that's most important to me. Does it really matter if I have to sleep in Viktor's bed, as long as I don't have to actually have sex with him?

"Fine," I bite out. "Whatever keeps the peace, right?"

"Precisely." Viktor smiles blandly at me. "Here we are."

The master suite, like everywhere else in the house, is decorated in a way that suggests Viktor had no hand in it. The furniture is all deep, dark wood, the bed a canopied four-poster with velvet swags and a heavy deep blue velvet duvet, along with quilted, crisp white shams to match the sheets and pintucked velvet throw cushions. It looks like a bedroom out of a magazine, right down to the cobalt, grey, and cream rug on the floor next to it and the blue velvet armchairs next to the fireplace.

"The bathroom is through there," Viktor says, inclining his head towards a half-open door. "There's a soaking tub I'm sure you'll enjoy. If the door is closed, I promise I won't intrude."

It's the kindest thing he's said to me since we got "home," and I manage a small smile. "Thanks," I say quietly, glancing at the door.

The truth is, I don't really want to fight with my new husband. I, too, want something like peace. But I'm also terrified of losing myself in this new marriage. I almost lost myself once already, with Franco. I'm very afraid of it happening again.

"Lunch will be served soon," Viktor says. "I'm not usually home, but I'll eat with you and the girls today. And then—" he shrugs. "I suppose you can occupy your time however you like until dinner. Tomorrow will be more normal. The beginnings of normal, I suppose."

I look around the bedroom, this new space that I'll be sharing with him. None of my things are here yet, they're all being brought over from my old house tomorrow, but even once I have my things here, I don't expect they'll make much of an impact on this room. I'm bringing clothes, some books, jewelry. No furnishings, no decorations. This room is never going to feel like my own.

I can't let it get to me, though. I force myself not to think about it as Viktor takes me to show me the outside, the back gardens, the pool, and the greenhouse, and by the time he's finished the remainder of the tour, it's time for lunch.

Lunch is delicious, baked salmon and fresh salad and crusty bread, and I'm impressed at the quality of Helen's cooking. I'm equally impressed by the fact that Anika and Yelena are eating the same food as us, only in child-sized portions. After they're excused, I mention it to Viktor while I'm still at the table with him. Neither child talked to me during lunch, although Yelena peered up at me through half-lidded, shy-looking eyes. Anika stubbornly ignored me, which I can respect.

"I've always believed in treating children as grown-up as they possibly can be," Viktor says. "There were no sippy cups in this household. We treated them as capable from an early age, so they've grown up to be quite capable children. That extends to their dietary habits. They've learned to enjoy real, quality food, and Helen works hard to make sure that it's all well-prepared."

"It was delicious," I agree. I pause then, realizing how little I actually know about the two children I'm meant to be a mother to now, besides their names. "How old are they?"

"Anika is nine and Yelena is seven," Viktor says. "Anika is—quite grown up for her age, though. She's the one you'll likely find most difficult. She's old enough to remember her mother even better than Yelena does."

"How long--?" I break off, worried that I might upset him by asking about his late wife, but Viktor seems to be in a better mood after the meal.

"Three years ago," he says quietly. "So Yelena was still very small. Anika only two years older, of course, but—it makes a difference." He pauses, not quite meeting my eyes. "I know both of your parents have passed. Perhaps you can connect over that."

They're dead because of you and because of Franco. I don't expect the sudden bitterness that wells up, but it's there, burning the back of my throat like acid. I suddenly want to be anywhere but there with him, at the long dining table too big for the two of us and two small children. He feels too close, too much, sitting to my right, looking at me as if he doesn't understand the expression on my face. As if he has no idea that my mother died because of the attack on the hotel that was his fault, part of his gambit with the Irish to bring Luca down. That my father's machinations, their fight over Sofia, and Luca's insistence on marrying her, led to my father's death. That the ongoing war with the Bratva caused Luca's father's death, and his mother's and Sofia's parents too. So many parents lost because of all of this, and I still don't even know why Viktor's first wife died.

I'm not about to ask right now, either.

This is why you did this, I remind myself as I try to breathe. *So that no more parents die. So that no more children like Sofia grow up without their fathers. So no more mothers struggle to raise families alone.* That *is the reason.*

"I'm very tired," I say quietly, pushing my chair back. "I'd like to go lie down, if you'll leave me alone for a while."

"That's fine," Viktor says, glancing up at me finally. "I won't disturb you."

I *am* tired. But as I walk into the bedroom and shut the door firmly behind me, I have no idea how I'm going to sleep. I walk into the bathroom, splashing cold water on my face, looking around this luxurious place that I now call home. The bathroom is gorgeous, with heated white honeycomb tile floors and marble countertops, a huge porcelain soaking tub, and a walk-in shower with dual showerheads. There are eucalyptus plants in the window, trailing down the tiled wall, and everything is cool and crisp, like a spa in my own home.

I just wish I could actually relax.

I'm no stranger to luxury, like Sofia. I've lived in it all my life. Viktor's home is beautiful, but it doesn't sway me from how I feel about all of this, which is that I steadfastly don't want to be here.

But in the end, I have no choice.

What's done is done.

I change into yoga pants and a loose t-shirt and lie down, but the bed feels unfamiliar and strange, and I can't get comfortable. I wind up lying on my back, looking up at the ceiling and thinking about last night, about Viktor and how different it had been from what I'd imagined, how it will feel to sleep next to him tonight, knowing at least that he won't touch me. But I'll still be sleeping next to him, remembering how good it felt, still humiliated that I enjoyed it. Knowing that *he* knows I enjoyed it. Which just makes me all the more determined not to let it happen again.

This is the right choice; I know it is. Last night was good in a way that could be dangerous if I let it. I won't be caught up by another man who will only hurt me in the end. I won't make the same mistakes twice.

CATERINA

*S*omehow, I finally manage to fall asleep. My dreams are a fractured mess of my wedding and the night that followed, of my looking over the balcony and reliving that moment where I imagined myself tumbling to my death, of waking up sweating in the bed only to realize I'm still dreaming and have it happen all over again. When I finally do wake up, I feel groggy and dazed, as if I didn't really sleep well at all.

It's still light outside, but the time on my phone tells me it's getting close to dinnertime. Viktor left me alone as he promised, but I can't imagine he'll stay out of his own room forever. I feel clammy after the bad dreams and restless sleep, so I decide to take a shower before I get dressed for dinner.

It's when I step into the shower that I see something that startles me.

There are products in the shower clearly not meant for Viktor—shampoo and conditioner in bottles clearly marketed to women, peach and almond shower gel, a fluffy loofah that's clearly never been used, a brand new razor. I stare at them for a moment, trying to make sense of it. They can't be his late wife's. It's one thing for the house to potentially not have been redecorated since she lived here, but keeping her toiletries would suggest a level of devotion that I haven't gotten any sense that Viktor feels towards her. And they're definitely not Viktor's. Besides the clear newness of some of the items, I can see his in the shower alongside them.

Which means one thing—they were purchased for me to try to make me feel more comfortable here. Maybe. And I don't know how to feel about that, how to reconcile it with the terse, almost angry man I've fought with twice today already.

He probably just had someone go out and buy things, I tell myself, reaching for the shower gel. But even if that's true, he still had to send someone out to get them. He still had to request it. Which means a part of him, however small, is concerned for me and my happiness. My comfort.

It's not enough. That's my first thought, and it's not. It can't make up for everything he and the Bratva have done, everything they've taken from me, everything they represent. It can't make up for the fact that I didn't want to marry him, that there's no love here, that this house can't and never will feel like mine. But it is a very small thing, one that tells me there's another side to the man I've married.

And it does, in fact, make me feel the tiniest bit better.

I linger in the shower, washing my hair and scrubbing until I feel clean and fresh again. I get dressed in the last outfit I brought with me, the same jeans and a sleeveless silk blouse, adding a diamond bracelet and stud earrings I inherited from my mother. I quickly braid my wet hair since my blow dryer isn't here yet, and when I look under the sink, it turns up nothing. Not something Viktor planned for, I guess.

When I look at my left hand, it's startling to just see the plain thin gold band. It's entirely different from Franco, who gave me a huge diamond for our engagement. But I can appreciate the lack of pretense. Viktor knows there's no romance between us, no love. He could have gone through the motions, bought me a giant ring I might or might not have liked, made a show of proposing to me. But none of that would change what this really is, and he knows that. The simple ring is proof.

M JAMES

Now, if only he could be that pragmatic about everything in our relationship, including sex. And different bedrooms.

I know I need to hope that the IVF works quickly. If it doesn't, Viktor will have all the excuse he needs to suggest we go about getting me pregnant in, as he put it, *the old-fashioned way.* And I know he'll enjoy that excuse.

The sooner I'm pregnant, the better.

Just as I'm finished dressing, there's a knock at the door. "Come in," I call out, fully aware of how odd it feels to be saying that in this room that doesn't even feel like mine.

The door opens and Viktor steps in, his gaze drifting over me. "You look very nice," he says noncommittally, but I can see the flicker of desire in his gaze.

"I wasn't sure how dressed up you get for dinner," I say quietly, feeling suddenly awkward. "But this is all I brought until my things come tomorrow. I hadn't—well, I hadn't expected us to really even be eating together."

Viktor smirks. "Did you think I'd keep you chained in the basement until I required your services in my bed?"

I flush at that. "No," I snap, my voice more cutting than before. "I just didn't expect family dinners around the table. You'll forgive me if the stories I've heard about the Bratva don't line up with that."

"Well." Victor smiles, and I see the small lines at the corners of his eyes, betraying his age. "You'll find that I am more domestic than most. Dinner will be served soon, if you'd like to come along?"

It's not really a question, but I nod, following him to the dining room. Once we're seated, one of the staff—a girl called Bianca, I think —starts to serve dinner, setting bowls of a summery salad and a cold gazpacho in front of each of us. I would have thought that Anika and Yelena would have balked at cucumber gazpacho, but Yelena just says cheerfully: "Green! My favorite!" and digs in. Anika dips her spoon but doesn't say a word.

"What have you girls done today?" Viktor asks, and Anika finally speaks, telling him about exploring in the garden and a story she's reading about a girl who does just that. She doesn't look at me as she speaks, seemingly pretending I'm not there, but I don't really mind. It gives me a chance to watch her and her father, and what surprises me is how intently he really seems to be listening, both to her and to Yelena, as Yelena starts to tell him, a bit quietly, about her dollhouse and what the residents have been up to today.

Like the items in the shower, it gives me an insight into a different side of Viktor. He's not a man I would have expected to find carefully listening to the details of garden explorations and dollhouse dramas. Yet, he soaks up every word, barely acknowledging when Bianca comes to deliver the next course, sliced roast, carrots, and potatoes, a surprisingly American meal.

"What?" Viktor asks, snorting a little as he sees my expression. "Did you think it was all stroganoff and borscht here? I enjoy a good Sunday roast as much as anyone."

"You're stupid," Anika says suddenly, looking at me. "I can already tell."

"Anika!" Viktor's voice deepens as he turns back to his daughter. "Apologize to Caterina. Right now. That's not how we speak to anyone at our table, but certainly not her. Do you remember what I said about respect?"

"Why should I?" Anika juts out her chin. "She *is* stupid. She doesn't even know what kind of food we like."

"Anika." Viktor's voice holds a clear warning. "Go to your room."

"But I'm hungry," she whines, looking at me accusingly, as if it's my fault. But I see in that glance a chance to possibly try to get an inroad with her, at least. And it's her and her sister I most want to make progress with, not Viktor.

"Viktor," I say gently, reaching out to touch his arm. I have a sudden memory of my mother doing the same thing with my father, reaching out over the dinner table to touch his arm, in reassurance, in apology, in supplication. For the first time, more so than at the wedding or during the night that followed, I feel as though I'm actually Viktor's wife. "Viktor, it's alright. This is difficult for everyone. I know Anika didn't mean to be rude. She's simply adjusting."

Viktor lets out a breath, and Anika looks at me warily. I can tell she's suspicious of my motives, and honestly, if anything, it makes me like her. She's a smart child, and in this world, that will serve her better than innocence or naivete.

"You can finish your dinner," Viktor relents. "But you still need to apologize to Caterina for speaking to her that way."

"M'sorry," Anika mumbles, stabbing a carrot with her fork. At best, it's a half-apology, but Viktor lets it go, turning his attention back to his own plate.

"It's okay," I say gently, watching the girls from across the table as I poke at my own food. I'm not really hungry. The stress of today has completely stolen my appetite. But I don't want the girls to see me not eating—something I often saw my own mother do, so I force the food down, bite by bite. It's good. Viktor has an excellent cook.

After dinner, Viktor and I wind up in the living room, where he sits down to work on a puzzle with Anika. There's *another* fancy, intricate dollhouse there for Yelena. After a moment's hesitation, I sit down next to her, asking her to show me what's happening in this one.

"Well," she says in her small, quiet voice, "These are the parents." She shows me a tall dark-haired doll and a pretty blonde doll in a fancy dress. "They're going to a ball. They're in love and they want to go dance."

"That sounds perfectly reasonable to me." I watch as Yelena picks out an outfit for the blonde doll to wear, explaining to me why the one she chose is the right one, and then follow along as she takes the dolls to the "ball" in front of the house, spinning them in circles as they dance.

"What are the doll's names?" I ask, watching her. She's warmed up to me faster than Anika has, which gives me hope. If both girls had hated me, I would have been more inclined to feel hopeless about the situation, but I can deal with Anika's stubbornness. Hopefully, we can form a truce in time, and if I don't have to fight both girls at once, that will make it so much easier.

"This is Viktor, of course," Yelena says, looking at me with surprise. "Just like my papa."

"Of course." The doll doesn't really resemble Viktor in any way beyond the dark hair. Still, I can appreciate her ability to pretend. "And the lady doll?"

Yelena presses her lips together, looking at me from under her lashes nervously, as if she's afraid I might be mad. "This is Vera," she says quietly. "Like my mama."

"Oh." I look at the blonde doll. "Well, I'm sure that you miss her very much. Does this help you feel closer to her?"

Yelena shrugs. "Sometimes. Sometimes it just makes me sad. Then I put her away and play with my other toys."

"That's a very healthy solution." I'm surprised, actually, that she's managing it as well as she is. Viktor's household isn't as dysfunctional as I might have imagined it. I'm also surprised by how attentive he is with his daughters. I don't doubt that my father loved me, possibly in the way you love a very expensive racehorse or piece of art that you can use to invest in later. He would never have been caught doing puzzles with me around the coffee table or listening to the sagas of my dolls. After dinner, he always went straight to his study, if he made it home for dinner at all. My mother was better about showing love, but hers came more in the form of preparing me for the life I would have one day—lessons of all kinds, teaching me to run a household, preparing me for the fact that my love life wouldn't look like that of some of my friends. She'd encouraged me to make friends with other girls who would live similar lifestyles, but that was hard. No one else was the daughter of Vitto Rossi. No one else had had the same weight on their shoulders since birth.

My father would have said that weight was nothing compared to the responsibility of running his branch of the Family. But he couldn't possibly have understood. He couldn't have understood how it would feel, as a young girl, a teenager, and still as a woman, to know I'd likely never fall in love. Never know what an equal partnership of marriage felt like. Never have the fairytale or ever dream of it. Never be able to aspire to a career of my own. While other girls were out getting internships in college and networking, I was just getting my credits, knowing that I was only putting off the inevitable day when I'd never actually get to use any of this.

"Mr. Andreyev?" I hear Olga's voice from the doorway and see her smile indulgently at both girls before she continues. "I've come to get the girls for their baths and bedtime. I'm sure Mrs. Andreyv isn't quite up to the task yet."

My first instinct is to be offended, but there's nothing in her tone that suggests she means it that way. If anything, she looks at me kindly as she comes to gather up Yelena, who is protesting about bedtime. I, too, want to protest because I'm not at all ready to go to bed with Viktor, even if all we'll be doing is sleeping.

But protesting won't do any good. Viktor already made it very plain how he feels about my sleeping in a different bedroom. While I hadn't thought he would be the kind of man who cared all that much about gossip, it's becoming more and more clear to me throughout my first day here that he seems to be a man who values domestic peace. It's strange, really, considering all the stories I've heard about the Bratva.

I can't help but wonder if, despite the tentative truce that we came to during our fight earlier, he'll still try to touch me. I have a single change of nightclothes with me, silky light blue pajama shorts and a tank top. Even that feels too revealing, considering that I want nothing more than for my new husband to keep his hands off of me. I catch a glimpse of myself in the mirror and see the edge of the blue silk clinging to my thighs, the tank top pressed against my thin waist, my nipples poking out of the lightweight fabric. It's hardly lingerie, but looking at myself in the mirror with my hair tumbling down around my shoulders and so much of my arms and legs and upper chest exposed, it suddenly seems far too sexy.

But it's all I've got, and being naked would be worse, so I just focus on quickly splashing water on my face and brushing my teeth, managing to slip into bed and tightly close my eyes before Viktor comes into the room.

"I know you're not asleep," he says in his deep, rumbling voice as he opens a dresser drawer. "But don't worry, Caterina. You might think I'm a brute, but I'm a man of my word. I won't touch you, and tomorrow there will be an appointment made with an excellent fertility clinic."

I let out a slow breath, cracking one eye open to see him striding towards the bathroom. There's an intimacy in sharing a suite of rooms that I don't feel prepared to share with Viktor, but I've been given no choice. I think about him seeing my things on the counter, my skincare and the splashes of water left over from me washing my face, him standing where I was a few moments ago as he brushes his own teeth. This man was a stranger to me yesterday morning, and now we're sharing a nighttime routine.

Now I'm a stepmother to his children. Thinking about it in the simplest terms, it's ludicrous. It only doesn't seem completely outlandish to me because I was raised to believe it was normal. To know that this was my future. But to anyone else, it would seem like a horror show.

I just know there are far more horrific things out there now.

Viktor barely looks at me as he switches on his bedside light, climbing into bed. I see to my surprise that he's holding reading glasses and a novel with a title in Russian. I can't hide the expression on my face when he slips into bed in his pajamas and glasses, opening his book to where he'd marked it.

Viktor Andreyev, the terror of the Italian mafia, *Ussuri* of the Russian Bratva, a man who I know from what I've heard strikes fear into men all over this country and Europe besides, is sitting beside me in bed with his glasses perched on his nose, reading a Russian novel.

I can't quite believe my eyes.

He narrows his at me when he catches sight of my face. "I like to read before bed," he says shortly. "It calms my mind. So you can stop looking at me like a zoo exhibit. Have you never seen a man read before?"

"Of course I have," I manage, still staring at him. "I just—"

"What did you think I do to relax at night? Shoot a few men in the back garden and leave their bodies for the gardener to bury before crawling into bed?" His mouth twitches and I realize he's having a joke at my expense. I clench my jaw, suddenly angry. I don't like being mocked. Franco mocked me often, and even if his jokes were much crueler, I'm not about to be the butt of another husband's humor.

"You know that's not what I thought. But enjoy your book," I snap. "I'm going to sleep."

"Suit yourself." Viktor shrugs, looking away from me as if it truly doesn't matter to him one way or another what I do. That stings, too, for some reason.

I should be glad Viktor doesn't care. The less he cares about what I'm doing, the more freedom I'll have. But something about his nonchalance almost hurts. As if I'm completely inconsequential to him.

Which, I will be as soon as I've given him a son. I focus on that, on what my life could be like raising my son and Viktor's daughters with minimal input from him into my day-to-day. It's not the freedom I'd hoped for, but it's something. It'll be freedom from the worry that he'll push me into his bed, freedom from his opinions and moods, of which I'm sure he'll have plenty. I might once have dreamed of doing more with my life than simply being a mother, but that at least I'll enjoy. And if I decide I want another child, once I've given him the requisite son, IVF usually produces more than one embryo. I won't have to go to bed with him even for that.

As deals go, Viktor might have gotten his, but I think I might have made a pretty good one for myself.

That thought, at least, ensures that I'm able to fall asleep.

VIKTOR

*M*y new wife is proving to be a handful in every way except the one I'd like her to be.

I wake up from a less than peaceful sleep, unused to having someone in my bed again after three years of sleeping alone. Caterina isn't a restless sleeper, but any slight movement seemed to jolt me awake as if she'd shaken the entire bed. At one point, I simply lay awake for a while, watching her in the moonlight bleeding through the bedroom curtains.

I could not have picked a more beautiful bride. I'd known she was lovely, but somehow seeing her in person seems to make the memory of every other woman I've ever found beautiful fade. Everything about her, even in her waifish thinness, is perfection. As I laid there, I found myself wanting to reach over and touch her face, push a curl of dark hair away from her cheek, run my finger over her nipple beneath the thin fabric of her top.

Of course, I did none of those things. I'd promised her that I wouldn't so much as lay a finger on her, and I am, as I'd said, a man of my word. I lay there with my cock hard and throbbing instead, cursing the fact that I couldn't simply roll over and take my new bride. At that moment, I began to regret denying her request for a separate bedroom.

Keeping my hands off her would be much easier if she were elsewhere, not sleeping beside me every night. But I made a promise, and I'll keep it until I have reason to do otherwise. For instance—I'd agreed to try IVF. I didn't promise how many failed months I'd let it go on before I insist that we try a more natural route. And looking at Caterina lying next to me, her chest lightly rising and falling with sleep, I have a distinct feeling that I won't last many months before I start pushing for her to come back to my bed in every single way.

I had intended on a marriage of convenience, not one of celibacy. I've never been a man meant for monkhood. I can restrain my desires, but I don't prefer to. Why, when money and power mean that I can satisfy almost every desire I could possibly have?

That power bought me a bride. But apparently, it doesn't frighten Caterina enough to make her open her legs for me after the first night. And while I should find that offensive, instead, it's arousing. I don't think any woman has ever told me no. I've never forced a woman, but I've never been put in a position to have to. Only Caterina has ever looked me dead in the eyes and told me she would not willingly lay down for me.

And that, in and of itself, has made me want her with a desperation that I've never felt before.

It's also why I'm in the shower, my hand wrapped around my cock while my new wife sleeps peacefully in our bedroom just beyond the door.

Just thinking about our one night together is enough to get me rock-hard, almost painfully so. Thinking about everything we didn't do, everything that we could still do if she'd just fucking give in, is enough to have me on the verge of orgasm in seconds. I'd planned to do so many things to her after the first night, from finding out how well she can suck a cock to taking that tight asshole of hers and showing her that pleasure *can* come from that, whatever she's been told. Even once she'd made her displeasure at being married to me known, I'd been aroused at the idea of breaking her to my will, forcing her to experience pleasure so great that she'd be begging for my cock before our first anniversary.

But I hadn't expected her to pull the card that she had, and now I have no choice but to let her call the shots. For now, anyway.

I run my hand down the length of my shaft and back up again, imagining that it's her hand, her mouth, her pussy. She felt so good when I fucked her, hot and tight and clenching around me when she came like she wanted to milk every ounce of cum out of my cock. The fact that she'd come despite herself, that her body hadn't been able to resist the pleasure of my thick cock whether or not it was attached to a man she claimed to despise, had made my orgasm all the better.

The princess thinks she's married the monster instead of being saved from him, I think bemusedly as I stroke myself, picturing Caterina's small, firm breasts and how I'd like to paint them with my cum. She has a ridiculous idea of me in her head, of a cruel and brutal man to everyone around him, shedding blood at a whim without thought. I've been cruel and brutal, though I never do anything on a whim. But I'd never hurt my family. And Caterina, whether or not she likes it now, is a part of that family. My wife. My *zhena*.

"*Fuck.*" I curse under my breath, jerking faster. I don't have all morning to hang out in the shower, and Caterina will likely wake up any moment. I need to come, and I slam my fist down my cock, biting back a groan of pleasure as I once again summon the memory of Caterina's tight pussy and the way the heat of it felt gripping every inch of my length as I'd fucked her on our wedding night, nice and slow, with long strokes that let me feel every inch of her—"Oh, *fuck, fuck, fuuuck—*"

I clench my jaw as I thrust my hips forward, the first spurt of my cum hitting the drain as my cock swells and throbs in my hand, my hips jerking with the need to fuck something, anything. Right now, unfortunately, it's my fist.

I'd give anything to be inside of Caterina, instead.

By the time I finish, I'm breathless, my cock wilting in my fist as I grit my teeth in frustration. I'll have to deny myself even this for a few days before our appointments at the clinic, and somehow that feels like adding insult to injury. I can't fuck my wife, and I can't even jerk off thinking about her until the appropriate time.

She quite literally has me by the balls.

*　*　*

There is, however, a tentative peace between us for the next few days until our first appointment. I left her in Olga's care while I returned to work the day after bringing her home, and by the time I returned that evening, I found our bedroom and bathroom well-stocked with her things. I saw the uncertainty in her face when I came in that evening as if I might be upset by the dresses in the closet and the new books on the shelves, the tampons under the sink, and the hair products in the bathroom but I found it oddly calming. Though I never would have said so out loud to her. For three years, the master suite has had the lingering feminine touches of Vera's decorating, but none of her things, which made it feel as if the room were missing something every time I walked in. Now, it feels as if an empty space in the suite has been filled.

I am the leader of the Bratva, a man of power. I was never meant to be a bachelor, and I never intended to be one. To have a wife in my bed and in my home is the natural order of things, and rather than be turned off by the sight of womanly things in my private rooms, it makes me feel, in an odd way, comforted. As if all is right with the world again.

If only my wife herself were so comforting.

"I've made an appointment at the clinic," I told her that night. "It's after lunch, two days from now."

"Good," was all she'd said in response, turning away from me and switching off her light.

It's a relief, at least, that she's not fighting the idea of carrying my child. *That* would be a war between us. I'm willing to make sacrifices to keep the peace in my own home and with the Italians and the Irish, but some sacrifices cannot be made. I need an heir, and Caterina's purpose was always to provide one for me.

Olga proves to be an excellent source of information on how things are when I'm not at home those first few days, meeting me when I walk through the door ahead of my wife and children. Caterina is always there, looking elegant and composed, her face unreadable. The only time I ever see her smile is when I'm interacting with the children or when I catch glimpses of her with them. In that, I find relief too. If she can be a good mother to my girls, and provide me with a son, then anything else in the marriage, I'm willing to write off as a loss.

But Olga is quick to tell on her when she thinks Caterina is spending too much time in her room or to let me know that Anika still doesn't like her and hasn't warmed to her in the slightest. "I told you bringing an Italian woman into the house was no good," she mutters as I come home two nights later, glancing sideways at Caterina, who is standing a little ways back and watching the girls instead of either of us. "Anika might have taken to a good Russian woman better. A blonde, like her mother."

"Anika is going to have to learn to adapt, as we all do," I tell Olga sternly. "And the more quickly you treat Caterina as befits who she is in this house—my *wife*—the sooner Anika will come around."

"I'm kind to her," Olga says, pursing her lips. "I haven't said an unkind word to that woman."

"The way you speak about her to me is enough." I glare at her, though not angrily. "Your attitude comes across, Olga. When you're *accepting* of her, the girls will follow suit. They need to see respect from you; they love you dearly."

"And I love them." Olga glances over at Caterina and the two girls. "Yelena has really warmed up to her," she admits. "I think the difference in ages changes things. Anika was always closer to her mother. And Yelena remembers less."

"Then hopefully, Anika will learn from her younger sister." I stride forward, greeting Caterina with a kiss on the cheek and then bending down to greet both of my daughters.

My new wife has been remarkably good at pretending that all is well in front of the staff, reserving her coldness towards me for when we're alone. But I catch the glances that she gives me occasionally, the curious looks, the way her gaze will catch on my face or my body for just a moment, and I know she's remembering that brief time during our wedding night when we both lost control.

It makes it even harder for me to keep that control now.

I spend the morning of our appointment in my study, working on ledgers from home and taking lunch in my office. When I finally emerge in time to have the driver take us into the city, I find Caterina already waiting in the living room, dressed impeccably in a dark red sheath dress with a black leather belt and leather pointed pumps. Her hair is pinned back with a diamond clip that matches the diamond solitaires at her ears and neck and the tennis bracelet on her wrist. She looks beautiful in diamonds, and I wonder where she acquired those from. She doesn't seem like the kind of woman to keep gifts from a former husband that she hated.

"Ready to go, I see." I smile tightly at her as I walk into the room. "Very punctual of you, my dear."

"I thought you didn't like to be kept waiting." Caterina's smile is equally as icy, her voice clipped. "So I made sure to be on time."

"And thoughtful, too. What a lovely bride I've chosen." As we walk towards the door, I offer her my arm, brushing my fingers over the bracelet as I open the door for her. "I don't recall giving you anything as beautiful as this."

"You didn't." Caterina gives me a tight smile as she strides out of the door towards the car. "Jealous?"

Without the servants around to hear, her tongue is as barbed as ever. *I can think of a few other uses for it.* If only. The fact that I'm driving my wife to a clinic to have someone else inseminate her with sperm I could so easily—and happily—give her myself feels more insulting by the minute. As I slide in next to her, I can't help but hope that every dime I spend will be wasted money, if only so I can enjoy filling her with my cum a few months from now without guilt.

"No. But I am curious. Gifts from Franco?"

Caterina opens her mouth as if to shoot back a response, but her shoulders sag a little, and she lets out a long breath. "They were my mother's," she says tiredly. "I have a decent amount of jewelry from her."

In her tone, I can hear everything behind those words that she's not saying—that her mother died because of her former husband's actions, because of *my* actions, because of so many other things. That she doesn't want or need gifts from me, she has her own things. *Good*, I think angrily in my head, looking at her elegant profile as she looks out of the car window. *I didn't intend to give her jewelry, anyway.*

"Thank you for making the appointment," Caterina says quietly, still not looking at me, and I wonder if that's her way of trying to stop the fight before it really begins. "I know you would have preferred to do things—differently."

That's putting it mildly. "I thought Catholics believed IVF was a sin," I say shortly, still irritable.

"I'll go to confession," she quips, her mouth twitching. "Besides, I'm hardly devout. I've only gone when absolutely necessary for a long time."

"Neither am I," I admit. "Church isn't exactly a place I feel comfortable, these days. And confession even less so."

I wonder if she'll ask about that, about what sins I've committed that make the inside of a church feel uncomfortably warm to me, but she doesn't. She simply continues looking out of the window, her hands folded primly in her lap.

The clinic is everything one would expect from a swanky downtown Manhattan fertility clinic, where couples undoubtedly pour thousands and thousands of dollars into trying to have a child of their own. It's full of airy windows and green plants, furnishings upholstered in soft pink, and soothing music playing from the speakers above. Caterina remains absolutely silent until we check-in, and then she simply gives the receptionist the information she requests and goes to find a seat.

After seeing the spitfire side of her on our first day together, her calm silence is almost unnerving. She stays that way, pale and tight-lipped, all the way through them separating us for exams, then when we reunite in the doctor's office, a dark-haired man who looks a few years older than I am. He looks at me warily, and I know then that he has some idea of who I am.

I can always feel that flicker of fear, the charge in the air when someone knows me. When they know to be afraid of me. Knowing what our family went through to get to this point, to command this sort of fear and respect, means that reaction never fails to send an almost arousing flush of power through me every time.

He flicks through our charts, frowning, and then looks up at us. "Mr. and Mrs. Andreyev, I have to say, this is unusual. There's nothing to suggest that you would have any trouble at all conceiving naturally. How long have you been trying?"

I feel Caterina flinch next to me. "We haven't," she says quietly. "We were married a week ago, and we've had intercourse once."

Intercourse. It almost makes me want to laugh. It's too clinical a word, too cold for what happened between us that night, for the way Caterina shook and trembled when her orgasm took over her body, the way it felt to thrust into her and feel her squeeze around me, the heat of her so intense it felt as if it was searing into my cock—no, *intercourse* isn't the term I would use.

The doctor's frown deepens. "I'm confused, Mrs. Andreyev. So you haven't even been trying to conceive for a full cycle, and you've only had intercourse once, but you want to pursue IVF? These treatments are very expensive, and I might suggest—"

"Money is not an object," I interrupt, my voice sharp. There's a condescending note in the doctor's voice as he speaks to Caterina that sparks a flare of anger in me. This might not be what *I* want, but it is what Caterina wants, and the decision should be between us. Not with the input of some meddling doctor who I'm paying handsomely to do as we ask. "We're here because we've made the decision—"

"IVF is an invasive process," the doctor says calmly. "Injections, hormones, mood swings—couples often find it to be a strain on their marriage. I would be remiss, Mr. Andreyev, if I took your money without going over all of the options with you first."

What will be a strain on my marriage is forcing my wife to have sex with me against her will. "I appreciate your commitment to your work," I tell him coolly. "But we're here because we've made this decision after our own discussions, and we simply would like to move forward with the proceedings."

Privately, I wish that the doctor's caution would change Caterina's mind. I can't quite believe that she's willing to go to such lengths to stay out of my bed, that she'd rather suffer through hormone injections and changes in her body before she even becomes pregnant to avoid sex with me. To avoid *pleasure,* because I know she enjoyed it. In fact, I'd be willing to bet that has something to do with this whole rigmarole.

Caterina doesn't want to admit she fucking enjoyed it. She doesn't want to go to bed with me again because her body would betray her, and she'd have to come to terms with the fact that she likes it. She might despise me, pretend to be disgusted by me, but deep down, she wants my cock, Bratva or not.

"My husband wants a child," Caterina says stiffly, as the doctor turns his gaze back to her, opening his mouth as if to begin trying to convince her once more that this isn't the path she should go down. "This is the way I've chosen to accomplish that."

"I'm paying you enough for this visit alone," I growl, still seeing the uncertainty in the doctor's face. "We'll do what my wife wants."

He lets out a long sigh, flattening his hands on the desk and looking down at our files again. "Fine," he agrees, finally. "This is all very—unusual, but you're right. You are the one paying me, Mr. Andreyev. So we'll do it the way you and your wife want."

"Correct," I growl, glaring at him. "And if you start having second thoughts, I suggest you ask around about the name Viktor Andreyev. I'm not a man whose time you want to waste."

The doctor's face pales slightly in a way that makes me feel that pleasant rush of power again.

We're given the rest of the information then, injection and appointment schedules, information about egg retrieval and embryo survival rates, and all kinds of other technical details that make my head swim. I can feel a rising frustration as the doctor goes on. This could all be avoided if Caterina would stop being so fucking stubborn, stop trying to prove a point, that she can have some power in this marriage. Caterina is listening to him intently, which of course she fucking is. If this works, she won't ever have to let me fuck her again, which is just confirmed when the doctor mentions *multiple embryos* and *future pregnancies* with the ones preserved from these rounds of IVF. I grit my teeth just listening to it, but I can see the smallest of smiles forming on Caterina's face as she takes in every word.

That, of course, only adds to the iciness between us on the ride home. "You'll have to help me with the injections," Caterina says, glancing at me blankly. "Unless, of course, you'd prefer I get one of the maids to help me."

"I'll do it," I bite out, my jaw working as I fight back everything I want to say to her right now. "We're keeping up appearances, remember?"

"How could I forget?" Caterina turns away, looking out of the window again.

It's hard to hold back the anger and frustration I feel boiling just beneath the surface. I want Caterina, now more than ever, and I'm self-aware enough to know that her stubborn refusal likely contributes to that a great deal. I'm not used to not getting the things that I want.

It's almost enough to make me regret marrying her. In the years since Vera died, I've managed to cultivate an internal peace that largely came from avoiding romantic entanglements with anyone. The passion, the anger, the arguments and makeup sex, the intense highs and even worse lows of my first marriage were all things I'd decided to put behind me. I'd thought that marrying a woman like Caterina would help me to maintain that peace. She'd been born into this life. She knows the rules, the expectations. She would be obedient, pliable, appropriate. I'd believed all of those things when I'd demanded Luca give her to me, and yes, a small part of me had desired her, too. But I'd desired the way taking her would make me feel more, the rush of demanding a woman and having her handed over to me.

But she's turned out to be none of those things. And it almost makes me wish I'd made a different choice—except that I still want her. And she's fulfilling the most basic tenets of what I demanded of her—in her own way.

She's going to carry my child, and she's good with my daughters. Ultimately, that's all I need from her, even if it's not all I want. And as I think about Vera and my first marriage and look at Caterina's pale face and set jaw as she looks out of the window, I know that I need to tread carefully. Caterina might be frustrating the hell out of me, but I don't want her to meet the same end. I don't want our marriage to drive her to that point—I'm not sure I could bear feeling that responsibility again. And the last thing in the world I want is for my children to lose another mother figure. I've already seen Yelena warming to her, even if Anika remains stubborn.

I could try to seduce her. I watch her from the corner of my eye as we drive, and I consider that idea. I consider romancing her, bringing her things she might like, treating her gently, with affection, and even love, however fake it might be. I consider teasing her, seducing her, making her want me until she can't bear to stay out of my bed a moment longer.

But we'd agreed not to lie to one another. And I'm not the kind of man who fakes things in order to get what he wants.

I simply take them.

Which means Caterina has a few months to have things her way.

And then we'll do it mine.

CATERINA

I CAN'T DO THIS.

That's my first thought when I wake up the next morning, Viktor has already gone, the sheets on his side of the bed rumpled where he slept.

I roll over, shoving my face into the pillow as I try to stop the tears, but I can't. Viktor gave me my first injection last night, and he was hardly gentle about it. I'd had some idea of what to expect. Still, I hadn't expected the sheer indignity I'd feel as I'd pushed up the side of my pajama shorts, baring the curve of my ass to Viktor's gaze as he readied himself to give me the shot.

I'd almost expected him to take advantage of that, to try to touch me in some intimate way, but he hadn't. He'd just jabbed it into my flesh, none too gently, and I'd bitten my lip so hard I'd tasted blood, refusing to give him the satisfaction of the pained noise I'd wanted to make.

I chose this, I'd reminded myself. *So don't make him think you're regretting it.*

The silence between us has become almost constant, cold and drawn out. Our interactions have even become stiff when we're around the staff or the children. It's hard to pretend to be a happily married couple when the disdain between the two of us feels as if it's growing by the day, and even Viktor seems to be getting tired of the charade. He makes it to dinner every night, but all of his attention is on Yelena and Anika. Any other time he's home, he stays in his study as much as possible.

For myself, I feel like a glorified nanny. I know I'm expected to be up by now, dressed and helping Olga get the children ready to leave for school. But I can't seem to get myself up. I shove my face deeper into the pillow, letting myself sob just a little—once, twice, and then deep gulping breaths as I try to pull myself together. I'm supposed to have lunch with Sofia today at least, the first time I've been out of this house, with the exception of the fertility appointment. The reminder of that gives me the boost I need to sit up. I rub my hand over my face in an effort to wipe the tears away and make it into the shower so that I can get ready and see what needs to be done before I meet her.

There's nothing to be done though, really. I don't have any purpose in this house beyond helping with Anika and Yelena. By the time I manage to get out of the shower, braid my wet hair into a single long braid that dangles over my shoulder, and put on a pair of jeans and a white t-shirt, Olga has already gotten them dressed and fed and bundled off to school. I can see what she thinks of that in her disapproving look as she walks through the dining room while I'm eating my breakfast, feeling adrift at the long table that's empty except for me.

"Mr. Andreyev expects you to be the one caring for the children sooner rather than later," she says, pausing at the table and catching me with a spoonful of steel-cut oats halfway to my lips. "I know you need time to adjust to this new role. But I am not their mother, Mrs. Andreyv."

Neither am I. I want to retort, seeing the stern, almost grandmotherly expression on her face. But the truth is, I wouldn't mind being a mother to them. It breaks my heart that they lost theirs, and it doesn't escape me that if their mother was still alive, I wouldn't be here. But I don't exactly know what to do. Yelena is warming up to me more quickly, but I'm at a loss about how to take care of her. I don't have any real experience with children, not in this kind of setting. And I don't know how to break past Anika's walls because they're all valid. She lost her mother, and her father has tried to replace her with someone nothing like her. I can understand Anika's bitterness.

Viktor had suggested I try to connect with them through the loss of my own parents, but that feels difficult too. I don't know if *I'm* ready to share that. I've barely spoken about that loss, even to Sofia. I don't know if I'm prepared to share it with children, children who will have questions, children who I will have to delicately tiptoe around the details of my parents' deaths with.

No, I don't think I'm ready for any of that.

"I'm doing my best," I say quietly. "Like you said, it's an adjustment."

Olga looks at me disapprovingly. "I don't think you are, Mrs. Andreyva. *Caterina.*" She says my name with distaste, her accent thickening. "I told Viktor he should marry a Russian woman. Someone who knows her place here. But he insisted on you. He insists that I model respect for you, too, for the girls. So I try. But the girls are not here right now, Caterina, and I will tell you that I think it was a poor choice for Viktor to bring you here."

I feel something knot in my stomach, burning acid climbing up my throat. I want to spit all kinds of things at her, all sorts of angry vitriol about how I don't want to be here either, what I think of the Russians and what they've done to my family and others over the years, how I feel about Viktor and her and everyone in this godforsaken house. But instead, I slowly set down my spoon, taking a deep breath as I meet her icy blue gaze.

"I didn't choose this marriage," I tell her calmly. "So I would agree with you that Viktor made a poor choice. I was not told I would be a new mother to two girls. But Anika and Yelena are very sweet, and I want to make the effort that is required of me. Viktor wants a son, and I am doing my best to provide that as well. Believe me, *Olga*, if I had a choice about being a part of this marriage, I would not be here right now. So, like I said before. It's an adjustment."

Olga is silent for a long moment, watching me keenly. "His first marriage was a love match, you know," she says quietly. "A tempest in a teapot, always. She didn't understand that you cannot change a man, and most especially a man like Viktor." Olga narrows her eyes at me. "I think you understand that. I think you know that Viktor has a nature that will not be changed. He is the man he was made to be and nothing less."

"I know that." I push my bowl of oatmeal away, my appetite gone. "He's made—some concessions, for me. I'm grateful for those. I know he's not—an easy man."

"He's not," Olga says quietly. "If he's made concessions for you, you *should* be grateful. That's unusual for him." She pauses, still watching me. "I've known him a long time, Caterina," she says finally. "I've worked for this house when his father was the one who ruled here. Viktor's family comes from a long line of hardship. They killed their way to what they have here, now, in America, earned it with blood and violence. That sort of thing is in his bones. That's what Vera, God rest her soul, couldn't understand."

"What happened to her?" I know I shouldn't, but I can't resist asking. I know from the shadow that passes over Olga's face when I do, though, that I won't be getting answers from her today.

"That's not my business to tell you," she says, her shoulders squaring. "Now, I have work to do, Mrs. Andreyva. But if you want to know that badly, ask Viktor. He should be the one to tell you such things."

I let out a sigh once she's gone, looking morosely at what remains of my breakfast. I should have known I wouldn't get answers from her. And regardless of her encouragement, I'm not going to ask Viktor —more than anything because I'm afraid of the answer.

Surely, if Viktor had killed his first wife, Luca would have known and not agreed to the marriage. Surely he would at least have warned me if he still felt he had no other choice than to go through with it.

I make up my mind to ask Sofia when I see her. Maybe she's heard something, or Luca has said something to her at some point. I also trust her not to say anything to Luca or anyone else, either.

She's already at the restaurant when I get there, a French bistro spot that we both like, idly fiddling with her phone while she waits. I'm astonished to see how good she looks when she stands up to greet me, a smile on her face. Her dark hair is in a high ponytail, her skin glowing, her figure filled out with her steadily growing pregnancy. There's still only the slightest of bumps under her form-fitting black sheath dress, elbow-length and belted at the waist, but everything about her screams that it suits her. She's wearing a long diamond lariat necklace and long silver earrings with diamond teardrops at the ends, and she touches her ears self-consciously when she sees me looking at them, a hint of the shy old Sofia returning.

"Luca's been spoiling me more these days," she says with a small laugh. "We came back from our appointment and he had these waiting for me, along with enough roses to fill half the bedroom. He's over the moon about the baby."

"That's got to feel good, after worrying about it for so long, though." I remember all too well how terrified Sofia had been when she'd admitted to me that she was pregnant. I'd been in the dark about it too for a long time and for the reasons why Luca had insisted she not get pregnant, at a threat to her life if she did. Yet again, another thing that was my father and Franco's fault, a contract that was meant to give our child—mine and Franco's—my father's seat at the head of the Family table one day. Sofia remaining childless had been part of the marriage contract my father had arranged between her and Luca, and she'd been terrified when she and Luca, during a night of passion, had conceived anyway. Her efforts to keep that child a secret had led down a dangerous path for everyone.

But now, everything is different. My father and Franco are gone and their reign of terror over Sofia is over. She and Luca are blissfully married, and she's accepted this life and the things that her husband sometimes does in pursuit of keeping her and their soon-to-be little one safe. And this baby is now wanted by everyone, no longer a secret.

Gingerly, I touch my stomach under the table, wondering how long it will be before I'll be harboring a small bump. My baby will be wanted too, and never a secret. In fact, the circumstances couldn't be more different.

There's a glass of white wine already waiting for me beside a glass of ice water, but I just sip at it lightly. The doctor had warned me it wasn't a good idea to drink, but after this morning, I feel like I need *something*, even if it's just a sip to take the edge off.

"How are things?" Sofia asks gently, looking up at me as she scans the menu. "You've been quiet lately. I've hardly heard from you, except to ask if we could get lunch today."

"It's been—difficult," I admit, glancing at the menu myself. It gives me an excuse not to look up and see the worry in Sofia's face.

"Has he been cruel to you? Hurt you?" Sofia leans forward, her eyes narrowing. "Because Luca—"

"No." I shake my head. "We've fought, but he hasn't hurt me. He hasn't even been particularly cruel, really. There's just—a lot that's been unexpected."

"Like?" Sofia asks and then quickly catches herself. "I mean, you don't have to talk about it if you don't want to. I just—I'm here if you do."

"I know." I push the menu aside. I'm not really hungry, although I'll order something and force myself to eat it. The doctor at the fertility clinic had commented about my being underweight and how that might impact my ability to get pregnant sooner rather than later.

I'd wanted to snap at him that I'd lost my parents and first husband in a matter of a few months to traumatic, violent circumstances, only to turn around and have a new marriage arranged for me before my first husband was hardly cold. So some weight loss seems normal when I'd never been particularly curvy to begin with. But of course, I hadn't, because staying silent these days seems like the safer option.

"Viktor was *very* insistent, on our wedding night, that he wants a son as soon as possible," I tell Sofia once the waiter has taken our order and left again.

"Is that a bad thing?" Sofia glances at me. "I know you like children."

"I do," I say, picking a bread roll out of the basket and putting it on the small plate in front of me, more to tear apart than to eat, really. "But that's not all. Viktor has two children already, from his first wife. Two daughters. No one bothered to tell me that."

"Oh," Sofia says softly. "So he wants a stepmother for his kids, and a new child too."

"Basically." I pick at the roll, feeling my stomach churn at the idea of taking a bite.

"So you've met them? Do they like you?"

"The younger one does. Yelena." I press my lips together, thinking about Anika and the first night I'd been in the house. "The older girl, Anika, is pretty resentful. She still avoids me as much as possible and doesn't want to talk to me. And it's hard to blame her, honestly. I know how hard it was to lose my mother as an adult. I can't imagine how I would have felt at her age." I pause then, looking up at Sofia, who is listening quietly. "Do you know how Viktor's first wife died?"

Sofia frowns. "No. How?"

"No, I mean, I'm asking you." The roll is now a pile of small pieces of bread, and I put one in my mouth, forcing myself to choke it down. "I don't know, and no one will tell me. And I'm not about to ask Viktor."

"I don't know, Cat. I'm sorry." Sofia shakes her head. "Luca's never said anything to me about it. I knew he was a widower, but I didn't think to ask—"

"I guess it must not be that bad then." I chew another piece of bread. "Luca would have told me if it was, don't you think? If he like— killed his first wife or something like that?"

"Of course." Sofia looks faintly horrified. "Luca wouldn't have given you to a man like that. I know he wouldn't."

I want to feel reassured. But it's hard because while I like and mostly trust Luca, I know from growing up in a mafia family, with my father at the head of it, how complicated these things can be. Even if Viktor *had* been responsible in some way for his first wife's death, there's always a chance that Luca might have gone through with the bargain anyway, for the promise of peace. He might have rested a great deal on that bargain, hoping that the threat of what would happen if it were broken would be enough to keep Viktor from harming me.

Luca promised I would be safe. But I can't help but wonder just how much I have to be safe *from*.

"What about the rest?" Sofia looks at me sympathetically. "He wasn't too—rough? On the wedding night, I mean?"

I can feel my cheeks flush faintly at that. My wedding night with Viktor is the last thing I want to think about right now. I have to avoid thinking about it every night when he comes to bed and lays down next to me. I remember the pleasure I'd felt that night, the way my body had given itself over to him despite myself. The way he'd lost control—

"It was fine," I say tightly, biting my lip. "But it won't happen again."

Sofia looks at me curiously. "But you said—he wants a baby."

"And he'll have one, hopefully." I swallow hard as the server comes back with our lunch, waiting until the plates are in front of us and they're gone again before continuing. "I convinced him to use a fertility clinic instead of the normal way. IVF."

A full moment of silence hangs over the table, and then another, as Sofia stares at me in shock.

"Oh my god," she says finally. "I can't believe you got him to agree to that."

I shrug. "I told him that if he forced me, I'd go to Luca."

"Would you have? Really?" Sofia looks at me curiously. "You know what it will mean if the deal Luca struck with him is broken—"

"I do," I say shortly. "Which is why yes, it was more of a bluff than anything else. But it worked. We had an appointment, and now my new husband is giving me fertility shots in the ass every night instead of taking me to bed."

"Wow." Sofia looks almost impressed. "I honestly can't believe—shit, Cat. You got the leader of the Bratva to agree to a fertility clinic instead of regular sex. That's pretty fucking impressive, honestly."

I have to smother a laugh. Sofia's eyes are wide, and she hardly ever curses, so I know she must be shocked. "I didn't think it would work either," I admit. "But I had to try."

"So, how does it make you feel?" Sofia asks curiously. "Having a baby, but not any kind of real marriage with Viktor. Does that make you happy?"

I have to think about it for a minute. *Am I happy*? That's not really a question I've been asking myself lately. I know, deep down, the answer isn't going to be a good one. I was crying into my pillow just this morning. But would a baby be enough to give me some happiness?

"I don't know," I say honestly. "I didn't expect to be *happy* with Viktor. After hoping to be happy with Franco and everything that happened, I didn't want to set myself up for that again. I thought going into it with low expectations would help. But sometimes, being in that house feels even worse. I don't belong there. Even the staff looks at me like I'm out of place. I hadn't really thought about babies when we were married. I don't know why—it's not like I shouldn't have thought that would be an expectation. And I do want children. I always did. I just—"

"Aren't sure about having them with Viktor," Sofia finishes. "It's understandable, honestly. I remember how scared I was with Luca. Everything was unfamiliar and unsure, and I felt so out of place. I'd never been somewhere like his penthouse, and for a long time, I felt like a prisoner there. Having a baby seemed like the worst kind of idea, then. But now—" she shrugs. "Now, I couldn't be happier."

"You're in love with Luca, though." I look at my food, wishing that I wanted to eat. Wishing that I could rewind time back to the night of Franco's funeral, just before Luca talked to me, when I thought I could be free. I wish I could stay there, in those few hours when none of this had even crossed my mind as a possibility.

"Yeah, but I wasn't then," Sofia reminds me. "Or at least I didn't know I was. All I'm saying is I know how terrifying the thought can be in an arranged marriage with a man you don't want to be married to. Even if our story turned out good in the end, it was still hard for a long time. But maybe—" she hesitates, looking at me with that same sympathy in her eyes. "if your marriage with Viktor isn't ever going to turn into love, then the baby could be a good thing. Someone for you to love."

I hate thinking of a baby like that, like a consolation prize, but I don't tell Sofia that. I know she's trying to be a good friend, trying to make me feel better, and it's not her fault that I feel like this.

I'd thought I'd known what I was getting myself into, agreeing to marry Viktor. But the reality of it seems so much harder to navigate.

"It's fine," I tell her firmly, hoping I sound more sure than I am. "Everything will be fine. Viktor might not be happy about using IVF for me to get pregnant, but in the end, when he has his son, he'll understand it was better this way. More clinical. We both get what we want, and in the end, that's what this is—a business deal. A bargain. We each get what we want this way."

"Of course." Sofia pauses. "Any chance you have for happiness, Cat, you should take it."

"I know." And I do, of course. I don't know how many of those chances I'll have now, trapped in this marriage with Viktor, 'til death do us part. There's never been any romance to wedding vows for me, no anticipation of binding my life to another's. It's always been shackles, a prison built for me since the day I was born.

"I have something exciting to tell you, though," Sofia ventures, and I look up, smiling encouragingly at her. I don't want this lunch to be all doom and gloom and talking about my misfortunes in marriage, and I don't want Sofia to feel bad for being happy.

"I *definitely* want to hear all about that," I tell her firmly. "So, what is it?"

"My first performance with the orchestra is next Friday night. I have some tickets to give to family and friends—and I'd really like it if you would come. I'll give you two, in case Viktor insists on coming—or you want him to. But whether it's with him or alone, it would really mean a lot to me if you could be there." Sofia is smiling as she talks, and I can see her eyes sparkling with excitement.

It's yet another difference between her marriage to Luca and mine to Viktor. Viktor is never going to let me go work as an elementary art teacher, any more than my father or Franco would have. But Luca apparently was wracked with guilt over stealing Sofia away from finishing her education at Juilliard and her chance at a top spot with an orchestra. Her plan had once been to go to London, to escape Manhattan and the mafia and all it entailed and play in the orchestra there. But of course, that hadn't happened—thanks to the Bratva and the threat they posed to her at the time.

It hadn't been very difficult for Luca to convince the head of Juilliard to let Sofia sit for her final exams. Then she'd moved directly into a spot in the New York Philharmonic. She wasn't a first-chair violinist, although Luca had wanted to strong-arm the director into giving her exactly that. She'd insisted that she start in a spot more appropriate to her experience. However, Sofia is still playing violin again, doing what she loves, using her talents that at one point earned her a spot at Juilliard. And now, she'll be performing for the first time outside of the school.

She has a level of freedom that I can't ever hope for. And while I would never resent my friend for her happiness, I can feel an ache in my chest that reminds me that I won't ever have that. Viktor might not be the cruel monster that he was always made out to be in the stories I and everyone else have always heard—at least not to his children and me—but that doesn't mean he's the kind of man who will ever give me that kind of freedom. He's made it clear that he chose me for two reasons—my pedigree and my ability to mother his children. *All* of them.

"I'll absolutely be there," I promise Sofia. "I wouldn't miss it for the world."

Telling Viktor, however, is going to be a whole different matter. So far, he hasn't insisted that I stay home or avoid my friends—in fact, he seemed happy that I was having lunch with Sofia today. "Public proof that the wife of the *pakhan* can have lunch with the wife of the Don," is how he put it, more precisely. But I'm not sure how he'll react to me going out to Sofia's performance at the orchestra.

When I pose it to him just before bedtime, though, after the injection that's administered every bit as bluntly as it has been since we went to the clinic, his response is similar.

"I'll attend with you, of course," Viktor says thoughtfully. "That will be good. The *pakhan* and his wife, attending a Philharmonic performance where the Italian Don's wife is playing. Luca may have invited Macgregor as well. It's good optics. It will be good for us to be seen there."

I feel a rush of bitterness as I stare at him. I'm not even astonished at the fact that he assumed he was invited, that I might not have intended to go to my best friend's performance alone and without my "husband." It's the thing that makes me lash out at him, even though I know a fight isn't in my best interest. The arrogance of it makes me too angry to stop myself.

"It's always astonishing to me to hear you use words like *optics*," I snap, glaring at him. "Aren't you Bratva supposed to use your fists instead of diplomacy? Torture instead of photo ops? Or are you, specifically, somehow above all of that?"

Viktor's eyes narrow, darkening dangerously, and I know that I've perhaps stepped just a bit too far.

"Oh, I've done my fair share of torture," he says, his mouth twitching as if it's somehow amusing to him. "Is that what you want to hear about, my sweet wife? All the blood I've spilled? The teeth and fingernails I've ripped out when I've been betrayed or crossed? The screams I've heard? Do you want a body count?" He moves towards me as he talks; his body is suddenly taut, muscles coiled. "If I tell you about the man I beat to death as a rite of passage when I was a teenager, will that satisfy the image of me that you have in your head?"

A cold rush of fear washes over me, my mouth going dry. *He can't be serious. As a teenager?* But even as I tell myself that can't possibly be true, I know it likely is. It fits with the stories I've heard of the Bratva, the horrible, cruel things they do. But what I can't make fit together is the cold, elegant man I married, the gentle and involved father, with the brutal Bratva leader that I know lurks inside of him.

How can one man have so many different sides to him?

It would be easier to understand Viktor if he were simply the cruel, violent man I'd heard about. But the man I'm coming to know—he doesn't make sense to me at all.

"No," I whisper, the word coming out halted from my dry lips. "I don't want to hear about any of that."

Viktor straightens, his blue gaze cold as he looks down at me. "Good," he says with satisfaction. "Then I'll assume you're pleased with the new leaf I've been turning over. The one where I make bargains with the Italian Don and the new Irish king instead of killing their families and stealing their territory. The one where I marry a mafia princess to bind our families together, and then take her on a lovely date to the Philharmonic where the Don's wife is playing a concert, so that we can show just how happy and well-adjusted the Manhattan crime families are these days." He raises one arched eyebrow, and I see the lines in his forehead deepen as he does. It's sexier than it should be, those lines and the creases at the corners of his eyes and the silver at his temples. It's a reminder that he's more than fifteen years older than me, a man at the end of his thirties when I've only recently been twenty-two, just before my engagement. I can feel my cheeks flushing at the reminder of how handsome my husband really is and the brief flash of our one night together, those blue eyes looking down at me as he fucked me deeper and harder than I ever had been before.

There's a beat of silence between us, and Viktor looks coolly down at me, that eyebrow still arched. "Which would you prefer, Caterina? The brute or the gentleman? I'm working very hard at trying to be the latter."

"The gentleman," I manage to whisper, my mouth still feeling as if it's stuffed with cotton. Even in our previous fights, Viktor had held back, but I can see a wave of anger in him now that is beyond anything he's shown me before. It's a reminder that I've married a bear on a chain, and the only one holding him back is himself. "Of course—we'll go together. A show of good faith for Luca and the others in the Family."

"There's my mafia princess." Viktor smiles, but it doesn't quite reach his eyes as he reaches out to touch my cheek, his fingers brushing over my burning cheekbones. "There's the woman I bargained for. I didn't just marry you for your fertile womb, you know. I also married you because you understand this life. The things we have to do. I thought you wouldn't shrink from them."

"Going to a performance with my husband is hardly something to shrink from." I force a smile, looking up at him as pleasantly as I can manage. I'm still seething, but this is one fight that I think Viktor has won. *You need to be smart,* I remind myself. *You need to be the woman you were raised to be if you're going to survive this. Not every battle is worth fighting.*

Viktor is still smiling coolly down at me. "Ah, yes," he says, his voice almost mocking. "There's the woman I married. My *printsessa.*"

I feel myself tense at the nickname, but I force myself to keep quiet. There's another moment of silence, a beat where I know he's waiting for my retort, for me to fight back. But I don't. I just turn away, walking towards our bed without another word.

Tonight he doesn't read in bed next to me. He turns out the light the moment we're both under the covers, rolling away. I can feel the space between us, the yawning chasm of the mattress that we leave so that there's no chance of us rolling into one another in the night, waking up in each other's arms. I can't imagine, at this point, how that would feel. I don't want to try.

That night, I dream about the fight we just had. But in the dream, I don't back down. Even as I look up at his handsome face, his silver temples and creased eyes, I spit into his face that he'll never be a gentleman, that a man like him, Russian and Bratva, can only ever be a brute. I can feel the fear rippling through me in the dream, waiting for him to react like Franco would have, to grab me and shake me, slap me, throw me across the room.

But he doesn't. In the dream, Viktor smirks down at me, running a hand through his hair as his eyes rake over my body. *"Your mouth says you don't want me,"* he growls, leaning towards me until there's almost no space left between our bodies. *"But your body says something different. Your body says that you remember that night. That you crave the pleasure I can give you."*

He leans closer to me, his face hovering above mine as he grabs my arms, pulling me into him, letting me feel the hard ridge of his cock pressing against my thigh. "*You make me hard, little* printessa. *You want me to be a brute? Then I'll show you just how cruel the Bratva can be.*"

I should be terrified. I *am*, even in the dream. But I'm wet too, as he lifts me and throws me onto the bed, following me down as he rips at my clothes, stripping me naked. His eyes are hungry as they rake over my naked body, without anything to cover me now, not like our wedding night. He reaches for my breasts, grabbing them in handfuls, squeezing them. "*Small*," he growls, pinching at my nipples. "*But still enough for me to grab. To squeeze. To punish.*"

I can hear myself begging for him to stop, but my body is screaming something else. When he slides his fingers between my folds, I'm dripping for him, my skin flushed and hot, aching for the deep, hard thrusts of his cock as he pounds into me. I want it hard, rough, for him to take me however he pleases, and the shame of it makes me burn bright red as he grabs my hips, forcing himself between my thighs.

"*Take that Bratva cock, little princess,*" he snarls, thrusting into me hard, his huge cock filling me to my limit, filling me to the point of pain laced with pleasure. "*Take it all. Don't you dare come on it until I let you. Don't fucking come until I give you permission.*"

But I do. I can't hold back, my body shuddering with waves of pleasure, with the incessant thrusting of his cock deeper than any man has ever been before, again and again, until I feel as if he's touching every nerve, pleasuring parts of my body he's not even touching. He fucks me harder, growling that I'm a slut, wet and dripping for him and his cock, but I'm beyond caring.

My body clenches a second time, coming again with deep, rippling waves of an orgasm that seems to come from my very core—and that's when I jerk awake, panting and drenched in a fine sheen of sweat.

Oh my god. I can feel the insistent throbbing between my legs, the pulse of arousal, the stickiness of it on my thighs. I can *feel* how wet I am from the dream, and my face blazes with heat so intense I'm sure anyone could see me blushing even in the darkness.

I squeeze my thighs together, wanting more than anything to get up and run to the shower, wash off the evidence. But I don't want to risk waking Viktor. I don't want there to be any chance that he might somehow know I was just dreaming about him, wanting him, having an *orgasm in my sleep* because of him.

Nothing like that has ever happened to me before. I feel hot and anxious, lying there, wondering what on earth is wrong with me that I'm dreaming about a man I despise, aching for him, that he can coax an orgasm from me even in my dreams.

I hate him, I decide as I look up at the ceiling, both wanting to fall back to sleep and desperately trying not to. The last thing I want is to slip back into another dream like that—or at least, that's what I tell myself.

The insistent ache between my thighs tells a different story, though.

VIKTOR

I handle things differently in my business than in my personal life.

Which is why Stefan, one of my lower soldiers tasked along with others to guard the girls at the warehouse, looks pale as death and as if his teeth might chatter out of his head when he approaches me on the docks.

"What's happened?" I ask immediately, my voice tight and cold. I can see the ripple of fear that runs through him at that. *Good*, I think grimly to myself. It feels good to be in charge again. It feels as if my domestic life isn't entirely in control at home, not unlike my first marriage. It's made my temper at work much worse, but if that inspires my men to do their jobs more efficiently, all the better.

Tonight is Caterina's and my "date" to the Philharmonic. While I hope that it will be an uneventful night, I've learned over the past two weeks of our marriage that Caterina isn't necessarily the pliable and easy wife I'd expected to be delivered to me. She's stronger than I'd expected, and while the challenge might be pleasant under other circumstances, the coldness of our marriage bed has left everything between us stiff, awkward, and constantly on the verge of a fight.

Our marriage isn't the only thing that's stiff these days, either, I think, remembering my shower this morning. It's become a habit to jerk off quickly before Caterina wakes up, imagining our wedding night over and over again until I could retrace every single thing we did. I imagine other things too, things I'd do to her—that I *will* do to her if the clinic fails and I'm able to find a good reason to order her naked into my bed.

It takes the edge off enough for me to get through my day. Still, it leaves me irritable and frustrated, a man who has never had trouble getting a woman, reduced to hastily jerking his cock in the shower while his wife sleeps.

"Let's go inside, boss. We'll talk there," Stefan says, his voice nervous despite what I'm sure are his best efforts.

"You can tell me here, now," I snap, my irritation growing by the second. "What's happened?"

Stefan glances at the water next to the dock, as if uncertain whether or not I might throw him in once he's done speaking. He's already on thin ice—he's partially responsible for Anastasia Ivanova managing to weasel her pretty way into the ranks of my brigadiers and fuck enough of them to uncover what Franco and I had planned together. It had turned out, of course, that Franco was double-dealing both sides. He paid for that. Stefan and the other brigadiers were punished too—I can see the gap where Stefan's tooth once was. But clearly, he's fucked up once again.

"One of the girls escaped, boss," he says, his voice cracking a little. It would almost be amusing how terrified he is if I weren't on the edge of exploding with frustration and anger.

What isn't amusing is that he's let part of my shipment escape.

"You're fucking kidding me." I stare at him, and I can see him shrink under the iciness of my gaze. "Are you eager to lose another tooth, Stefan? Perhaps two? Should I have one of the men beat all of them out of your mouth?"

"No, boss." He's shaking now. "No, please. I—she tricked me. I let her out to use the restroom like you said we should let them. And she—"

"She came on to you, didn't she?" I can feel my jaw muscles working. "How many times have you incompetent fuckers been warned not to let your dicks do the thinking when it comes to *my* merchandise?"

"She said she'd suck me off for some extra food. We just needed to go into the corner, and—" he shifts uncomfortably, and it takes only a second for me to put two and two together and come up with Stefan possibly never getting an erection again.

"She bit your fucking dick, didn't she?" Again, I'd almost laugh if I weren't nearly incandescent with rage. "And then she escaped."

Stefan nods miserably. "Yes, boss."

"Where were the other guards?"

"They were, ah—"

I don't need him to finish the sentence, and now I'm fucking furious. I push past Stefan, nearly shoving him into the water without meaning to as I stride into the warehouse. "Alexei!" I shout out, my voice echoing in the huge metal building. "Alexei, get the *fuck* out here!"

When Alexei emerges, Mikhail is with him, one of my other brigadiers. Alexei is tasked with overseeing the warehouse operations, and clearly, he's doing a shitty fucking job of it.

"Yes, Viktor?" His tone is cool, almost insubordinate, and I narrow my eyes. I've heard rumors lately that Alexei has been complaining about my leadership, about the way I'm handling things. If he goes too far, I'll have no choice but to bring down the hammer on him. And that would be a shame since he's an excellent brigadier.

"I heard one of the girls escaped last night."

"That's correct." Alexei frowns. "We've got men after her, and they took dogs with them. She won't get far."

"If she got into the city, she could. And if she does that and fingers us as the ones who kidnapped her with intent to sell—" I let out an angry breath. "I can grease plenty of hands to keep us from being held responsible for that. But I'd rather not have to, especially when I have plenty of men tasked with guarding them. Men who, apparently, can't keep from getting their dicks wet long enough to stop themselves from sampling the merchandise."

"If you'd listened to me about not allowing them out of their cages—"

"If my men could avoid fucking them, it wouldn't matter!" I raise my voice, and even Mikhail flinches back at the anger in it. "These women are meant for sale to rich and powerful men. You think those men would be happy if they found out the cocks of the lowest Bratva had been in their new purchases only days before?" I grit my teeth. "If they touched one of the virgins—"

Alexei swallows hard, and I know then that today is going to be a bloody day. "What do you want me to do, Viktor?"

"Collect every man who was on guard duty that night. Bring them in here and line them up. We'll handle this the old-fashioned way."

Bloodshed doesn't usually please me, at least not when it comes to matters like this. I don't relish punishing my own men, certainly not torturing them or killing them. But in times like these, they leave me no choice. It's the unpleasant part of my position, a necessary evil. If they believe that this kind of behavior can go unpunished, my Bratva will descend into chaos.

A leader who cannot keep his men in line is no leader at all.

The fear in the room is palpable when Alexei has assembled the men. Most of them are pale, a few are sweating for reasons that have nothing to do with the humid interior of the warehouse, I'm sure. I can feel the cold sense of duty settling over me as I survey them, any emotion I might have had pushed aside in favor of what I know needs to be done.

"You know why you're here," I growl out as I pace in front of them. "Who gave you permission to steal from me?"

The men look nervously at each other, a few clearly not catching on. "Sir—I don't know—" one of them speaks up, I'm sure he thinks bravely, but it's only foolishness on his part. "We haven't stolen anything from you, boss," another manages, clearly bolstered by the first man speaking up.

"Yes, you have." I face them, squaring my shoulders as my gaze drifts from man to man. "What are the girls in this warehouse?"

There's a moment of silence, all of them trying to decide what the right answer is. In the interest of moving things along, I decide to help them out.

"The girls here are property. *My* property. So when you decide to give in to their attempts to seduce you and escape or fuck them for your own pleasure when you're supposed to be guarding them, or worse still, ruin one of the virgins, you are stealing from *me*. Do I seem like the kind of man that you want to steal from?"

"No, sir," they all stutter out, nearly in unison.

"It seems that you think I am, though. That you don't have the respect for me that I'm owed. Your *pakhan*. You call me *Ussuri*, but you think I am a toothless bear? Without claws?"

"No, sir!" One of them nearly screams it, the fear in his face evident. They all know the punishment for theft. Not one of them wants to endure it.

But there's dissent in my ranks because Alexei thinks I'm too soft. That I treat the girls too gently, that I'm too forgiving with my men. So that stops here. If the stories about me need to be true in order to command the respect of my men, then I will simply have to be the thing they fear.

"Stefan allowed the girl to escape. He succumbed to her attempts to seduce him and then failed to keep her from running away. For that, Alexei will take him to Oleg for a beating. Make sure he's not damaged too badly to be back to work within a few days."

Alexei nods, and Stefan immediately starts begging, apologizing, but I ignore him. Oleg is one of my enforcers, a huge man who enjoys using his fists and meting out punishment. Stefan won't be likely to repeat his mistakes.

"The ones who fucked the girls without permission," I continue, "will receive the punishment for theft. Only one finger, on the left hand, since I need them not to be too badly maimed. They will be expected to continue work as normal once the doctor has seen to them."

Some of the men are silent, others start begging just as Stefan did, but I raise my voice, speaking over them until silence falls again.

CAPTIVE BRIDE

"Except," I say coldly, scanning the line. "Except the man who fucked one of the virgin girls. Mikhail, bring him forward."

I don't know the man's name. He's new, I think, one of the recruits who joined the guard ranks recently. He's pale as death, and his eyes dart nervously around, unable to meet mine. The cowardice makes me even less inclined to show him mercy.

"You haven't only stolen from me and cost me money," I tell him coldly, my blue gaze boring into his. "You've also damaged this girl irreparably. Before, she would have been sold to someone who would have been willing to pay a price you can't dream of for a virgin girl to do as they command. They would have treated her well, given her luxuries and comforts. Now, because you've stolen her virginity, not only do I have to renege on a sale, but this girl will go somewhere less pleasant. A brothel, maybe, or to someone else for a lower price, someone less inclined to treat her as an expensive commodity." I glance at Mikhail. "Bring her out, too. She should see this."

The girl Mikhail brings out is extraordinarily beautiful, which only makes me angrier. We doubtless had a buyer lined up for her already, someone who would have paid an outstanding price for her. But now, she'll fetch only half. Maybe less. Beautiful girls are still worth a decent amount, especially one as striking as her, with strawberry blonde hair and flashing green eyes. But her virginity would have made her worth millions.

She's got fire in her, I can tell. She's glaring at me when Mikhail drags her out, her gaze shifting across the line of men suspiciously. "Are you about to give me to the rest of them?" she spits, twisting in Mikhail's grasp, and he rears back, slapping her hard across the mouth.

"Enough!" I shout, and everyone goes very still, even the girl, who is looking at me with bitter hatred etched in every line of her face. "Mikhail, she's damaged enough. Don't touch her like that again."

"Sorry, sir." He's holding her bound wrists, and when I walk towards her, she starts to struggle again.

"Easy." I croon to her like a nervous horse, reaching for her chin gently. "You're not going to be passed around. Nor is anyone going to hurt you. In fact, I wanted you to get to see what happens when someone *does* hurt one of Viktor Andreyev's girls."

She presses her lips together, looking at me through narrowed eyes, and doesn't say anything. *A smart girl who knows when to keep quiet.* It's a fucking shame she was ruined. A girl this beautiful and a virgin, who knows how to be silent for her master, is priceless in my world.

"Is this the man who raped you?" I point at the man standing at the front of the line, now shivering with fear as he looks at the girl. "Who took your virginity?"

The girl swallows hard. She looks at him and then back at me, as if unsure. Like a rabbit wondering if she's walking into a trap.

"Tell me the truth, and nothing will happen to you," I assure her. "If he did this, he is the one who will be punished."

She bites her lower lip, worrying at it, and for a second, I think she'll refuse to speak. I can't have her damaged further, so there's not much I can do to force her to tell the truth, either.

And then, the fucking idiot seals his own fate.

"She's a lying little bitch, whatever she says," he hisses, his eyes narrowed. "Don't fucking believe that whore."

The girl jerks back, flinching. I can see the moment of decision in her eyes when her face hardens, and she stands up straighter, squaring her shoulders. "He's the one," she says, her eyes flashing fire. "He took my virginity by force, fucked me in every way a girl can be fucked. It was him." She lifts her chin defiantly. "If you don't believe me, he has a black mole on his fucking balls."

"She's got a foul fucking mouth," Mikhail comments, tightening his grip on her wrists. "Want me to check for the mole, boss?"

"He can take down his pants himself." I nod at the man. "Go ahead. Take them down. If I have to have someone do it, you'll regret it, I promise you. I can make things much, much worse for you than they already are."

From the fear in his eyes, he knows I'm telling the truth. I can feel myself relaxing into the renewed sense of strength, of power over my men. It feels good to have it once more.

Slowly, he unbuckles his belt, undoing the fly of his black cargo pants and pushing them down his hips along with his underwear. His cock is shriveled from fear, and I nod towards it, my mouth twitching with cold amusement.

"Move that fucking dick, so we can see." Mikhail barks, saving me the trouble.

He obeys, his hands shaking. He knows what we'll see, a huge black mole on the right side of his balls, just as the girl said.

"Get your pants up." I look back at the girl. "What's your name?"

She's trembling now, although her expression is as defiant as ever. "It's Sasha. Sasha Federova."

"It seems you were telling the truth, Sasha. So this is how it will go." I glance at Mikhail. "Undo her restraints."

He hesitates, but one look at my face has him undoing the plastic cuffs that hold her hands behind her back. She jerks her wrists forward the moment they're free, rubbing them as she looks at me uncertainly.

Slowly, I pull out my pistol.

The girl makes a small, frightened noise. And then, as I raise it, I hear the sound of urine hitting the concrete floor and smell the acrid scent of it as the man in front of me pisses his pants.

"Sasha." I look at her, my gun still leveled at the man in front of her. "As recompense for what was done to you, you will no longer be for sale. You'll work in my house, as part of the staff. I'm sure my house-keeper could use the extra hands."

Her mouth drops open. "Thank—thank you," she manages, but I'm already looking at the man now, who is starting to cry, blubbering sounds that aren't even words.

"For theft of property in excess of millions and the violation of a woman without permission, I sentence you to death." I click the safety of my gun off, and the man starts to scream, a plea for his life. But it's too late.

I'm finished with him.

M JAMES

The sound of the shot cracks through the warehouse, and the stench of piss only grows as more than one man in the line next to him loses control. Sasha, to her credit, doesn't make a sound, although she's trembling when I look at her.

She's looking at the body on the concrete, blood pooling around his head.

"Have the other men clean this up while I take her back to my office," I tell Mikhail. "And then find Oleg when he's finished with Stefan, to take the fingers of these men for their theft. Let me know when it's done."

"Yes, sir."

There's not a sound from anyone in the line, despite what's about to happen to each of them. They're all shaking, pale and trembling, but no one protests. They all know now what could happen if they do.

For now, all thoughts of rebellion have been clearly quelled.

"Come with me." I jerk my head at Sasha, and she follows. She's in need of a shower and clean clothes, both of which she can get at my home, but I don't want Caterina to know anything about my business. For that reason, I stop her just before we get into the car.

"Where are we going?" she asks nervously. "Are you going to—"

"I'm not going to touch you," I reassure her. "You're going to work in my house, just as I told you. But I need to make something very clear to you. If you breathe a word, ever, about how you came to be here or anything in that warehouse, you will end up exactly where the man who violated you did. I don't like to harm women. In fact, I won't even pull the trigger myself. But I have men under my command who don't have the same scruples and will be happy to carry out that order. Am I understood?"

She swallows hard. "Yes, sir," she manages and then pauses. "Should I call you sir?"

"My name is Viktor Andreyev, but yes. 'Sir' is the proper address for me, especially in my home." I open the car door, gesturing for her to get in, and after a moment's hesitation, she does.

"As to where we're going, I'm taking you to my office, where you'll be cleaned up and given appropriate clothes. One of my trusted men, higher in rank than the man who dared to touch you, will take you to my home and introduce you to Olga, who is in charge of the house. She'll take over from there. My wife will likely be home as well, and she especially should hear nothing about the warehouse or anything that takes place there. Do you understand?"

Sasha nods. "Yes—sir. Yes, of course."

She remains silent all the way back to the building where my office is housed. I turn her over to one of the men, who promises to show her where she can get cleaned up and find her a change of clothes. I retreat to my office, where I know Levin will be waiting for me with any pertinent updates.

"I heard about what happened down at the docks," Levin says as soon as I walk in, headed straight for the sideboard where a bottle of vodka is waiting. "I also heard you handled it with remarkable—"

"Brutality?" I finish. I shrug, downing the first glass and pouring another. "It's been years since I've had to be so heavy-handed with them. But Alexei is stirring up trouble. Dissent in the ranks. I can't have it."

"Of course not." Levin hands me a file. "The information on the next shipment. The one you'll personally oversee while in Russia a few weeks from now."

I groan, taking another deep drink. I'd almost forgotten about that business trip. "Have you heard anything I should be aware of? Among the men?"

"Not really." Levin leans back against the wall as I flip through the file. "There are rumors floating around about your marriage, though. That your wife refuses your bed, that there was an appointment made at a fertility clinic. Which, of course, leads to rumors about your own virility, *Ussuri*. Questions about how much of a man you are. Questions which," he adds hastily, "I'm sure you put to rest today."

I grit my teeth, anger welling up again. "If I find whoever is spreading rumors about my marriage, what happened today in the warehouse will look like child's play."

"I don't doubt it," Levin says mildly. "Those rumors are feeding

Alexei's willingness to sow discord. And since you've made no move to punish him—" he shrugs.

"He's one of my top men." I rub a hand over my mouth in frustration. "If I'm too harsh with him, if I don't handle this gently, he could defect. He could make things worse."

"If you don't handle it at all, he *will* make things worse."

I let out a breath. "I'll think on it, Levin. Is there any other advice you'd like to give me?"

"Ah—" he catches my sarcasm and shakes his head. "Not at all."

"It seems like you want to say something." I narrow my eyes at him. "Go on. Say it."

Levin lets out a breath, watching me warily. "Just that—if your wife is the root of these problems, perhaps it would be best to lay down the law at home, as well. Cut out the problem at the source, and then Alexei will have nothing to go off of."

I toss back the rest of my vodka, eyeing Levin. "Don't think I haven't considered it. But Caterina is the lynchpin of the bargain I've made with the Italians. I can't force her. It could very well break the agreement we have, and that's tenuous at best. Not to mention—" I look away, unsure of how much I want to say to Levin. We're close—he's been my right hand for as long as I've had this seat. He worked for my father before that. But there's only so much of myself that I'm willing to allow out into the open.

But Levin catches on without my having to say much. "Vera," he says simply, and I nod.

"I don't want the same thing to happen to her. And not only for her sake." I glance back at him, and I can see the understanding in his face. "My children can't handle that again."

"Of course. You know best how to handle your family."

With that, Levin drops the subject and moves on to other things. But as we discuss business, I can't help hearing his last words over and over in my head.

You know best how to handle your family.

I just hope, this time, that it's actually true.

CATERINA

*V*iktor is unusually quiet, even for him, when he comes home from work.

I've spent most of the late afternoon getting ready for the performance tonight. This is the first time I've been out of the house for something like this since our wedding, and I'm cognizant not just of wanting to look good for myself, but because I know Viktor will expect it. He'll want me to be one of the best-dressed women in the concert hall tonight, not for his personal pleasure, but because of how it will reflect on him. His *business*, his standing with the other families.

It's nothing new to me, and I don't know why it grates on me so much with him. I was raised as a trophy for a man, an ornament in a pretty dress, to talk sweetly to others, organize the dinner parties and look pretty on the arm, to lie down and spread my legs later and never complain about any of it. I'd always known this was how it would be. I'd thought I was okay with it. I had been when I'd married Franco.

But it's as if something broke loose inside of me during my first marriage, and it's still rattling around inside of me, chipping away at those old ideas and ways of doing things. It's as if that one moment of possible freedom after Franco's death lodged inside of me, and now all I feel is restless and dissatisfied.

I wonder, if Luca had married me off to Viktor in the first place the way he'd tried to demand before Franco and I were wed, would I feel the way I do now? Or would I have settled into the role of wife to the *pakhan*, content to be ornamental and only moderately useful?

Or am I rebellious because I've been married to a Russian, the leader of the Bratva, and not to a ranking mafia man as I'd always believed?

I know there's some mocking there when Viktor calls me *printcessa*. It's a reminder that I was, and am, a mafia princess that was given to him, someone all Italian mafia consider beneath them, for his pleasure. To bear his child, live in his house, take his cock.

There's plenty of women who pity me, I'm sure. Women who will be in that concert hall tonight with their husbands, whispering about the poor Rossi girl who was sacrificed to the Bratva leader. Women who will laugh behind their hands at how far they think I've fallen. Who will say *poor Luca* for having to make that choice, and *poor Caterina*, for everything that's befallen me.

I don't want their pity. So it's for me, as much as for Viktor's whims, that I've dressed tonight. Because I want them to be envious when they look at me, not pitying.

The dress I'm wearing tonight is new, one that I chose and had delivered when Sofia first told me about the performance. It's a floor-length, crimson red Dior, with a stiff v-neckline that comes to a point at the base of my cleavage and curves over the top of each breast, into thin straps that cling to my shoulders and dive down into the impossibly low back, which stops at the base of my spine. I'm not sure what Viktor will think of it. It's sexier than what I usually wear and accentuates how thin I am. However, I've gained a little much-needed weight eating Helen's good cooking these past few weeks. I never want the girls to see me pick at my food, and so I force it all down whether I feel like eating or not.

I've paired it with my hair up in a perfect chignon. My makeup is light and understated, with crimson lips to match the dress and six-inch nude Louboutin stilettos. But the final touch is my jewelry, more of it that belonged to my mother, not gifts from any man.

The rubies I wore to my engagement party to Franco, blood-red against my skin, from the heavy necklace to the drop earrings to the huge cocktail ring on my right hand. I expect Viktor to say something when he walks in, whether it's to be angry over the sexiness of the dress or the expensive jewelry or to look at me with appreciation in his eyes.

But he does neither of those things. He simply pushes past me, headed straight for the bathroom without saying a word, the door closing sharply behind him after he grabs his own tux off of the garment rack.

I stare at the closed door, shocked and a little unsure as to what to do.

We don't have long before we're supposed to leave. I wind up pacing for a moment, checking my clutch purse to make sure everything I need is inside of it, and finally going downstairs without Viktor to wait for him. The last thing I want is for him to come out of the bathroom and see me hanging around like a puppy waiting for its master.

I want to feel powerful tonight. I want to feel like myself again, like I did once, before Franco. Happy, carefree, sure of my place in the world. It's going to be difficult, with Viktor at my side, a constant reminder that I'm none of those things now. But for one night, I want to feel something like happiness. I want to *enjoy* myself again.

His gaze lights on me for just a moment when he comes down the stairs. Olga walks into the room just then with Anika and Yelena to have them tell their father goodnight before we leave, and Anika ignores me entirely. *Like father, like daughter,* I think. But then Yelena squeals, pulling away from Olga and running towards me, and I feel my heart melt in my chest.

She skids to a stop a few inches away, looking up at me with those wide blue eyes that seem to take up most of her face. "You look like a princess," she whispers, her expression awed. "Like—like—" she screws up her face, clearly trying to think of a princess to compare me to. "You look *beautiful.*"

I reach down without thinking, scooping her up into a hug. "You're the real princess," I whisper. "The little princess of this house. You and your sister."

Anika makes an unpleasant noise. "She's not as beautiful as *our* mother was."

I hear Viktor reprimand her, but I'm too busy letting myself enjoy this moment, Yelena clinging to my neck, her warm little body in my arms. At that moment, I feel a rush of love that makes me want to be a mother to these girls and to have a child of my own.

Before long, I might have exactly that. The next appointment at the clinic isn't that far off.

"We need to go," Viktor says, cutting through my thoughts as Olga gently pries Yelena away from me. "Goodnight, girls. Be good for Olga. I'll see you in the morning."

He opens the door then, and we walk out into the warmth of the evening together, the car waiting in the driveway for us.

"Yelena seems to have taken a liking to you," he says, sliding in first as the driver holds open the car door, and I follow. "It's good that one of them has, at least."

"Anika will come around," I say quietly. "It's harder for her."

"Because of her age, yes." Viktor frowns. "She needs to learn to accept it, though. This is how things are, now."

Something about the way he says it makes me think he's not only talking about his daughter, and I glance sideways at him. "And how is it that things *are* exactly?"

"You're my wife," he says simply. "We are married and will remain so. You're the only mother these girls will have now, besides how Olga cares for them. And soon, God willing, they'll have a brother. Another child to liven up the household."

He sounds genuinely pleased at that, and as always, it surprises me how much Viktor seems to care for his children. In my experience, men in this world seem to view their children as commodities, pieces on a much larger chessboard. Boys to inherit or hold ranking positions, girls to marry off and strengthen bonds, more children to fill those roles in the future. They're not little people to be loved and cherished. They're pawns in a greater game.

But Viktor doesn't seem to think of his daughters that way. Whatever else I might think of him, he seems to really love his children. It makes a small part of me wonder what he'll be like with *our* child, what it would be like to see him hold our son in his arms. It almost makes me want to soften towards him, to give him more of a chance, and I have to pull myself back from that thought. Viktor might be a surprisingly good father, but that doesn't change the core of him.

Something that, as Olga said, can't be changed. He'll always be Bratva, always be a brute deep down. A man without the same kind of honor as the men I grew up with. A man looked down on by other men, who took his power by force and violence.

I know he'd say that so many of my family, and the other Italian families, did the same. But from all I know of the Bratva, it's different. It always will be.

"It's good to be out," Viktor says, surprising me when he breaks the silence again. "I haven't gone out much in a long time."

"No?" I glance at him. "I suppose it loses its shine after a while."

"I wanted to be with the girls as much as possible after their mother died." He sounds pensive, and I watch him curiously, wondering why he's saying so much. Viktor isn't the type to open up, or at least not from what I've seen of him so far. And certainly not to me, based on what I've seen so far as well.

"You're a good father." The words slip out before I can stop myself, and I can see from the expression on Viktor's face that it surprises him as much as me.

"You think so?" His face is carefully blank. "I would think a good father would have made sure that their mother lived."

I feel my heart skip a beat in my chest. There's no emotion in his voice, no way to tell what he means by that. My only consolation is my deep-held belief that Luca would never have given me to a man who murdered his own wife. Still, there's always the lingering question in the back of my head—*what if he didn't know?*

There's no point in letting your imagination go wild, I tell myself firmly as I fold my hands over my clutch in my lap, watching the city go by as the driver makes his way through downtown Manhattan towards the concert hall. There's certainly nothing I can do about it now, except to be careful.

In more ways than one. Setting aside my concerns about how his first wife died and my deeply ingrained hatred of the Bratva and all they stand for, I find Viktor more than a little intriguing. He's a more complicated man than I'd thought he would be, with layers that I find myself wanting to uncover, even as I tell myself that at his core, he'll be nothing but a Russian thug.

That's not the man that I see at home, though. Not the man who loves his daughters, who seemingly has regrets about the past that he can't keep from slipping out, even though I know he wants to keep his distance from me.

A man who could give me pleasure if I'd let him. But as much as I want to think I can keep my body and my heart separate, I'm not so sure that's true. If I give Viktor my body willingly, and then see him with his children, *our* child, eat dinner with him every night and see his small kindnesses, I'm afraid that my heart might follow where I've given my body. I'm so scared that I might want this to be a *real* marriage, not just a bargain.

I'm terrified that I might actually fall in love with a man who is everything I should never want to love.

I can feel his gaze on me as the car winds through traffic, running over my bare arms, my cleavage in the deep neckline of the red gown, the nape of my neck just below where my hair is swept up. I force myself not to think about how his lips would feel there, brushing over the soft fine hairs, down the back of my neck to that spot between my shoulder blades that he kissed on our wedding night, back when he was trying to pretend that this could be more than it is.

Viktor isn't a man capable of love, of a real marriage. How could he be? I think if I asked him, he'd say the same. So I have to protect myself. And the only way to do that and be sure is to remain cold to him in every way.

I just hadn't thought it would prove to be so difficult.

I sneak a glance at him and see him turned away, his profile silhouetted in the passing streetlights. It gives me a chance to look at him, just for a moment, without him noticing, to take in his features. His strong jaw, lightly stubbled, the silver at his temples, the lean, hard lines of his body in the tux. He's an astoundingly handsome man, with a cold elegance that's all the more attractive for the way I've seen it melt and burn on our one night together. And I suspect that was only the barest glimpse of what Viktor would be like in bed if we ever both let ourselves go entirely. I felt how leashed his control was, even then.

"We're here," Viktor says as the car pulls up to the curb, and I look away quickly before my husband can catch me studying him. He remains still until the driver comes around to open the door. Then he slips out, reaching for my hand to help me as I slide across, careful not to let the slit on one side of my skirt fall open.

I let him take it. My hand feels small in his, and I suck in a small breath as his broader hand wraps around mine, sending a shiver down my spine. I can't tell if he noticed. His face is as carefully impassive as ever, but I can feel my skin prickling, my heart starting to beat faster as we walk towards the concert hall, hand in hand.

So much pretending. I force a smile onto my face as we walk up the steps, trying not to think about how warm his hand is around mine, the calluses that I've always been curious about rubbing against my skin. Ranking men in the mafia don't have callused hands. It would detract from the elegance, the sophistication that the Italian men cling to with such fervor. What does Viktor do to have those rough spots on his fingers and palms?

I remember how they felt, running over my skin, and it sends a quiver through me that I hope he doesn't notice. When his hand slides to the small of my back, pressing against my bare flesh as he guides me towards our seats, I know he can't help but feel it.

When I dare a glance at his face, I expect to see mocking humor in his eyes, amusement at the fact that his touch is affecting me like this. But instead, all I see is heat in those blue eyes, melting the ice in them until I can feel the warmth of the desire in his gaze all the way down to my toes. I swallow hard, looking away from him as I take my seat between him and Luca.

Get yourself together, I shout in my head, clenching my teeth as I smooth my skirt out. *Nothing good can come of you mooning over him like a schoolgirl. You're supposed to hate him, resent him at the very least, not get damp between the thighs because he put his hand on your back.*

"Caterina!" Luca's voice is warm and pleasant as he looks over at me. "Sofia is going to be so glad that you came. I'm so happy to see you here. And you, Viktor," he adds, with just enough emphasis to make it clear that his pleasure at seeing Viktor comes a far second to seeing me.

"I wouldn't miss the chance to show off our newfound friendship," Viktor says, with that smile that doesn't reach his eyes. It's a smile that always chills me because it's hard to know what's lurking behind it, if there's something darker than even I'm aware of. I can't help but feel that there's something to him that I don't know about, something that would make all the stories I've heard about him and the Bratva make sense. Because right now, the man I see and the man I've heard tales about don't match up.

"I hope congratulations will be in order for the two of you soon," Luca says, glancing at me. "Sofia and I are so excited for our own child. Nothing could cement the bond between our families more than a child of the Bratva and the mafia coming together."

Viktor smirks. "We're doing *all* we can to hurry that along," he says coolly, and I can hear the veiled threat beneath his words. If he wanted to, he could complain to Luca that I'm not doing my duty, that I've demanded we take a more complicated route. Then, of course, I'd argue that forcing me to his bed constitutes harm, and it would be up to Luca to decide who is in the wrong—Viktor or me.

I'm not entirely sure, in that situation, whose side he would take. The last thing I want Viktor to do is suggest to Luca that I'm not fulfilling my part of the arrangement.

"I'm glad to hear it," Luca says, glancing away as Liam Macgregor's arrival interrupts the conversation. "Alone again?" he asks with a laugh, as Liam takes his seat and looks out over the balcony towards the stage.

"Aye," Liam says, his thick Irish brogue warming the room. "Perhaps your wife will have a lass or three she might be able to introduce me to after the show?" He winks at Luca, who frowns.

"Shouldn't you be looking for a wife and not a threesome?" Luca asks disapprovingly, and Liam lets out a deep belly laugh, loud enough that several other patrons in the audience look over at our group with an expression similar to the one on Luca's face.

"Ah, marriage has made you dull, aye?" Liam grins. "I remember the days when your exploits with women were the talk of the Northeast, from Jersey all the way down past Boston. A threesome was a slow night in your heyday, or so I hear."

"I'm a married man now," Luca says with a laugh, loosening up a little. "Devoted to one woman, and all of that."

"And quite a woman she is." Liam leans over, glancing towards Viktor. "I hope you're taking care of this princess, too? Quite a treasure Luca's entrusted you with."

I don't miss the warning in his voice, and I'm reminded of the wedding when Liam made it clear to me that he wouldn't tolerate any mistreatment of me on Viktor's part.

The tension between Viktor and Liam is palpable as Viktor's eyes narrow. "I think my marriage is none of your business, Irishman. *Aye?*" I can hear his accent thicken as he speaks, and to my absolute shame, I can feel my skin flush, that shiver running down my spine again.

I don't want *to want him,* I think desperately, and I hope that no one else can see the flush on my cheeks or that if they do, they attribute it to how warm it is in the concert hall.

Which, admittedly, isn't very.

"Not tryin' to start a fight," Liam says, raising his hands good-naturedly. "Just making sure that Caterina is safe, that's all. We all know what you Bratva are capable of."

I can feel Viktor's rising anger next to me, and my heartbeat quickens in my chest, anxiety rising. *I wish he'd just let me come alone,* I think miserably. I wanted to enjoy tonight, to have a night out in Manhattan, see my best friend play at her first public performance, and try to have a moment of peace and happiness. Viktor insisted on coming along, and now I can feel the rising tension between him and Liam.

"Enough," Luca says tersely, and I can feel the air rush out of me like a pricked balloon. "We're here for Sofia, not to fight. Caterina is fine, I'm sure?"

He turns his gaze on me, and I can feel the weight of it. Now would be the moment to speak up, to express any fears or unhappiness I have, but there's nothing I can say. Here is hardly the place, and besides, the only complaint I could muster is that I don't like being married to Viktor—which is no surprise. He hasn't harmed me, and my fears about him being complicit or responsible for the death of his wife are just those—fears. I have no proof, no real reason to think that.

"I'm fine," I say quietly. "Viktor and I are adjusting to married life."

"I'm glad to hear it," Liam says, but I can tell he doesn't entirely believe me. His voice is taut, mirroring the rigid set of Viktor's shoulders, but he leans back in his seat as the lights flicker and our attention turns to the stage.

My heart aches for a different reason when the audience lights dim and the stage lights brighten, and I see Sofia walking out to take her seat with the rest of the strings. I remember all too well when she'd thought that marriage to Luca meant she'd never play again, that the part of her life she'd worked so hard for was gone forever. And it's surprising to everyone. A wife of a high-ranking mafia member doing something like this is almost unheard of. But despite his firm hand with everyone else, it's clear that Luca is madly in love with Sofia now—that he'd give her just about anything to make her happy. And I'm happy for her, even if I am a little bit jealous.

Viktor doesn't bother to hold my hand through the concert. He sits ramrod stiff next to me, his jaw set, and I wonder if we'll end up having a fight tonight after we leave.

I don't want to. But I know that what I *do* want, right now, is something I shouldn't have. I let myself imagine, just for a moment, that we're happy tonight. That Viktor is holding my hand, his calluses warm against my skin, that we're going to laugh together later tonight and have drinks at some swanky Manhattan bar and then make out in the back of the car on the way home, stumbling into the house and trying not to wake the girls as we make our way to our bedroom, ripping off clothes as we go.

It's a ridiculous, even childish fantasy. Viktor and I don't have that kind of marriage—in fact, I'm not sure I would believe that *anyone* does, if not for Sofia and Luca. *She got lucky,* I tell myself as I sneak a glance at Viktor while the music swells, my chest constricting. Things could have gone so very differently for them. Luca hadn't wanted a wife or children. The connection they'd had that had turned a burden into a love story was one in a million.

There's no way that's in the cards for me. And imagining it, fantasizing about it, is only going to make it so much harder to live the life I actually have.

I close my eyes, trying to let the music sink in, to let it soothe me. But I can't lose the awareness of Viktor right next to me, the presence of him, this man that I'm now married to and will lie next to tonight, and every night after that.

I tried with Franco. I'd tried to be happy, tried to make it as real of a marriage as it could be. And hasn't Viktor shown himself to be a better man than Franco, in so many ways? Even if he is Bratva, he hasn't hurt me. He hasn't even really threatened me, beyond the reminder of what could happen if the contract between families is broken.

It could be so much worse. I *know* how much worse it could be. And there's a small part of me that thinks I shouldn't be fighting so hard to keep as much distance as I can between Viktor and me.

CATERINA

"You should come to the afterparty," Luca says when the concert is finished, and the lights come up again. "I know Sofia will want you to be there, Caterina. And of course, Viktor, you're welcome to come as well."

'I would hope so since I'm with Catarina tonight." Viktor's voice is still tight, rasping, and accented, and I swallow hard as I force myself not to look at my husband. I don't know if I feel desire or disgust right now. Not being able to differentiate between the two is one of the more confusing moments of my life.

The afterparty is at a downtown wine bar, and most of the orchestra is there. Sofia is in the midst of them when we walk in, still in the black velvet dress she wore to perform, her dark hair swept up and her eyes shining with pure happiness. She has a glass of water in her hand, and as she talks to a petite, pretty blonde woman, she touches her stomach gently.

It's such a sweet, automatic gesture that it makes something inside of me ache. I can easily imagine that being me. I think about the injection Viktor will have to give me later tonight and how much easier it might be if we did things his way—in one respect, anyway. For me, I don't know how much easier it would be. I can't let myself be hurt by another man who can't ever give me more than duty and bargains.

Even if he isn't hurting me directly, the way Franco did.

"You were amazing!" I tell Sofia enthusiastically when she makes her way towards us, hugging her tightly. "I'm so glad I was able to come and see you tonight."

"I am too!" Sofia returns the hug, squeezing me before taking a step back. "Oh my god, Cat, you look fucking *gorgeous*. That dress was *made* for you." She glances at Viktor, who is standing silently behind me, before taking in the dress one more time. "And that jewelry. You look like a princess."

I can't help but flinch inwardly at that, even though I know she means it as a compliment. "They were my mother's," I say softly. "I'm sure she'd be happy that I'm finding an occasion to wear them."

"I'm sure you must be very proud of your wife," Viktor says to Luca, ignoring both Sofia and me. "She played extraordinarily well."

"I am, and she did," Luca says with a smile, reaching for Sofia and sliding a hand around her waist. "But you're welcome to tell her that yourself. She's the one who worked so hard to be there tonight, after all."

I look at Luca, surprised, and even Sofia has a glimmer of startlement on her face. Men belonging to any crime family aren't known for being the most progressive, and for Luca to so pointedly hint that Viktor should be addressing Sofia and not him is unusual. I can see Viktor stiffen at the underlying rebuke, and my breath catches in my throat again. The last thing I want is for an argument to erupt here, especially, and ruin Sofia's night.

But Viktor turns towards her, a pleasant smile on his face, though I can still see a hard edge in his eyes. "You played exceptionally well tonight, Sofia. *Luca's* decision to let you accept the invitation to join the orchestra was well-founded. Tonight would not have been nearly as lovely without you as a part of the strings."

Sofia smiles, and I can see a tightness around her mouth, too. "Thank you," she says simply, and I can see that the mention of Luca "allowing" her to play galls her. But she can't exactly deny it—Luca was the one who gave her permission to accept. "It was more encouragement than permission, though," she adds, and I glance at her. Her face is fearless; she's clearly not afraid of Viktor, and I feel a sudden rush of affection for my friend. I remember a time when she was terrified of him, and of Luca and everyone else in the families too, but she's grown so much since then. She's truly flourished in her marriage.

I feel that small flush of jealousy again and do my best to push it down.

For the rest of the party, I stick to water as well, not wanting to give Viktor a reason to scold me. He drinks vodka while Luca sips red wine. The two of them discuss some mild business matters—a few shipments that they don't disclose the nature of, business trips in the future. Nothing particularly interesting or even all that damning—I've always known that the mafia deals in guns and sophisticated party drugs. My father, Luca, and all the rest are hardly blameless when it comes to illegal business.

It makes me wish that I knew more about what Viktor really does. I'd heard rumors about the sex trade, about filthy parties and slave trafficking, but I can't square that with what I've seen of Viktor. I know how easily rumors can spread—my father had more than a few about him over the years. Although, he successfully quelled them, usually through violence that put a swift end to it, and any others that might have sprung up shortly after. But I don't actually *know* what Viktor does—and part of me hasn't wanted to ask.

If I'm honest with myself, it's because I'm afraid some of it might be true.

It's a little after midnight when Viktor suggests we head home. I hug Sofia again, promising to make plans with her soon for lunch. I feel a knot in my stomach as we get into the car. Viktor is very silent next to me as the driver pulls into traffic.

"I'm surprised Luca allowed her to accept the invitation to join, honestly," he says, drumming his fingers on his thigh. "But I suppose after so much work on her part, it was best to let her get it out of her system before the baby comes."

I look at him with surprise. "You think Luca will make her quit after the baby? Because she hasn't said anything like that to me."

"Why wouldn't he?" Viktor glances at me. "She'll have a child. Her job will be to be a mother and a wife, supporting her husband in his position. Not—"

"Not using her talents?" I glare at him. "Not enjoying the fruits of years of work and study? A child doesn't take up every second of every day. My mother did nothing else, and there was still a nanny to make sure that she got plenty of 'me time.'"

Viktor shrugs. "It's very unusual, that's all. She clearly has Luca wrapped around her finger."

"Well, she's lucky then." I look away from him. "No girl born into this life expects to have a husband who gives a shit about what she wants out of her own life."

I feel Viktor flinch slightly next to me, probably surprised to hear me curse. It doesn't happen often. But he says nothing, and I can feel the space between us grow cold as the driver makes his way back to the house outside the city.

There's silence all the way until we get back to our bedroom. He closes the door behind us, and I let out a breath, which sounds very loud in the close, dim quiet of the sleeping house.

"I might need help with my necklace," I say finally, hating that I need to ask. But the clasp gave me trouble when I was putting it on this evening, and the last thing I want to do is break it.

"Of course," Viktor says neutrally, walking up behind me and reaching for the clasp. His fingers brush over the nape of my neck as he touches it, and I repress another shiver, not wanting him to see.

He pauses, his fingers lingering there. "Are you truly unhappy, Caterina?" His voice cuts through the silence, low and gruff, and I go very still, startled by the question. I can't help but feel that it's a trap, which makes me even more uncertain of what to say.

"I was born knowing that marriage would not make me happy," I say carefully. "I was always raised to know it would be arranged. I didn't expect a fairytale."

"So why is this so hard for you?"

I pause, choosing my next words very carefully. "Because I expected my marriage to be arranged with an Italian man. A mafia man. Someone who might not love me, and who I might not love, but who would at least be familiar. Who would know my family, and I theirs. Who was not my enemy, and my family's enemy."

"And I am?"

"The Bratva have been our enemies for decades. You know that, Viktor."

He undoes the clasp of the necklace, letting it slide down. I catch it in my hand, striding away from him towards the dresser where my jewelry box sits and taking longer than strictly necessary to put it away. I don't want to turn around and see his face, and yet at the same time, I do.

"We don't have to be enemies. You and I." He comes to stand closer to me, behind me, and I feel my breath catch at the nearness.

"I think it's time for my injection. Can you?" I'm not excited about getting yet another of the shots that will hopefully soon help me fulfill the one thing Viktor requires of me. Still, I also desperately want to change the subject.

Viktor lets out a sigh. "Of course."

Slowly, I push the skirt of my dress aside, the slit parting as I bare the side of one cheek. I bend over slightly, leaning against the dresser, very aware that this is much more sexual than my usual flowered or silky pajama shorts that I wear to bed. I can feel my heart speeding up a little in my chest when Viktor approaches, and it's all I can do not to let out a small gasp when his hand rests on the small of my back, holding my skirt aside.

The injection fucking hurts. It always does. I grit my teeth, glad for the momentary pain this time to distract me from the growing tension in the air between Viktor and me. It burns, but it's a better burn than the flush of my skin from him touching me or the heat in my blood from remembering the one and only time we did much, much more than dance on the edge of the tension between us.

I expect him to step away, but he doesn't. His hand stays there, resting against the silky material of my skirt, and I feel his thumb brush over the spot where the needle just sank into my skin.

MY SKIN FEELS as if it's burning where he's touching me. All night I've felt the tension growing between us, the touches and looks, the shivers down my spine, and the awareness of how handsome my husband is. I wish we'd never had to sleep together on our wedding night, because now I know how good it can be, that it could be even better if we learned each other, if I let him do what he wanted to that night and seduce me. Pretend, just for a little while, that we aren't a mafia princess and a Bratva *pakhan*. Two people who should be enemies but have been pushed into an uncomfortable marriage for the sake of peace.

A peace that I can't feel because everything in me feels like turmoil, like torment, like I'll never feel comfortable and safe and at home again.

I so desperately want to forget everything I was taught about what marriage would be for me, everything I've ever known about it, everything that marriage to Franco showed me about not trusting men, not putting hope in them. The small part of me that still craves love and happiness despite it all wants to believe it can be different this time. And that's the part of me that makes me turn around, knowing how little space there is between Viktor's body and mine, knowing that when I turn around, he'll be nearly touching me, up against the dresser.

My skirt falls back into place when I turn, his hand dropping to his side. His face is a hand's breadth away from mine, his blue eyes darker than I've seen them before, and I feel my heartbeat quicken when they drop to my lips.

I could let him kiss me. One kiss, to feel something again. I still remember how his mouth felt on our wedding day, cool and firm, his lips brushing over mine. They would feel different now. Warmer, maybe, full of desire instead. That kiss had been one for others, to seal our vows. What would it feel like for him to kiss me with passion, a kiss just for him and me?

Viktor takes a step forward, moving closer to me. I step back, but there's nowhere for me to go. I feel the knob of one of the drawers pressing against the small of my bare back, the metal cold against my skin as Viktor closes in on me, his hard, muscular body brushing against mine as he raises a hand to my face.

Those calluses. The roughness of his palm. I've never felt anything like it. He presses that palm against my flushed cheek, his thumb brushing over my cheekbone, and I can see the desire in every taut line of his face.

"You'll have to ask for me to kiss you, *printcessa*," he whispers. "I won't have you accusing me of forcing it. So kiss me first, or ask me." His thumb is pressing against my cheekbone, and I know he can feel how hot my skin is. "You feel so warm." His fingers slide down my jaw, his thumb pressing against my lips, pushing against the seam. I feel a sudden throb of desire at the thought of his cock there instead, the head pressed against my mouth. Franco had loved me sucking him before our wedding, but after he mocked me, telling me I wasn't good enough. Telling me how the other girls he fucked sucked him better.

Somehow, for all the cruelty I know he must possess deep down, I know that Viktor wouldn't do that. He'd groan instead, tell me how good it feels, urge me to take it deeper. He'd be rough, dominant, pushing all of that hard thickness that I saw on our wedding night down my throat, but he'd praise me for it. The thought sends another rush of desire prickling over my skin, and I can feel the damp silk of my panties clinging to me. I'm wet, aroused, aching for him.

And all I have to do is ask—or kiss him first. One word, one motion, and his mouth will be on mine, his hands. I can make him stop anytime, unlike Franco. I have that power over him, the power of threatening to go to Luca, to break all of this apart.

If you kiss him, you won't stop. As much as I want to deny it, I know it's true. I'm aching for something to make me feel again, to give me a rush, to pull me out of the dull routine every day that's become my life since I was married again. If I kiss him, if I feel his hands on me, I'll want to keep going. I'll want to feel his hand between my thighs, his cock, want him to make me come again, to give me a few blissful moments of pleasure.

"Caterina." He breathes my name then, not the nickname I hate so much but my actual name, and I feel my heart flutter in my chest.

Don't fall for it. It'll hurt so much more when you remember that there's no future in wanting more than what this is.

His hands drop to my waist, catching on the fine red silk of my dress. "I didn't tell you how beautiful you looked tonight. I should have."

"It's okay." I feel my breath hitch in my throat, the words a whisper. "We agreed not to pretend."

"It's not pretending for a man to tell his wife how beautiful she is. Especially when it's true."

The words hover in the air between us. *Just a kiss*, I think, looking at his mouth, a breath away from mine. *Just a kiss.*

I lean forward, my hand reaching for his face. I feel his stubble scrape against my palm, and my heart skips a beat in my chest again when I see Viktor's eyes close at my touch, hear his sigh as my fingers slide back into his hair. It feels soft to the touch, and I know I'm lost even before my face tilts up as his mouth leans towards mine, and I feel the hot brush of his lips.

It's all I can do not to arch into his body, not to pull him closer to mine. His mouth is as warm and soft as I'd imagined, not firm and tense the way it had been on our wedding day. I hear the groan deep in his throat as his hands tighten on my waist, feel the warmth of his tongue brushing over my lower lip, and I want more.

"Viktor—" his name slips from my mouth before I can stop myself. I feel my heartbeat in my throat, everything in my head screaming at me to stop, everything in my body screaming at me to keep going. His lips feel so good on mine, the slide of his tongue, warm and firm and making me think of what it might feel like to spread my legs and let him kiss me this way lower down, something Franco never did, something I've never experienced.

His hand slides up my waist, presses against my ribs. I breathe in, and then his hand slides higher, his thumb pressing against the boning in the neckline of my dress, his palm rubbing over my stiffening nipple, and alarms go off in my head.

I have to stop this. I have to stop it now, or I won't stop it at all, and then I'll have no more defense, no more high ground.

There will be no more fertility treatments, no way to stay out of Viktor's bed, no way to keep him from wanting this night after night until I fall into the trap I've been so desperately trying to avoid.

Before I can let it go any further, I bring my hands up, shoving them against his chest hard. "No," I breathe, breaking the kiss, turning my face away, and praying he doesn't choose this moment to lean forward and drag his mouth down the sensitive skin of my throat. "No, Viktor."

For a moment, he doesn't move, and I have a flash of fear, a memory from my marriage to Franco, of me saying no and him laughing in my face. *You're my wife. You can't tell me no.*

The fear is enough to push back my desire, to stop me cold in my tracks. I shove harder, pushing him a step back with sheer force, which is impressive in and of itself.

"Stop, Viktor!" My voice rises, and then to my surprise, Viktor takes several steps backward, putting an arm's length between us and then more as he retreats towards his side of the bed.

"Alright." He's still breathing more heavily than usual, and I can see the thick ridge of his erection, pressing against the trousers of his tux. "I'm not going to force you."

He looks so handsome, so devastatingly *sexy* in that moment that it's all I can do not to change my mind, not to follow him and push him back onto the bed. The thought of hiking up the silk skirt of my dress, straddling him, and guiding his thick cock into me makes me feel a rush of power—that I could have it if I chose. His hair is mussed from my fingers running through it, his lips reddened from the kiss, his eyes still full of heated lust as they rake over my body again despite his words. *I could have anything I wanted tonight.*

But that power would be fleeting. And once it was done, Viktor would have reclaimed all the power in our marriage that he'll ever need.

I spin on my heel, tearing my gaze away, and flee to the bathroom. The moment I slam the door shut behind me, I lean back against it, closing my eyes and wishing for my heart to stop racing.

I can't let that happen again.

CATERINA

I've never been so relieved to wake up to an empty bed the next morning. Going to sleep next to Viktor last night was excruciating. He'd made sure to have his light off by the time I'd come back into the bedroom, probably wanting to avoid me as much as I wanted to avoid him. For the first time, I'd considered ignoring his clearly stated wishes and going to sleep in a guest room.

Only the thought of his reaction and how little energy I had to fight about it or deal with any gossip that might happen, as a result, kept me from actually doing it. Instead, I'd curled up on the very edge of my side of the bed and listened to Viktor's soft snores as I stared at the closet door until exhaustion finally claimed me.

Now, getting dressed to go downstairs, I'm glad that I at least don't have to deal with him this morning. I throw on jeans and a t-shirt, scraping my hair up into a high ponytail, and head downstairs to have breakfast, trying not to think about how my days stretch out with so little to fill them. Olga still hasn't entirely trusted me to take care of Anika and Yelena, and they're at school for a good part of the day. The hours feel empty, and although I know I should join a gym or find some other hobby to fill them, I can't really find the desire to.

I'd thought that I would feel better once Franco was buried and I could make my own life. But now I'm just waiting again for the fertility treatments to be finished and to, with any luck, be pregnant. That at least will give me some kind of purpose. Something to focus on, something to do.

I'm barely paying attention to anything around me when I walk into the dining room, but then the moment I walk in, something stops me in my tracks. A girl is standing at the mantle of the fireplace, dusting it slowly, looking for all the world like she has absolutely no idea what she's really doing.

She's also not someone I've ever seen in the house before. I'd have remembered her—the girl has lovely strawberry blonde hair, more red than blonde really, which is currently braided back with flyaways escaping everywhere. She's staring at the mantle intently, so much so that she doesn't hear me come in until I clear my throat. She spins around, looking as guilty as if she were chipping away at the wood instead of cleaning it.

"I'm sorry!" she chirps, her eyes skittering over me. "I didn't hear you come in, miss.—Ms.—Mrs.—"

"I'm Mrs. Andreyva." The name sounds strange on my tongue; I'm not sure if I've referred to myself that way before. It hadn't felt so odd to change my name to Bianchi from Rossi. That had been another good Italian name, the syllables and rhythm of it comfortingly familiar. But there's nothing familiar about my new, longer last name, or how it changes from Viktor's to reflect the feminine, or the...*Russianness* of it. It feels as if it should belong to some other woman. Certainly not me.

"Are you having your breakfast in here, then?" Her voice has a lilting Russian accent, her voice more melodic than Olga's, making it prettier. "I'll go, so I don't bother you."

"No, wait." The moment I speak, she freezes in her tracks, like a deer in the headlights. "I like to know the staff. What's your name? You must be new."

"I am." She inclines her head, looking up at me through pale lashes. "I'm Sasha. Sasha Federova. Your husband hired me recently—I am new. New staff, that is. I'm sorry if I've done anything wrong—"

"You're fine," I tell her gently. "But I'm sure Olga has something for you to do if you want to stop polishing that mantle."

"Of course, ma'am!" She bobs a *curtsy* of all things, as if she really doesn't know what to do, and flees the room before I can say anything else, ostensibly in search of Olga.

There's nothing really strange about it on the surface. I have no idea, really, how Viktor's household is run, how the hiring of staff works, how often they bring on someone new. I haven't been here long enough to really figure it out, and Viktor doesn't exactly talk to me much about the running of the place. Neither does Olga, who I privately think doesn't want me taking over much of her duties from her, regardless of whether or not I *should* have more of a say in the running of things technically, as Viktor's wife. I've been fine with that because I was raised to run a good Italian household, to know how to behave and speak to and defer to the Italian men. These mafia men would come to dinner and expect to be served. How to entertain *their* wives, what to talk about, what to do. I don't know how any of that is meant to work in the Andreyev household, and Olga doesn't seem inclined to teach me.

But something seems off about Sasha. I can't put my finger on it, and I don't know really what *could* be wrong, but it's just a gut feeling that something isn't quite right.

What if Viktor has her here for himself? What if her being part of the staff is just a front for him to have an outlet for pleasure since I won't have sex with him?

The idea that he might have some girl here, coerced into sleeping with him, makes me feel a deep wave of guilt. Would he be doing that if I *were* fucking him? I have no idea what Viktor's ideas about fidelity within marriage are, particularly a marriage of convenience. Would he do something like that even if I *was?*

Stop, I tell myself firmly, forcing myself to take a bite of my breakfast and then another. *You have no idea if that's even what's going on. There's no reason to believe that. She could just be nervous about a new job.*

The pit of anxiety stays in my stomach, though, all the way through breakfast and until Olga comes to find me to tell me that

Viktor wants me to pick up the girls from school before lunchtime and bring them to see him at his office.

"Why?" I look at her curiously, and she shrugs.

"Sometimes, he likes to have lunch with them. He's already called the school to say they're being picked up."

"And the school was fine with it?"

Olga smirks. "No one tells Viktor Andreyev no. Not even you," she adds, with a hint of warning in her tone.

I feel a small rush of satisfaction at that because the fact is, I *have* told him no. Just last night, in fact, and he backed down. It makes me wonder if he feels something more for me than just duty and obligation because everything I hear tells me that there's a side to Viktor that I don't see. That I don't know about. I don't know if it's terrifying or encouraging that he's clearly made concessions for me that he won't make for others.

A little before noon, I go to pick up Anika and Yelena—or rather, I sit in the back of the car as the driver takes me to go and get them. It's not unusual for me—a driver came and got me from my private Catholic school when I was a child. Still, I can't help but wonder what it would have been like to be a normal child, riding a bus or being picked up by a parent, or to pick up my child on my own. I've never really craved a more ordinary life, but sometimes I think it must be simpler to not have so many restrictions on what you can and can't do. To not have the weight of so much expectation.

To have more freedom. A thing I'll never really have—and neither will Anika, nor Yelena, or my as-of-yet-unconceived child, no matter how much I love them or their father loves them.

The girls are both smiling ear-to-ear when they pile into the car—at least until Anika catches sight of me, and her face falls. *"You're coming along?"* she asks, her voice suddenly brittle, and I'm amazed at how much she sounds like her father when he's angry.

"I'm glad she's here," Yelena says, pushing her lower lip out and glaring at her older sister. "Why are you so mean?"

"I'm not mean." Anika looks stubbornly out of the window. "She just doesn't belong here, that's all."

It's hard to argue with that. *I don't really feel that I belong here.* "You know," I say gently to Anika as the driver pulls away from the curb, "this wasn't my choice. Your father picked me, and I didn't really get a say in it."

To my surprise, Anika actually looks at me then, her face pensive. "You could have told him no."

I hesitate, unsure of how much to say. I don't want to be the reason either of the girls think differently of their father. "Someone that I couldn't say no to asked me to agree to marry your father," I tell Anika carefully. "It's very complicated. It wasn't as simple as just saying no."

She wrinkles her nose at me. "Is this where you tell me I'll understand when I'm all grown up?"

I have to stifle a laugh at that. "No," I say gently. "It's something I hope you don't *ever* have to understand. But I don't know what your father's plans for that are when you're older. And that's something you have a long time before you need to think about."

"I wouldn't marry anyone I was told to," Anika says, lifting her chin. "I don't even want to get married. Boys are gross."

I don't argue with her. Far be it from me to be the one who tells Anika that most likely her father will marry her to someone that is advantageous for him, just as I was married to Viktor because it was beneficial for both of our families. One day, if it happens, I'll be there for her to comfort her and help her through it, just as my mother tried to do for me when I was growing up. But for now, I want to let her believe that choice will be hers to make.

The girls scramble from the car when it pulls up to the curb at a high-rise building, one that I assume holds Viktor's offices. "Wait for me, Anika," I call out, holding Yelena's hand tightly as we slide out of the door the driver is holding for us. Yelena clings to my hand, and a warm feeling washes over me, reminding me that things will be better when I'm comfortable taking care of the girls and when I have a baby of my own.

They need me. My own child will need me. And that should give me a purpose, at least.

"Girls!" Viktor meets us at the elevator when it opens at his floor, his smile bright and all for them. He glances at me but quickly gathers Anika and Yelena up, telling them that he has lunch all set up in the conference room as soon as he grabs something from his office.

I follow them in, looking around as I take in my surroundings. The office is simple, with a long desk near the window, clear except for a calendar and a stack of files, with two more boxes of files next to it. There are leather chairs for seating, a bookshelf, and a bar cart, but it's hardly a homey space. I can see why Viktor prefers to be home instead of long nights at the office when he's able.

"I can see *everything!*" Yelena pulls away from my hand, tearing towards the floor-to-ceiling window that makes up the back of the room. I hear footsteps come in behind me just as she pulls away, and Viktor says: "Alexei—" just before she knocks into the boxes of files next to the desk, sending them sprawling everywhere.

"Yelena!" Viktor snaps in a voice I've never heard him use before. But I can't move because all I can see are the files and papers spread across the floor, scattered by Yelena's clumsiness.

There are pictures of girls on the front page of every file, with their details—names, height, age, weight—and below that, I see numbers. Figures. Projected sale prices.

My stomach turns over, and I back up, nearly running into Alexei. I see his smirk, and I push past him out into the hallway, unable to breathe.

"Alexei, go look after my wife," I hear Viktor say from a distance, my ears ringing as if I'm hearing him from the end of a long tunnel. "Girls! Sit down, right now, while I clean this up. Don't move!"

"Mrs. Andreyva?" Alexei's voice is behind me, and I straighten slowly, meeting his pale blue gaze. I can see the mocking expression on his face, the smirk on his lips. He doesn't like me, I can tell. Maybe he doesn't like me because I'm Italian, or because he thinks I'm not good enough for Viktor, or because he hated my father—who knows? I don't, and at this moment, I don't even particularly care.

"I'm fine." I lick my dry lips, trying to *look* as if I'm fine because I'm not really. But I don't want Alexei to know that, or Viktor either.

"You didn't know what your husband did for business, did you?"

His smirk grows. "You've been in the dark this entire time about the man you married."

"I've heard rumors." I force out the words through a mouth that feels as if it's filled with cotton. "I didn't know how true they were."

"What are you going to do now? Run back to Romano?" The taunt in Alexei's voice is clear. "It won't help you. He knows what Viktor does. He thought he was saving Sofia from that fate when he shot up a hotel room to bring her home."

Luca knows? *Of course, he does,* I tell myself. *Don't be stupid.* Liam probably knows too, my father probably knew, and anyone else who does business in our world. It's just that I was shielded from it, insulated, and I'd let myself believe that it was all rumors. That something so awful couldn't really be true.

Viktor steps out, motioning for Alexei. "Caterina, take the girls for a minute," he says, as coolly as if I didn't see anything at all. "I need to speak with Alexei."

My heart is racing in my chest as Anika and Yelena step out into the hall. "I'll be with you in just a minute," Viktor says, stepping into the office with Alexei and shutting the door.

I still feel as if I can't breathe. How am I supposed to sit here and have lunch with my husband and his daughters as if everything is okay, as if I didn't just see files of other daughters that Viktor is selling to the highest bidder?

I have to get out of here. I need air. I need something familiar, somewhere that I can think for just one goddamned minute. But I'm not about to abandon Anika and Yelena in the hall, either, or send them back into the office where I'm sure Viktor and Alexei are dealing with the scattered files right now, where they could see the truth of what their father does.

Who he really is.

"Come on, girls," I say with authority, speaking like their mother for the first time. "Your father is busy. Let's go. We'll see him at dinner tonight."

"He said to wait." Anika narrows her eyes. "We should stay."

"We're going." I don't let her pull her hand away. "Come on. Your

CAPTIVE BRIDE

father wants me to take care of things when he's not able to. He's said so himself. I'm supposed to take care of the two of *you*, especially. So that's what I'm doing."

"What about lunch?" Yelena is pouting, clearly on the verge of tears. "I'm hungry."

"We'll get lunch. Anything you want," I promise.

"Even hot dogs?" Yelena is perking up at the sound of that, although Anika's spine is ramrod straight, her small nails digging into my hand in an effort to pry herself away still. "Papa never lets us have hot dogs."

"Hot dogs it is," I promise. "But come on, now. We need to go."

Anika is still having none of it, but she's a child, so it's not that difficult to hurry her along. My heart is in my throat as I take both girls towards the elevator, waiting for Viktor to step out and shout after me, asking me where I think I'm going. I know he's going to be angry with me later, but I can't bring myself to care. All I know is that I have to get out of here. I can't stay in this building another second, or I feel like I'll go insane.

I don't want to use Viktor's driver, either. He'll either tell me I can't leave or refuse to take me anywhere other than back to the house, citing Viktor's instructions. So instead, I pull out my phone, calling an Uber.

"What are you doing?" Anika asks suspiciously. "The driver is right downstairs."

"We're going to have an adventure," I tell her cheerfully. "You like adventures, I know that. Just like that girl who explored the garden. We're going to have a fun afternoon, take a drive through the city, eat hot dogs, and you'll get to see a very old house." I'm sure Yelena, at the very least, will be fascinated with my parents'—and now my—mansion just outside of the city. Anika is a tougher nut to crack, but she might like it too. My parents had a much more old-fashioned style of decorating, and I hadn't had a chance to update the house since they passed.

"As long as we get hot dogs," Yelena insists, now fixated on that for lunch.

I manage to get the girls out of the building and away from where the driver is waiting, slipping into the Uber without being seen. Viktor must still be upstairs because my phone hasn't started ringing, nor has anyone come after us. But I turn my phone off, just in case. I need time to think, and I can't do that with him trying to get in touch with me.

He wants me to take care of the girls, so he's going to have to trust me to do that, just for one afternoon.

I try to keep the girls from seeing how distraught I am, and lunch proves to be a decent distraction. Yelena is in her own happy little world with the junk food, and even Anika seems somewhat mollified by it, all the way until the Uber drops me off at my old house.

"We should go home," Anika says firmly. "This isn't home."

"This is *my* old home," I tell her, squatting down so that I'm at her eye level. "I just need to get some things from here, that's all, and then we'll head back. Would you like to see the garden? There's a beautiful one out back."

Anika narrows her eyes, but I can tell that she's tempted. "Okay," she finally relents. "Show me the garden."

Her tone is a little demanding for a ten-year-old, but I don't fight it. The last thing that I need is her angry with me, which will just make all of this so much harder. I know Viktor will be furious, and a knot of dread is steadily settling in my stomach, reminding me that this was probably a bad choice.

But it's too late now. And I just couldn't face going back to him, or back to the house that doesn't, and will probably never feel like mine.

Anika is temporarily placated by the garden, which is as beautiful as ever despite the fact that I don't live here any longer. The trust my parents left me, which I hardly need after my new marriage, has been going towards the upkeep of the house until I can decide what to do with it. My mother loved roses, and there are still sprays of them everywhere, climbing lattices and blooming on bushes. The garden is immaculately manicured, and Anika runs up and down the cobblestone paths, pointing out the names of flowers she knows and asking me to identify ones that she doesn't. It's the most she's ever opened up to me, and I feel a warm flush of happiness that it's here, in my mother's garden, a place that always used to bring me so much happiness too.

"I have something fun for you girls upstairs," I tell them, when Anika is finally starting to tire of the flowers. Yelena is clearly tired, and I need a moment to myself. I have the idea that I can put Yelena down for a nap and ask Anika to keep an eye on her while I make some excuse to slip away, and there's a room already perfect for that. I'd started working on a nursery from the moment Franco and I had begun trying for a baby. There's already a room with a daybed and toys that I'm sure either of them will be happy to play with.

I just need a minute to think, alone. To decide what to do next.

Anika is less than pleased, as I'd imagined she would be, but I manage to convince her to settle in with some of the dolls and keep an eye on her sister, who is already yawning and curled around a stuffed bear on the daybed. "I'll be back in a few minutes," I promise her. "I just need to look for some things in my old room."

The moment the door shuts behind me, I let out a sigh of relief. The room—*my* room—feels like home, more so than it ever did before I'd left for my marriage to Viktor. It smells like my perfume and the familiar scents of the lavender drawer sachets I always used, like the detergent used on my sheets, like the candles I picked out, rose and honey-scented and still sitting on my bedside table.

The sudden feeling of home, of safety, overwhelms me along with all of the feelings I've been shoving down since I walked out of the building, feelings about what I saw in Viktor's office, grief and guilt, and fear and disgust. I sink onto the edge of my bed, pressing my face in my hands.

For the first time since that first afternoon in Viktor's house, I start to cry.

Here, with no staff to eavesdrop, I let myself go, crying in great, huge gulping sobs, gasping for breath between each one. I'd married one violent man only to have him die and go straight into the arms of another, and now all my fears about what he might have done to his first wife come rushing back, overwhelming me with the force of them.

Can I be married to someone like this? I don't know what choice I have, really—Alexei was telling the truth, I'm sure, when he'd said that Luca would know about this. That, in and of itself, feels awful. But what hits me hardest, right at this moment, is the question of how I can bring a child into this world, a *son* especially, who will inherit that terrible business from his father.

I can't understand how a man who loves his daughters as much as Viktor does can sell the daughters of other men, traffic in human flesh, and then come home and look his children in the eye. But even more awful than that is the thought of raising a son who will believe that it's okay, that it's his birthright, a son who will carry on that horrific trade.

The betrayal feels fierce and painful, like Franco all over again, only somehow worse because it's not just me that will be affected by this. It's the child Viktor has demanded, too. And I don't see any way out of this, not without causing bloodshed that will affect other children, other families, cause more death, and more grief.

There's no good solution, and suddenly this new world that I've married into feels even more terrible than the one I inhabited before.

I curl into a ball on my bed, pushing my face into my pillow and breathing in the familiar scent of my own bed as I cry and cry, wishing I could disappear, stay in this room forever, never go back.

I don't mean to fall asleep. I don't even realize that I have until the pounding on my bedroom door jolts me awake, sending a bolt of pure fear through me as I hear Viktor shouting my name on the other side, his voice so full of vicious fury that I feel like I might throw up.

That's the moment when I know I've fucked up.

And I have no idea what's going to happen next.

VIKTOR

I can't remember the last time I was this angry. The absolute, incandescent rage that I feel in this moment goes beyond what I'd felt even in the warehouse when I'd discovered what the traitorous guards had done with the women held there. This feels different, even more intensely personal, and worse still because of who is at fault.

Caterina.

My *wife*.

The woman I'd chosen to be a mother to my daughters, to protect them, to take care of them. And she pulled *this shit*.

I'm so angry that I know I shouldn't be standing here right now. I don't have enough of a hold on my emotions to keep from doing something I might regret later, but at this moment, I'm to lost to care.

I'd thought, for one terrifying second, that she'd taken my children and run away with them after seeing the files scattered on the floor. I'd feared all along that it would be too much for her, which is why I'd done my best to keep it from her as much as possible. But I hadn't expected her to scoop up the girls and take them with her.

Losing my wife would have been one thing. But there's a small dark part of me that thinks I might have killed her myself if she'd tried to run farther than this with them.

As it is, I'm going to punish her for what she's done. And I don't intend to be gentle or merciful about it.

But no matter how hard I pound on the door, she doesn't answer. "I know you're in there," I growl, banging my fist against the heavy wood. "It'll be worse for you the longer you hide from me."

Silence, and then I bang on the door again. "Caterina, you can come out, or I'm coming in there to get you. It's your choice."

I hear what sounds like a small, gasping sob from the other side, but I'm beyond feeling sorry for her. I take a step back, my body tensing as I lash out, kicking the door latch as I feel the rage pulse through me, a feeling of absolute, complete loss of control. All I can think about at this moment is breaking down the door, dragging her out, and making it clear to her beyond a shadow of a doubt that what happened today can never, ever fucking happen again.

Caterina clearly thinks that she has more freedom in this marriage than she does. But after today, it's going to be very clear who has the power. Who is in charge.

If she believes I'm nothing but a Bratva dog, then I'll treat her like my bitch.

The door creaks with the first kick, splinters with the second. The third breaks it open, sending it swinging into the room and giving me a clear view of the bed and the tear-streaked face of the woman atop it.

"I told you I was coming in here to get you," I snarl, striding for the bed and reaching out to capture her even as she starts to squirm backward, trying to get out of reach. I manage to grab her wrist, and I haul her forward, dragging her across the bed as her face turns white with fear.

"What the *fuck* did you think you were doing, running off with my children like that?" I stare down into her dark eyes, wide and terrified, and I know that I'm frightening her as much as her first husband ever did, maybe even more. But I can't bring myself to care right now. All I can think about are Anika and Yelena, what they must have thought when Caterina brought them here, what she might have told them.

I'm not even sure she fully understands what she saw. But she must have gotten a pretty good idea, considering her reaction.

"I just needed some space!" Caterina's voice is high and breathy, full of fear. "I didn't mean to fall asleep. I was coming back, I swear!"

"Why should I believe you?" I glare at her, feeling my face reddening with anger. "You didn't bother telling anyone where you were going. Does that sound like someone I should trust? Someone who's word I should believe?" I grit my teeth, feeling my chest heave as I try to catch my breath. "*Fuck* you, Caterina. You've behaved as if I were beneath you from the moment you agreed to be my wife. You think I'm nothing but a beast? Nothing but a Russian dog? Then I'll show you how brutal the Bratva can be with those who cross us."

"Viktor, I—" Caterina starts to speak, but I grab her chin, pulling her forward as I stare down into her eyes.

"There's nothing you can do to escape punishment now, little *printsessa*," I growl. "But you can learn a lesson from it, perhaps."

"What—what are you going to do?" Caterina's voice is small, barely a whisper.

Mine is low and deadly, almost mocking. Darker than even I've ever heard it, as if I've found a devil inside of myself that I didn't know existed.

"Wait and see."

I grab her shoulder, twisting her so that she's flipped over on the bed, bent over the mattress with her feet pressed against the carpet. I half-climb onto the mattress myself, pushing my knee into her back so that she can't escape as I grab her jeans and yank them down. She's still too thin, thin enough that I can yank them down without unbuttoning them. Caterina lets out a yelp of protest as I pull her panties down with them, leaving her small, pert ass bare to the cool air of the bedroom.

"Put your hands flat on the bed in front of you," I tell her, my tone low and threatening. "And don't move them. If you do, it'll be worse for you. This is your last chance to keep me from sending you back to

Luca. If I do, I'll make him regret ever bargaining with me in the first place."

"Viktor, please—"

"Shut up!" I can feel myself almost shaking with rage. "You made me wonder where my children were, Caterina. You made me fear things that I have gone to great lengths to never have to fear. You've been playing your own game with me since the day we married, but that stops now."

I step back, unbuckling my belt and pulling it out of the loops, and I hear her soft sob of fear at the sound. But I'm past caring. "I've been too soft with you," I growl, looking down at her pale, trembling body, her fingers clutching at the duvet in front of her. "I've allowed you too much freedom, too much trust—and look at what the result was. I tried not to be as brutal in my home as I so often have to be in the outside world." I fold the belt in my hand, feeling the warm leather against my palm. "But that changes now."

And then I bring the belt down across her ass, leaving a red mark in its wake as it strikes her lily-white skin.

Her cry awakens something in me, something deep and dark and primal. Over the course of my life, I've very rarely explored this side of myself, rarely even let myself fantasize about it. My first wife would never have entertained even the slightest idea of such a thing. I'd never punished her like this—I'd never felt the need to. She was spoiled and bratty at times, but it had been more of an annoyance than anything else.

She'd never driven me to this point. And she'd never aroused anything like this in me.

With the first yelp from Caterina, the first red mark across her ass, my cock is instantly erect, hard, and throbbing, nearly painful with the sudden rush of violent lust that I feel as I bring the belt down across her ass again and again.

"Viktor, please!" She reaches back as if to stop me, her toes digging into the carpet as she tries to arch away from me, and I bring the belt down on her upper thighs, lashing it across the spot where she won't be able to sit down tomorrow.

CAPTIVE BRIDE

"Put your hands back on the bed," I hiss, my voice choked with anger and lust. I've never felt such a complicated rush of emotions before, fury and desire and need and violence all tangled up until I can feel my pulse throbbing with it, making me almost dizzy as I bring the belt down again. "If you try to get away again, or move your hands, we're finished, Caterina. I'll send you back to Luca, and I'll destroy every fucking thing you love."

"You already have," she sobs, but her hands go back in front of her, fingers spread and digging into the duvet as I lash the belt across her ass once more. "You—this life—it's all destroyed everything I loved. Everything I hoped for. Everything—ah!"

She cries out again, and I feel my cock lurch in my trousers as I see her thighs spread just a little in anticipation of the next blow, the puffy, pink lips of her pussy showing at the apex of them. And then, just as I'm about to bring down the belt again, I see something that pushes me to the edge of nearly losing control, my cock throbbing until I think I might come then and there from the sheer eroticism of it, appealing to the darkest corners of my nature.

She's fucking *wet*.

I can see it, glistening on her skin, her folds swollen and damp with arousal. She's nearly crying into the duvet, her flushed cheek pressed against the mattress, but I can see the undeniable evidence that this is turning her on, too.

"You fucking like this, don't you, *printsessa?*" I croon, my voice still full of anger but with a mocking note now. "You claim you don't want to come to my bed, you claim that I'm hurting you, but your pussy tells me a different story. You're dripping like a needy whore after a few good strokes." I reach down, adjusting my painful erection. "You crave this cock, even if you don't want to admit it. This thick Bratva cock that made you come on our wedding night despite yourself." I bring the belt down across her ass again, and this time her body jerks, her thighs squeezing together as she lets out a whimper that's nearly a moan.

Christ, if she keeps this up, I'll come on the spot. The sight of Caterina squirming half-naked on the bed as I spank her, her reddened ass and dripping pussy, and the sound of her squeals and cries has me wanting things I never knew I desired, craving dark and depraved acts with my wife that I would never have imagined before.

She's awakened a beast inside of me, and I've never felt so hungry as I do right now.

"No," Caterina whispers. "I don't want it. I don't!"

"Either your mouth or your pussy is lying." I bring the belt down again, hard, and she nearly screams, shoving her face down into the duvet to muffle it. "And I think I'd wager I know which one it is."

"Viktor, please!"

"You keep saying that." I feel my cock throb at the sound of leather hitting flesh once more. "You've used up all my patience, Caterina. There's no more mercy for you from me."

I take a step back, my cock nearly tearing through my fly by now, my fist wrapped around my folded belt. Her ass is red and flaming, her thighs squeezed together so that I can barely catch a glimpse of that sweet, swollen pussy. Her face is invisible to me, buried in the duvet as she sobs with a muffled sound.

Finally, she lifts her head, turning her face towards me with an accusing glare as she sees my erection, a thick and straining ridge against the fabric of my pants. "So what?" she asks, her voice pained, but still defiant despite it all. "What are you going to do now, Viktor? Force me to fuck you? Take me here on the bed while your daughters are a few rooms away? Spread my legs and force your way into me?"

I smirk. "For one, the girls are already headed back to *my* home. I had Alexei collect them and take them back while I—tended to you. But as for your other questions, no." I step towards her, and I see her flinch, her thighs tightening in anticipation of another stroke. But I'm done spanking her—for now at least.

"I'm not going to force you," I continue, reaching out to touch her thigh, the skin warm where I brought my belt down on it. "But you'll come to see the error of your ways, and quickly, if you want to keep the deal that Luca brokered. I bargained for a wife, not a science project." My hand slides upwards, pressing against the firm, soft flesh of her ass, and despite herself and the pain she must be in, I can feel her arching upwards into my touch.

She wants me. She just refuses to admit it.

"We're done with this fertility clinic shit," I tell her firmly, my voice deep and rough. "I won't take you now, but you'll come to bed soon, willing and ready to fulfill your duties in our marriage. You'll be my wife completely, or not at all, and if you can't keep that part of the bargain that was struck, then you need to decide once and for all what your decision is. You can go back to Luca, plead your way out of this, have the marriage annulled. But the consequences of that will be on your head and no one else's."

I don't wait to hear her response. There's a small sob, her body twitching under my touch like a fly-bitten horse, and I jerk my hand away. I won't force her; I refuse to cross that boundary. If I remain in the room another moment with the heat of her freshly-spanked ass against my hand and her hot, drenched pussy so close, I know that I won't be able to stop myself.

So I turn on my heel, my belt still gripped in my hand as I stride towards the door. "If you come back home, I'll know your choice is made," I tell her darkly, my voice rough and brooking no argument.

Truth be told, I don't know what she'll choose.

But I know that I've never wanted anything so goddamned much as I want her in my bed, naked and wet and willing, begging for me to fuck her.

It's not all I want, either. She's awakened something in me, and I feel a hunger that, if left unchecked, feels as if it could drive me mad.

I want to break her, own her, *possess* her.

I want to make her mine.

CATERINA

I lay there, facedown in the blankets, for what feels like a long time after Viktor leaves the room.

I've never felt so humiliated. So ashamed.

I'm hurt. I'm afraid.

And I'm also terribly, terribly aroused.

"What is *wrong* with me?" I let out a small cry, my mouth against the bunched-up duvet as I lie there, my ass red and throbbing and my thighs sticky with the arousal that Viktor glimpsed and threw in my face. *How could that have turned me on?*

I've never been spanked in my entire life, not even as a child. To have Viktor throw me across the bed like that, using his belt again and again until I felt like my skin might catch fire, should have been nothing but the most humiliating pain.

And it was.

But it also turned me on in a way that I've never, ever felt before.

"What is wrong with me?" I ask again, mumbling to the empty air, but of course, there's no response. I'm alone in the house again, which should be a relief, but it isn't. I can't stay here forever.

I have a choice to make.

Tell Luca that I'm done with my sham of an arranged marriage, or go back to it and everything that entails. No more fertility treatments, no more doctor's appointments, no more injections. Just Viktor doing his best to get me pregnant the old-fashioned way, and I have no doubt that he'll try as often as he's able.

Between our wedding night and what happened today, I have no doubt that I'll enjoy it no matter how hard I try not to. That Viktor will pull me down into some dark spiral, arousing my body to want things that it shouldn't, dragging me into his depravity along with him.

Slowly, painfully, I push myself up from the bed. It's not the first time I've had to pull myself together from the aftermath of violence. Not the first time that I've been terrified of my husband, shivering with fear while I take the punishment for my perceived flaws.

But something about this time was different.

For one, I know I was in the wrong, deep down. I needed to get away from Viktor, but I also know I shouldn't have taken the girls with me. I think some small part of me wanted to scare him, to make him feel the same fear that the fathers of those women that he sells must have felt when their daughters went missing, but I also know it was wrong to use Anika and Yelena in that way. They're innocent in all of this—they never asked to be born into this life, or to lose their mother, or to be given a new one from a fraught marriage of convenience. I shouldn't have involved them.

So in a way, for the first time, I actually deserved what my husband meted out.

But also, Franco punishing me never *turned me on.*

Franco never spanked me. He would grab me, slap me, throw me around, punch me, force me to bed with him. But it had never occurred to him to spank me. If he had, I still don't think it would have had the same result.

Viktor turned me on because, deep down, the same brutal depravity, the Bratva in him, the things I most despise, I'm also aroused by.

I'm terrified of and horrified by and attracted to my husband all at once. It's the most confusing fucking thing I've ever had to confront in my entire life.

And now I have to decide whether to go back to Viktor and truly face it, make a marriage with him regardless of the consequences and regardless of my own emotional turmoil, or I go to Luca and tell him I want it annulled.

There will be consequences to that, too.

Bloody ones.

If I leave Viktor, he'll be furious. He won't hesitate to go to war with Luca, with Liam even, to resurrect all the old grudges and all the old hate. And that will be my fault because I couldn't deal with what it meant to be married to a Bratva *pakhan*, a bargain that I agreed to. I made vows, and even if I didn't know the full extent of who my husband was, what he did, I knew the rumors. The stories.

I knew that there were parts of him that were not good. Dark corners, terrible sins. But there's not a man I've ever known in this life who doesn't have some of that haunting him. Certainly, my father did. Even Luca does.

So what do I do?

How can I forgive Viktor for any of it? Go to bed with him, be a wife to him, live out my days married to him? Knowing what I know, how can I not resent him for it, even hate him?

But at the same time, how can I walk away?

And why the *fuck* do I want him so badly, even after all of this?

It feels like he's awakened some desire in me that I didn't know I had. Something dark and wicked that makes me wonder how I could want something like that, as if it was always inside of me somewhere deep down, waiting for a man like Viktor, brutal, handsome, and dominant, to come along and wake it up.

I look over at the door where it's been splintered, the knob and latch broken, and I remember how I'd felt when I'd heard him kicking it down. I'd been more terrified than I ever had in my entire life—but at the same time, I'd felt a sort of fearful lust that I'd never known I could experience. At that moment, I'd known he was coming for me, and there was nothing I could do to stop him. I hadn't known what he had planned, exactly, but a part of me had hoped that it would involve him inside of me, fucking me the way he had on our wedding night.

I'm not supposed to want him. It makes me feel as if there's something broken inside of me, something that makes me crave things I shouldn't, want things that should make me ashamed of myself. And I am deeply ashamed of so many things. The way he made me respond on our wedding night, the night of the concert when I let him kiss me and kissed him back in return, the way I handled the situation at his office, the way I can still feel the pulse between my legs every time I shift my weight and feel the sting of the marks on my ass.

It feels as if my life has been turned upside down since the day I said "I do" to Viktor. And with every day that passes, it feels like it's spinning more and more out of control.

But I don't see how I have any choice other than to go back.

There's a tiny part of me that whispers, as I walk towards the broken door, that deep down, I *want* to go back.

That I want to know how this will all play out to the bitter end.

That I can't run away now.

Viktor is nowhere to be seen when I get back to the house. I took another Uber, knowing better than to call and try to get the driver to come for me. I'm left at the driveway of a house that's supposed to be half mine now, but after being back at my own home, it's never felt less like it belongs to me in any way.

But I'm here nonetheless, and I need to make the best of it.

Whatever that currently means.

Olga is talking to Sasha near the foot of the stairs when I walk in, and she gives me a look so ugly that I know Viktor must have told her what happened with Anika and Yelena. A flush of shame washes over me, and I look away, unable to meet her eyes. I can feel Sasha's nervous gaze on me, and I wonder all over again how she ended up here. What plans Viktor has for her.

I should have gone alone. I wish I had, now. I can't stand the idea that anyone would think I'd actually harm the girls. If there's one good thing about this entire fucked-up marriage, it's my two stepdaughters. But I don't know how to even go about helping to raise them or protect them when their father does such terrible things—let alone my own child.

I go into one of the guest rooms to lie down, past caring what anyone in the house thinks. If Viktor has allowed my fall from his good graces to spread by telling Olga about the children—or maybe she figured it out on her own—then it doesn't matter anymore. And frankly, I don't care. What else can he do to me that he hasn't already?

I'm sure there's something. But the fact that I'm lying on my stomach to protect my sore and bruised ass makes me feel very differently.

Exhaustion overwhelms me, and I fall asleep again.

* * *

I'M NOT sure how long I sleep for, exactly. Long enough that it's dark outside, the house is quiet, and my mouth feels sticky and dry, my eyes are swollen from too much crying. A quick glance at my phone tells me that it's nearly midnight, well after most of the house has gone to sleep, including Viktor.

A small, rebellious part of me wants to stay in the guest room tonight. He's going to demand that I fuck him, probably sooner rather than later, so my first thought is that he ought to concede that I don't actually have to sleep beside him as well.

But I think my days of Viktor making concessions for me are over. And I don't want a repeat of today's punishment so soon, just because I didn't want to sleep next to him in bed.

I slowly get out of bed, feeling stiff and slow, and walk to the adjoining bathroom to splash some water on my face. With any luck, he'll be asleep when I go to our room, and I don't want to wake him up by going into the bathroom in there.

Looking in the mirror feels like a shock. My face is paler than usual, my eyes swollen and red-rimmed, and the cold water on my face helps a little, but not much. *Why do you even care?* I ask myself as I toss the washcloth in the hamper, running my fingers through my hair so that it's less of a rat's nest. It's not like I need to impress him. He's already married me, and he's going to fuck me one way or another. Some reddened eyes and tangled hair aren't going to dissuade him.

The house is dark when I step out into the hall, and I creep down towards our bedroom, walking softly in an effort to make it there without waking anyone up, especially Viktor. I manage to push the door open almost silently, and it's then that I catch the glow of his bedside light still on.

But it's not the only thing I see and not the thing that makes me stop in my tracks, my heart suddenly hammering in my chest.

Viktor is lying on his back, shirtless, his pajama pants unbuttoned, his head thrown back as his hand grips his thick, hard cock, stroking it feverishly as he groans, low and deep in his throat with pleasure.

A rush of arousal like I've never felt washes over me as I stare at him, fascinated. I've never seen a man masturbate before. Something about the way Viktor looks in this moment, his jaw tense and neck muscles straining, back slightly arched, forearm flexing as he grips his thick length, is the most erotic thing I've ever seen. I stand there in the doorway, frozen as I watch him rub his thumb over the swollen head, glistening with his arousal as he strokes it down the shaft, squeezing and slowing his movements as his hand flexes around his cock, another groan of pleasure slipping from his lips.

I don't know how long I stand there, watching him pleasure himself, feeling the steadily growing wetness between my thighs at the sight. It's pornographic in its intensity, watching the handsome man on the bed stroke himself closer and closer to climax. Part of me wants to join him, while another part wants to flee back to the dark safety of the guest room.

And while I'm standing there frozen with indecision, Viktor opens his eyes.

It's impossible for him not to see me standing there. I'm in the middle of the doorway, staring. A cruel smile curves his lips as he stops stroking, holding his rigid cock as he teases the head with his thumb and lets his gaze rake over me, lust plain in his eyes.

"Come here," he says simply, the order clear in his voice.

I feel like I'm in a dream as I walk towards him. My heart is pounding in my chest, my skin prickling with a desire that feels almost electric, my eyes shifting nervously between his face and his hard cock. I know what's about to happen, or some of it anyway, but I still can't figure out how I feel about it.

In my head, that is. My body feels as if every nerve is aroused, my blood throbbing through my veins, my heart racing until I can hear it pounding in my ears. I take another step towards him, and another, until finally, I'm standing at the end of the bed, waiting for Viktor's orders.

He stands up smoothly, his pajama pants hanging on his lean hips, his cock jutting forward all on its own, thick and huge and glistening. His gaze rakes over me mercilessly, taking in my rumpled clothes, and his lip curls as he looks at me.

"Take those off," he says, reaching for his cock to run his fingers lazily down the shaft again. "All of it. Strip for me, like you did on our wedding night."

He'd stripped me then, more than anything else, but I don't dare argue. My hands are shaking when I pull my t-shirt over my head, from fear or desire or some combination of the two, I don't know. I suspect it's that latter, but that doesn't make it easier as I see him look at my breasts, his gaze heating as I reach down to undo my jeans.

He doesn't say a word until I've stripped down to my bare skin, my clothes fallen in a pile on the floor as I stand there completely bare to him for the first time. At least on our wedding night, I'd had the lingerie to help cover me, but there's nothing like that now. I'm acutely aware of my nipples, how they're stiffening under his gaze despite the warmth of the room, the concave slope of my belly, the fact that he can see the soft hair between my thighs, damp from the arousal that's been growing since the moment I opened the door.

Viktor steps closer to me, his eyes narrowing as he raises one hand to my breast, his finger outlining the curve of it, tracing beneath and around, up to the nipple. When he pinches it, I gasp; I can't help myself. It sends a bolt of sensation through me, straight down between my legs, my clit suddenly pulsing with the need to be touched *there* too, maybe even pinched, certainly stroked the way he's stroking my nipple now, making circles around it with the tip of his finger until my breath is ragged and I'm biting back a desperate, needy moan.

"You like that, don't you?" His voice licks over my skin, makes me shiver with a need I don't want to feel. "What about this?"

His hand slides from my breast, down my stomach, and I suck in a breath as I realize where he's going to touch me next, right where I feel as if I need it the most. My cheeks are already burning, knowing how wet he's going to find me, the slick heat that's going to coat his fingers when he dips them between my folds.

"*Bladya*—fuck—" Viktor curses beneath his breath as his fingers slide against my hot flesh, and I can't stifle the moan this time. It slips from my mouth, my lips parting as my eyes close, unable to look at him as he circles my clit, his fingers gathering my wetness as he does so. "Christ, you're fucking soaked." His palm presses against me, cupping my pussy as he strokes my clit, back and forth and then in circles, until my hips are pushing against his hand, wanting more.

"I want this shaved before the next time." His voice is sharp, cutting again. His fingers move between my folds, his middle finger suddenly at my entrance, piercing me. He pumps it in and out of me once, twice, a third time as I gasp, my eyes rolling back at the sudden pleasure of the intrusion.

And then, just as quickly, he jerks his hand away. "Do you understand me?" he asks, lifting his hand to his lips. He breathes in, and I feel my face go hot, my mouth dropping open as he slides his fingers between his lips, licking away my arousal.

"Mm." He groans. "You taste delicious, Caterina." And then, before I can speak or move, he steps forward, his hard cock brushing my bare belly as he grabs my hair, running his fingers through it and fisting a handful as he tilts my head back.

It pulls almost uncomfortably at my scalp, but that's not enough to stop a fresh wave of arousal from washing over me, trickling down my thighs as I bite my lower lip to stop myself from moaning again.

"On our wedding night, I wanted to taste that sweet pussy of yours," he growls, his face looming above mine. "I wanted to make you come, to bring you pleasure, to make it good for you. But you've refused every effort I've made to do exactly that. So, then, we're going to do this a different way."

His gaze rakes over my face, blue and piercing and heated with lust. "Until you learn to behave, to be a proper wife to me, I won't be making you come with my tongue or my fingers. There will be no orgasms for you, my pretty little bride, unless you're sheathed on this cock." Viktor reaches down, squeezing himself, his fist pressed against my belly. "That's the only way you may come, *printsessa*, until you learn your place."

I can't think of anything to say. Not even when he lets go of my hair, his hand resting on my shoulder as he presses down.

"Your first lesson is this—get down on your knees, mafia princess, and suck the cock of the man who owns you now."

I feel like I can't breathe, afraid and aroused all at once, my thighs slick with it as I start to sink to my knees. I feel ashamed and turned on, my body aching for him even as my mind screams that I'm not his princess, that he doesn't own me, that he can't force me to do any of this. But the truth is that he *can*, and it's not even really forcing if I *want* to. As I sink to my knees, a cock bigger than any I've taken in my mouth an inch from my lips, I want to taste him, feel him, to give in. It would be so much easier to give in, to let myself want my husband. To stop fighting him.

It's going to hurt so much more when he's *the one who doesn't want you anymore if you do.*

But I can't think about that now. I feel him pressing the head of his cock against my lips. Without thinking, I flick my tongue out, swirling it over the smooth flesh and tasting the saltiness of his own arousal.

"More," Viktor growls. "Open your mouth, *printsessa*. Let me see how you suck a cock."

I know I'm good at this. Franco might have been an asshole to me about it after we were married. I still remember how much he liked the blowjob I gave him in the back of the limo after he proposed to me. And as angry as I am with Viktor for the way he treated me earlier, I also want to please him at this moment.

CAPTIVE BRIDE

. . .

HE'S BIG, so much bigger than what I'm used to. I can feel my lips stretching around him as I take him, inch by inch over my tongue, teasing the underside of the head and then running my tongue down the length of his shaft as I fight to take every inch of it. Viktor's hand wraps in my hair again, his face twisted with pleasure as he watches me slide my lips down his cock, the head pushing against the back of my throat as he urges me downwards.

"That's it, *printsessa*," he groans. "Take it all. Take that fucking cock."

There's another gush of arousal between my thighs as I hear him say that, and I choke as I slide down the last inches, his cock wedged fully in my throat as my lips brush against his groin. Viktor moans, his other hand sliding down to cup his balls, lifting them so that they brush against my chin and bottom lip.

"Lick me," he orders. "While your throat is stuffed with that filthy Russian cock you hate so much."

This is the Viktor I didn't see at first, the brute, the beast, the man I feared and hated. But now that he's here before me, all of the careful gentlemanliness washed away in the tide of his rage today. It's arousing me as much as it is terrifying me. And I have no idea what to do with that.

Except, for now, to follow his orders.

My tongue flicks out, sliding over his balls as I choke on the cock in my throat, and Viktor groans, his hips thrusting forward and pushing even more of him further down. For a moment, I feel like I can't breathe, like I'm going to suffocate on his huge, throbbing cock, that this is how I'm going to die.

And then Viktor's hand in my hair yanks my head back, pulling my mouth off of him, now shiny and glistening with my saliva as I gasp for breath, my eyes watering as I look up at him.

"Fuck, yes," he growls, shoving the head of his cock against my lips. "Take it again, *printsessa*. All the fucking way."

I've never felt like this before, ashamed and demeaned and aroused all at once. With Franco, I went from desire to pure revulsion quickly. His treatment of me killed any attraction or affection I had for him. But he never could have dominated me the way Viktor is in this moment. He'd been a silly boy, childish in his desires and his behavior, but Viktor is a man. A hard, cruel, brutal man, and as he looks down at me, naked on my knees with my mouth full of his cock, I feel like bursting into tears and begging for him to fuck me all at once.

The emotional whiplash of it is exhausting.

"Once more," Viktor says as he pulls free, and I gasp for breath again. "Take it one more time, and then I'll let you lie back on the bed while I give your sweet pussy the fucking it deserves."

My pussy clenches at that, tightening all the way to my core. I take him in my mouth and throat one more time, my nose brushing the soft hair at his groin, my tongue laving his balls, tasting the warm muskiness of him as I choke on his cock, feeling him thrust into my throat, and then when I come up gasping he grabs me, hauling me to my feet and tossing me bodily onto the bed.

I wince when I feel the embroidery on the duvet scrape against the tender flesh of my ass. Viktor is already pulling me forward, moving me so that my ass is on the edge of the bed, his hands pushing my thighs apart so that he can see me, vulnerable and exposed.

He slides one finger between my folds, pressing the tip of it against my entrance and then dragging up so that the callused fingertip scrapes over my clit, making me gasp and moan despite myself. My flesh feels swollen and hot, aching for the slightest bit of friction, and Viktor laughs as he circles my clit once more with that rough fingertip, and my hips jerk under his touch.

"So horny for the man you despise," he murmurs, his tone slightly mocking. "So wet. Your pussy is dripping for me, *printsessa,* and yet you insist that you don't want me. If I ate this sweet, hot pussy, though, you would be screaming my name in moments." He spreads my folds with his fingertips, looking down. I flush hot at the realization of how exposed I am, how he can see every inch, every inner crevice of my body, displayed lewdly for his pleasure. I can imagine how his tongue would feel, how he would swirl it around my clit, finger me while he sucked at my swollen flesh, and I moan again, the sound ending on a high and nearly desperate whimper, my body almost trembling with the need for more.

"If you want to come, you do it on my cock." He jerks his hand away, wrapping it around his rigid shaft. "You haven't earned the right to orgasm for your own pleasure alone, Caterina."

He looks like a cruel god as he looms over me, standing between my thighs as his cock presses between my legs, the head pushing against my entrance. I'm too wet to give him much resistance, and I cry out as it slips inside of me, the fullness of even just that pushing me closer to the edge of climax. Viktor's jaw is tight, his sharp, handsome face taut with pleasure, every inch of his muscled body rigid and flexing as he thrusts into me, his cock filling me to the limit as my body clenches around him. He lets out a groan that sounds almost painful, his hands gripping my hips as he holds himself inside of me, his cock throbbing.

It feels like our wedding night all over again, me struggling to hold onto my pleasure as Victor grips my hips and thrusts into me—only this time, I'm entirely naked, every inch of me bare as his gaze rakes over me hungrily. His strokes aren't long and slow but fast and hard, thrusting into me almost angrily. My sore, bruised ass scrapes over the embroidered duvet again and again, until my cries are mingled pleasure and pain. But even that only seems to push me closer to orgasm until I'm panting, forcing myself to leave my legs dangling open for him, not wrapped around his hips the way I so desperately want right now.

"That's right." Viktor looks down at me with a cruel satisfaction in his eyes, his lips curving in a heated smile. "Come on my cock, Caterina. You know you want to. It feels so fucking good, doesn't it? You might want to hate me, but you love how it feels when I fuck you. You love how I fill you with this big...fucking...cock—" The last words are punctuated with his groans as he shoves himself into me hard each time, pulling me downwards on each stroke. I cry out, my hands clenching the duvet as I feel the pleasure start to unfurl through my body, my thighs quivering, the climax coming whether I want it to or not.

"Come on my cock, *printsessa*," he growls, and I'm helpless to do anything but obey.

I swivel my head sideways, my hand coming up to muffle the moan that escapes my lips, the cry of pleasure nearly a sob as my back arches, my body shaking with the force of it as I clench down around him, so hard that he can barely thrust as my hips move with him, my body forgetting who he is, why I'm here, only wanting, wanting, wanting. The moment the force of how tightly I'm gripping him lets up, he starts thrusting again, harder than before, his face twisted with pleasure as he pounds into me. It pushes my climax into a second, smaller one that ripples through me until I'm left gasping and shaking underneath him.

And then Viktor pulls himself free suddenly, leaving me to feel hollow from the sudden absence of him, and I look up, confused.

The confusion only lasts a moment when he turns me, using his grip on my hips to flip me over so that I'm on my belly, his palms sliding over my red, sore ass.

My first thought is that he's going to take me from behind as he pulls me backward so that my feet are flat on the floor, his palm pressing into my lower back so that it arches, my ass upturned for him. But then I feel his fingers slide between my cheeks, probing at the one spot where I've never had a cock before, and I twist around wide-eyed to look at him in shock.

"Viktor, no!"

"Yes." His voice is rough, so full of lust that it's practically dripping with it. "You came back, Caterina. There's no more argument, no more fighting me. I'm going to take you in every way that a husband has a right to take his wife, including in this tight virgin hole of yours." His finger presses against me there, sending a shiver through me, and he chuckles. "You *are* a virgin here, aren't you?"

I'm tempted to lie and say no, that Franco fucked me in the ass, just to deny him the pleasure of being the first. But that would mean he'd be less gentle with me, either because he'd think I wouldn't need it or out of spite. The thought of him shoving his massive cock into my ass without preparation makes me shudder with fear.

"You'll learn to take my cock in all of your holes, whenever I please." Viktor's fingers dip between my folds, dragging through the arousal there, coating them in my wetness. "You'll learn to be a good wife, my little princess, to submit to my desires. You did a good job sucking me earlier and taking me in that tight, wet pussy. Now you'll take me in your ass, and if I choose, you'll come with my cock in your ass too."

I want to tell him that no, I won't, that I'd never come from something so disgusting, but I can feel my clit throbbing, aching for him to touch it, his fingers so close. I know that even if he filled my ass with his cock right now, in one painful thrust, if he touched my clit I'd likely come again, almost immediately. I feel as if every nerve in my body is raw and vulnerable, aching for the pleasure I know he can give me.

"You wanted to play games with me, *printsessa*," Viktor murmurs, leaning forward so that his mouth is close to my ear. I can hear him behind me, stroking his cock, lubing it with my own arousal. "So we'll play games together. I fuck you in the ass, and if you don't come with it stuffed full of my Bratva cock, then I won't fill your ass with my cum."

I moan, and he laughs. "Little mafia slut," he whispers and shoves two fingers into my pussy, thrusting them in and out until his hand is drenched again. "Get ready to take my cock in your ass."

He presses the head of his cock against my tight opening, pushing forward against the resistance, and I cry out. "It's too big." I shake my head, looking back at him with frightened eyes. "It won't fit, Viktor, stop!"

"Oh, it'll fit." He grimaces, his hips bearing down, and I feel the tip of him slip inside.

A burning pain washes over me, and I stifle a shriek as he pushes forward another inch and then another. He's slick and wet, but not enough, and I arch my back, trying to make it easier, anything to stop the burning pain.

"Relax," Viktor grinds out through his teeth. "This cock is going in your ass one way or another, Caterina, so fucking *relax*."

That's easy for you to say. I don't know how to think past the pain, how to do anything other than clench the duvet in my fingers, my eyes watering as Victor shoves himself in an inch at a time, stretching me past the point of being able to bear it.

"Alright." He groans, panting as he suddenly stops moving. "It's in. Christ, your ass is fucking tight." His hand smooths over my flushed cheek, still reddened and sore from the spanking. "I should spank your ass every fucking day, *printsessa*. It looks so fucking good, red like this, with my cock buried in it."

I feel as if I can't breathe, and then suddenly, his hand slides around my hip, reaching between my legs as he starts to thrust.

It's excruciatingly painful, but the feeling of his fingertips rolling over my clit, teasing it, playing with it, is so good that it detracts from the pain. So much so, in fact, that I can feel the pleasure starting to build, tensing every muscle in my body until I'm shaking. I can feel myself clenching around Viktor, his thrusts stuttering as he tries to keep going, his fingers digging into my ass as he groans.

"Remember, *printsessa*," he murmurs beside my ear, his voice taut with pleasure, "if you don't come, I won't fill your ass when I do."

Oh god. His growling Russian accent in my ear, telling me *not* to come, does the exact opposite. His fingers are rubbing my clit faster now, harder. I moan helplessly, knowing that I'm going over the edge, that I can't stop, that I'm going to come shamefully with a cock in my ass. There's nothing I can do about it.

"Yes, Caterina, fucking *come*," Viktor snarls as he feels the first shudder of pleasure through my body. Then I feel his fingers pressing harder against my clit, rubbing and circling and pinching, his cock thrusting deep in my ass, and I lose what little control I have left.

"Oh my god!" I nearly shriek as the orgasm bursts over me, my back arching, driving myself backward onto his cock despite the pain. I hear Viktor's growl of pleasure as he starts to pound into my ass harder, fucking me as my body twists with the sensation of his fingers on my clit, not stopping, still rubbing and rubbing until I think my

CAPTIVE BRIDE

own orgasm will never stop either. I claw at the duvet, throwing my head back, my hair cascading over my back, and I hear Viktor moan with appreciation as he thrusts into me again, hard. His hand leaves my clit, at last, his fingers digging into my hips as he rocks himself even deeper, letting out a guttural groan that lets me know he's reached the end of his control, too.

"Fuck, I'm going to fill your ass with my cum, *printsessa*," he moans, the words choked as I feel him start to shudder, his cock rock-hard and swelling even larger inside the tight confines of my ass. I can feel the hot rush of him as he starts to come, his hips grinding against me as his cock throbs with every pulse of his orgasm.

The feeling of it ripples through me, and I drop my head forward, moaning helplessly, my face flushed with humiliation as my husband pumps my ass full of his cum, rocking against me as he savors every last drop of the pleasure he's extracted from me.

When he finally slips free, Viktor slaps his half-hard cock against my ass, letting out another moan. "Fuck, that was good." He stands up, and I slump to one side, looking at him with wide, exhausted eyes as the sensations start to fade, leaving only embarrassment and anger. "I should fuck you like that more often, wife."

"I thought the point was to get me pregnant," I snap, narrowing my eyes at him. "You can't knock me up by coming in my ass, Viktor. Or did they not teach you about the birds and the bees in school? Clearly, this is about your pleasure, not getting a child from me."

Viktor smirks. "Spread your legs then, and I'll give you another load where you seem to want it so badly, if you're that hungry for my cum. I can be hard again in moments."

"I doubt it, old man." I glare at him, but he only laughs, his eyes cold.

"Not so old that I can't fuck my lovely wife all night long. Not even forty yet, in fact. But if you don't believe me, I'd be happy to show you and prove you wrong."

"You took advantage of me."

"You came back to this house, knowing what it meant. You stood in that door, watching me stroke my cock, and you didn't run when I saw you. You wanted it, Caterina. Stop pretending that you don't. It's infantile, and I married a woman." Viktor shakes his head, turning away. "I'm going to shower. You can use it when I'm finished unless you want to get fucked again in there."

"*Stronzo!*" I spit out as he starts to walk away. *Asshole.*

I expect him to say something in return, but he only laughs, striding into the bathroom and slamming the door shut.

I want to follow him—I desperately want a shower after all of the events of the day, but I don't doubt that he'll follow through on his threat if I do. So instead, I lay on the bed, aching in every inch of my body, struggling with coming to terms with everything that's happened.

I hate him, I think to myself, burying my face in the blankets. And maybe that's true. Maybe I do hate him.

But I also want him, more than I've ever wanted any man.

And I hate that most of all.

VIKTOR

Never in all my years have I experienced pleasure as great as taking Caterina in the ass for the first time. I'm far from inexperienced—I've had plenty of sexual experiences over the years that might be termed *adventurous,* even exotic. Still, none of those pleasures, however delicious, could have compared to the sweet tightness of her ass clenched around me, her heated skin under my palms, the way her body writhed and twisted as she fought the orgasm that she couldn't escape.

Not to mention the exquisite bliss of filling her ass with my cum.

She was right, of course, I won't get her pregnant that way. Which means for all my threats, I don't plan to take her there often. But nothing was going to stand in my way last night. *Nothing.*

Caterina came back home. That means one thing, whether she wants to accept it fully or not—she agrees to be my wife in all ways. To fulfill her role without trying to bargain further on her own behalf. It's intoxicating to have that power over her at last, especially after she tried so hard to keep it from me. I've possessed her now in a way that no other man ever has, and all it's done is make me want more of her.

Which is why I tell her, over dinner the next night, that she'll be coming with me on my business trip.

M JAMES

"We leave tomorrow," I tell her, stabbing a small roasted potato with my fork. "Sasha can help you pack if need be. The girl needs practice taking orders around the place."

I can see Caterina's face darken at the mention of Sasha, but I ignore it. I've purposefully never addressed how she came to be here, and Caterina has never asked, although I'm sure after the explosion of files in my office that she has a reasonable idea. It should make her softer towards me, to think that I saved one of the girls from the fate Caterina finds so despicable, but it hasn't seemed to have that effect. If anything, I see her glancing suspiciously between the two of us whenever Sasha is in the room, which is easy enough to figure out.

She thinks I've brought Sasha here for my own pleasure, which couldn't be further from the truth. What I find amusing about it, though, is that if she truly wants to stay out of my bed, she ought to be glad to have another woman take her place.

Caterina would say it's about *morals*, about Sasha being kidnapped and *forced* to serve, but I know the truth. It's about the simple fact that deep down, Caterina wants me. And she can't bear to admit it.

Somehow, it brings me even more pleasure in our coupling. Shaming my princess, fucking her with the cock she claims to be disgusted by, turns me on more than I would have ever thought. She can't escape it, not now. She can believe that she's better than me as much as she wishes, just like every other fucking Italian in this city, but at the end of the night, she has to spread her legs for me.

She's contractually bound to do so. And it fucking turns me on like nothing else.

"What?" Caterina lowers her fork, looking at me with the wide, shocked expression that I'd expected. "What do you mean, I'm going with you? A business trip? Where?"

"Russia," I say casually, slicing into my meat and enjoying the sudden expression of horror on Caterina's face. "I wish to have my wife with me, that's what. Your job is to be on my arm when needed, an ornament for me to impress my betters with, and that's exactly what you'll do."

"I don't want to leave the girls here," Caterina says, shaking her head. "You wanted me to take care of them, to take some of the pressure off of Olga. How will I do that if I'm in Russia with you?"

I can feel my expression darken. *How dare she bring up the children after what she did.* "I think you've done *quite enough* for the girls," I say tightly, glaring at her. "You can prove yourself to be better at being a wife than you have at being a mother, if you do well. It's time you learned to honor the *obey* part of your vows, Caterina, or have you forgotten about those?"

Her cheeks flush, the high points of her cheekbones reddening, and she drops her gaze to her plate. Across from her, the girls are very silent. Anika has a small smile on her face, but Yelena looks miserable.

"I don't *want* Caterina to go," she says, dropping her spoon onto the floor. "I want her to stay here and play dolls with me."

"I know," I tell her gently, with as much patience as I can muster. "But I have things that I need her for as well. She'll be back soon, I promise."

Yelena purses her lips. "Pinky swear?"

It's hard to keep a straight face, but I manage somehow. "Pinky swear," I affirm, and Yelena's face relaxes a little.

"You should leave her in Russia," Anika mutters. "I can't believe she's still here after she tried to *steal* us."

Caterina's head snaps up at that, her expression wounded. For a moment, I consider letting it go—after all, I'd believed the same thing when Caterina had taken the girls to her former home. But Anika's stubborn refusal to accept Caterina is helping no one.

And besides that, some small part of me revolts at the idea of Caterina looking so miserable, particularly over something that I know isn't true.

"She didn't try to steal you," I tell Anika, still forcing patience into my tone. "She just made a mistake and didn't tell me before going back to visit her old house, that's all. She wanted to show you around a place that means something to her, that's all."

It's not quite the truth, but I can't explain more to Anika without telling her things that she's both too young to hear and that I hope she'll never know. Caterina is looking at me, her face faintly shocked, and I glance over at her.

"Thank you," she mouths when Anika drops her gaze back to her plate, sullenly glaring down at her dinner. There's a small, grateful smile on Caterina's face, and it warms my heart in a way that I don't entirely understand. I shouldn't care—she's caused me more trouble in the past days than I've had to deal with under my own roof in a long time. But she is my wife. And more than anything, I want a peaceful marriage, if not a happy one.

"I expect you to be packed and ready to go tonight," I say curtly, ignoring her thanks. "The plane leaves in the morning. Pack a few dresses appropriate for formal events, and jewelry, etcetera."

"Alright." Caterina's gaze drops back to her plate, and I let out a small breath of relief that she's decided not to fight me any longer on it. That, at least, is handled for the evening.

She's still packing when I come up for bed, folding clothes into a black monogrammed suitcase, and I watch her for a moment before she realizes that I'm there.

"I'm almost done," she says stiffly, looking away. "You didn't tell me how long we'd be gone."

"Only a few days," I tell her reassuringly. "It's a quick trip, Caterina. I'm not trying to keep you away from home for weeks or months on end. Nor is it a punishment, as much as I know you think that it is. It will simply be helpful to have my wife with me for this particular trip."

"So that I can be a trophy on your arm." Caterina frowns. "But that's all I was ever meant to be, I suppose. A trophy and a broodmare."

"Did you expect more?" *Did you* want *more,* is the question that I want to ask, but I don't. I'm not sure what I would do with the information, even if she said yes, that she wants more. How would I give it to her? After Vera, I'm not sure that I have any love left over, except for what I give my daughters. For Caterina, a woman I chose at least partially *because* of her lowered expectations, I don't know what I would have to give.

"No," she says curtly, turning away. "I knew not to expect more."

But it still stings. I can hear the words she's not saying, and that makes me wonder. I'd never thought that Caterina and I had that kind of connection, the kind that makes you able to hear the unsaid words, the unfinished sentences, anticipate the other person's needs. And yet, I know what she's thinking, as clearly as if she'd written it out for me in black and white.

She glances up and sees me still standing there. "What are you doing? Thinking about fucking me again?"

I'm tempted to tell her yes, and to stand up and bend over. The thought of having that power makes my cock throb, stiffening a little. But the idea of throwing her off her game by refusing to play into it is more enticing. "Get some sleep as soon as you can," I tell her, ignoring the question and striding towards the bed. "The plane leaves early."

* * *

To my surprise, Caterina is awake even before I am, dressed and already eating downstairs with her bags by the door. "You said to be up early," she says with a shrug when she sees the surprise on my face, turning back to her bowl of oatmeal and fruit. "So here I am."

I can feel the tension in the air between us as we finish breakfast and head out to the car, the bags already loaded up as the driver prepares to take us to the hangar where my jet is waiting. I'm sure it's not the first time Caterina has flown on a private jet. Still, I'd expected to see some surprise on her face when she caught sight of mine, even if just surprise that I have such a luxury at all. But she just boards the plane without a word, silently taking a seat as she wraps a dark cranberry sweater around herself, looking out of the window with the same icy silence that I've become accustomed to when we go anywhere together.

"It can't be that bad, can it?" I ask with a hint of humor in my voice, trying to lighten the mood. "A trip to Russia?"

"I clearly didn't have a choice," Caterina says tightly. "So no, I'm not particularly inclined to be happy about it."

I frown. "And if I had given you a choice?"

"I wouldn't have come."

"See? And I need you here with me. Thus—no choice." I let out a sigh. "Things would be much easier, Caterina, if you'd stop resenting your duty to me so much."

"I resent that duty being to *you*." She refuses to look at me. "It was bad enough when you were just Russian, Bratva, a man whose entire family is steeped in the blood of mine and those that worked for mine. But then I find out that you're a man who buys and sells women. And you want me to give you a son to take over that same business." Her voice cracks slightly at the end of the sentence, her jaw tensing. "So yes, I resent it."

Ah. There it is. I hadn't thought about the greater implications of Caterina discovering my business and how she would feel about providing the next generation to keep it going. "I respect women, Caterina. I always have. I tried to treat you with kindness. I love my daughters, I treat Olga and all of the staff with respect—"

"And yet you sell women into sex slavery. They don't choose this. What about Sasha?" She finally looks at me, her dark eyes wounded. "What is she doing in *our* house? Was she meant to be a sex slave too? Or did you bring her home to be yours after you're done putting a baby in my belly?"

I shake my head. "No, Caterina," I tell her firmly. I'd wondered if she might think such a thing, but I'd hoped not. "No to her being in our home for my pleasure, that is. I have no interest in her."

"So, what is she doing there?"

I let out a sigh. "She was one of the women slated for sale. A virgin. One of the guards raped her and took her virginity for himself. Rather than sell her to a lower bidder and a less desirable situation, I tried to make up for the abuse done to her by giving her a place in our home, on the staff, where she'll be housed, fed, well cared for, and well treated."

"But not free." Caterina stares at me. "Or will you let her leave if she decides she no longer wants to work for you?"

I pause. "To tell you the truth," I admit, "I hadn't considered it. I rarely have staff leave—precisely because they're treated *well*, Caterina. But if she wanted to—" I shrug. "She's not a slave, whatever you insist on thinking. If she wanted to go elsewhere, I see no reason why I would stop her."

Caterina purses her lips, but just nods, looking out of the window again as the plane starts to taxi down the runway.

"You still see me as this evil man." I shake my head. "Everything I just said to you, and still—"

"She wouldn't have been in that situation at all if you hadn't kidnapped her!" Caterina glares at me.

"I shot the man who violated her. He's dead." I grit my teeth, looking Caterina dead in the eyes. "I killed him the moment she identified him as her rapist and freed her. What more do you want?"

"You to not abduct unwilling women in the first place and sell them."

I let out a breath through clenched teeth. "You know nothing about the darker side of this world, Caterina. You were born into this life, but you're a sheltered mafia princess, pampered and spoiled and bred to warm the bed of a man like me. No one has ever told you about the dark and evil corners of the world because there was no need for you to know." I narrow my eyes, glaring at her in return. "Sasha was a foster child aging out of the system. They hadn't expelled her yet, but they would have soon. She was already a few weeks past her eighteenth birthday. Do you know what happens to very beautiful, very poor virgins without families in Russia?"

Caterina doesn't say anything, but I can see a dawning horror in her eyes.

"Someone else would have picked her up, not long after she went out onto the streets, penniless. They would have sold her to a brothel or or pimped her out themselves. Pumped her full of drugs so that she could fuck ten, fifteen men in a night, one in each hole until she was so used up that they could barely wring a penny from her. When she reached the point where no one would fuck her any longer, they would have taken her out back and shot her, like a dog or a racehorse that's outlived its usefulness."

"And that's better than what you were going to do to her how?" Caterina is still defiant, but I can see it wavering.

"Sasha was a virgin and extraordinarily beautiful. I had a sale lined up for her to a prince of a small Middle Eastern country, where she would have been a part of his harem, pampered and cherished for the rest of her life. He might have had her trained as a dancing girl or perhaps elevated to one of his concubines to have his children and be given even more luxuries. He was willing to pay millions for her. He would have treated her like something that *cost* millions. She would have lived in luxury for the rest of her life, instead of dying in a cold Russian alley that stank of piss, her body used up by callous, filthy men."

"And you lost millions because of that man." Caterina's voice is very quiet. "So why didn't you kill her?"

For a moment, I'm so taken aback that all I can do is stare at her. I'd known she believed me to be brutal and cruel, but I hadn't known it ran that deep. That she would think such a terrible thing of me.

"It wasn't her fault," I tell Caterina, unable to hide the surprise in my voice. "She did nothing wrong. I would never harm a woman like that. I killed the one responsible for stealing from me and gave her something in recompense for what she lost."

"And if he hadn't raped her?" Caterina asks quietly. "If she'd seduced him instead, to choose who she gave her virginity to? What would you have done to them then?"

I grit my teeth with frustration, letting out a long sigh. "Caterina, there are penalties for breaking the rules in our world. You *know* that. None of this is strange to you. Do you think Luca would behave differently if a woman stole from him? Cost him money and reputation?"

"He wouldn't murder her."

"Maybe Luca wouldn't," I concede. "He is, at times, far too soft for the position he holds. But your father? He would have. For fuck's sake, he would have killed Sofia if she hadn't agreed to marry Luca. Simply to keep her out of the Bratva's hands. Did you hate your father?"

"No," Caterina says softly, looking away. I catch a glimpse of the pain in her eyes, and I hate being the reason for it. But this stubborn refusal to face the facts of our life has to come to an end. "I loved my father. But I know that in many ways, he was an evil man."

"So you can forgive his sins and love him, but not mine."

Caterina glances back at me. "There was never any talk of love between us." Her hands knot together in her lap, and she looks out at the passing sky, the clouds puffy below us. "I didn't have to go to bed with my father, Viktor. I didn't have to provide him with a son to carry on those same atrocities. My love for him and my hatred of some of the things he did could live side by side. But you are my husband, Viktor. It's different."

"And Franco?" I dig deeper, even though I know it's salt in the wound. "After Ana? Sofia? Could you have lived with that? Given him children?"

"I hated Franco before I knew about any of that," Caterina says quietly. "He hurt me in ways that I know you will not, Viktor, and I'm grateful for that. But you can't expect me to be happy about this lot. You can't expect me to bear you a son cheerfully, knowing that you will teach him to exploit women, to buy and sell them, to hand them over to other men to choose how their lives will go."

"Your life has always been determined by men," I point out. "And you've lived a generous, comfortable life because of it. That's all I'm doing for these women. To say that your comforts have not come because of the men who provided them to you is a lie, Caterina, and to argue that these women are exploited, and you are not is hypocritical."

"I know I am, too," Caterina says, looking away again. "And I know that I've benefited from it. I thought for a moment that I'd be free of it after Franco died. But then you demanded my hand in marriage, and I knew that was a silly dream."

"And that freedom?" I shake my head. "It would have come from the money your father left you, the house that he gave you, the money your dead husband gave you. None of it would have been your own doing, Caterina. You can't change that."

She bites her lower lip, refusing to look at me again.

I let out a long sigh, resting my head against the back of the seat as I close my eyes. I hadn't intended to fight with her. But her stubborn refusal to open her eyes and admit that her life has not been so different, that what I do isn't black and white, is frustrating me beyond my ability to keep quiet.

Vera hadn't been able to live with it, either. And in the end, that's the reason that she's gone. I don't want the same to happen to Caterina, no matter how much she frustrates me. No matter how difficult our marriage has been from the start.

My hope is that this trip might change things. That she might be able to open her eyes and see some of the truths that I'm trying to explain to her.

But the stubborn set of her jaw, even after all of that, tells me that it won't be easy.

At least I've never shied away from a challenge.

* * *

"You have an apartment in Moscow?"

It's the first surprise that I've heard from her, and I allow myself to enjoy it a little as I show her up to the flat that I keep here for business trips. "It's not as luxurious as our home in New York, but it's comfortable enough."

"It's beautiful," Caterina says as we step inside, looking around wide-eyed, and I smile with pleasure at her tone. I'd hired a decorator for this flat myself. It's simply done, in cool tones and filled with plants and wooden fixtures, as well as imported rugs and furnishings, with an abundance of art on the walls. There are large doors in the living room that lead out to a balcony, and Caterina goes straight for them, opening them and stepping out to take in the view of Moscow.

It reminds me of the night of our wedding, seeing her out on the balcony of our hotel. I'd worried then that she would jump, and I feel a small pang of fear now, but I don't think she would, not in front of me.

All I want is to find some way to convince her that we can have a

CAPTIVE BRIDE

normal, even pleasant life together, that it doesn't have to be like this all the time, the two of us always battling, always at each other's throats.

I want this trip to show her the better side of what our life can be.

* * *

SHE LOOKS every bit as gorgeous as I could have hoped, dressed up for the gala tonight. It's chillier in Moscow, even in late spring, and Caterina is wearing a deep green velvet gown, off-the-shoulder, with a neckline that curves beautifully over her breasts. It nips in at her waist and flows over her slender hips, stopping just above the black heels that she's wearing. There are diamonds at her ears and neck and wrists, and I can't help but lean in as I escort her out to the car, my mouth very close to her ear.

"You would look even better dripping in emeralds tonight."

"I don't own any," Caterina says, her voice cool and smooth as she darts a glance my way, sliding into the dim leather interior of the car.

"Perhaps I'll have to give you some." The banter surprises even me; after Vera, I'd told myself I wouldn't spoil a wife again the way I'd spoiled her. But something about seeing Caterina looking so beautiful tonight, her hair swept up and pinned up with pearl-tipped gold pins, her face so lovely that I can't help but think every man there will envy me, makes me want to give her things I never have before.

We could be so good together if only she'd stop fighting me. And tonight, I want her to see that.

The gala is being held at the Kremlin, and I see Caterina's eyes widen when the car pulls up. She seems a little stunned by the grandeur of it as we step out of the car, and I smile at her, reaching for her hand. "This is the heart of Moscow," I say simply, as we start to ascend the steps.

I don't come here often. Usually, I send some of my trusted men, Alexei or Mikhail, to handle the shipments. It was requested that I come and personally oversee this one. It's not necessarily an unusual request. Sellers sometimes like to be reminded of exactly who they're selling to. Especially shipments like this one, that contain several very valuable girls.

It's a reminder, being here tonight, of how far the Andreyev family has come. There was a time when my grandfather could only have dreamed of being inside a place like this, of attending a gala with a woman like Caterina at his side. She, as much as anything else, represents the power that our family has built. Once upon a time, the Rossi family and the other members of the Italian mafia spit on us.

Now I demand their princess, and they hand her over.

I wondered at first how Caterina would handle the gala. She doesn't speak Russian, of course, although most of the people she will meet tonight speak English, as well as several other languages. But she's made her distaste for Russians, and Bratva especially, more than clear to me. I wonder if her stubbornness will persist, if she'll be angry and sullen, refusing to play the part she's meant to.

If that's what happens, I'll have no choice but to punish her. I've been given a spirited filly, and if I have to break her, that's what I'll do. But that's not how I want tonight to go.

Caterina surprises me, though. From the moment we enter the crowded gala, and I begin introducing her to business associates and their wives—a few of them mistresses—she's charming and pleasant, her hand tucked in the crook of my elbow as she talks about our recent wedding, my beautiful home, my lovely daughters. To hear her speak, you'd never know that just this morning she was lashing out at me on the private jet here, tight-lipped and resentful. There's not a trace of that in her face or voice, only the perfect, smiling wife that I'd hoped I'd married.

She's doing exactly what she was born to do, taught to do since she was young. It both impresses and turns me on—not least of which because in the moments in between guests, I can tell that she's more than a little intimidated. I can read people well, and I catch her gaze flicking around the room, singling people out, the quick tensing of her mouth when someone approaches us. All through dinner, she stays poised, making small talk between bites and smiling her way through the meal. I've shared enough dinners with her now to know that the way she's picking at her food is a sign of anxiety, that this entire night has her on edge.

And yet, she's playing her role to absolute perfection.

"I'd like to have this dance with my wife," I tell her when the band starts to play, a slow song reminiscent of the one that played for our first dance at our wedding, though it's not exactly the same. Caterina stands up gracefully, her hand in mine, and I lead her towards the dance floor, her palm warm against mine.

"I hope you're pleased," she says, her gaze cool as my hand slides against her waist, my fingers laced through hers as we start to dance. I'm acutely aware of how little space there is between our bodies, how close she is to me, the scent of her perfume and her hair, and I can feel my cock starting to stiffen, ideas of what I'd like to do to her when we get back to the apartment tonight flooding my head.

"You've been a model wife tonight," I tell her sincerely, swaying across the dance floor. "Everything that I could have hoped for, truly."

"I wouldn't want you to be disappointed." Her tone is still biting, but there's something softer there, something that I find myself wanting to latch onto.

"You were made for this, Caterina," I tell her, pulling her closer as the music intensifies. "if you would just see my side of things, trust me, we could be so good together. This could be a real marriage, one of equals, if you wouldn't fight me so." I pause, my gaze fixed on her dark eyes, her perfect, delicate face. "I wanted you because you were raised as a mafia princess. You were born to do exactly this, to stand at the side of a man like me. Not cowed, not broken, not behind the way Franco wanted you. You were meant to be elevated one day to be someone's queen."

"And you fancy yourself a king?" Caterina's tone is lightly mocking, but it's more teasing than anything. I don't hear the condescension that's so often been there. I grab onto it, hoping that she's beginning to soften, to relent.

"I'm a king of my own territory," I tell her with a smile, spinning her and then pulling her back into my arms. I hear her soft gasp when her body brushes against mine, and my cock throbs, my suit trousers too tight and uncomfortable to get an erection here. "I wanted *you*, Caterina. I want you to be more than a broodmare, as you said, more than a glorified nanny. I want a wife."

Even as the words spill from my lips, I'm not entirely sure where they're coming from. I had told myself exactly the opposite when I'd gone to bargain with Luca and kept telling myself that—that I wanted a mother for my children, an heir, and nothing more. Not an equal, not a love match, not a partner. Not a woman that I couldn't keep my hands off of, who drove me mad with desire.

A marriage of convenience. A deal to be brokered and kept through whatever means necessary.

Not a marriage of passion.

I've seen how that ends.

But what can I call the feelings I've had for Caterina, the way I've desired her, the way I desire her right now, if not passion? I want nothing more than to take her out of this room, back to my flat, and strip her bare before we even get to the bedroom, to cover her pale skin with kisses and taste the sweet core of her, to bring her pleasure again and again until I finally thrust myself into her and take my own pleasure, until we're both sated and exhausted.

I don't want a cold bed or rote coupling. I want Caterina, and all her fire and stubbornness, bound to me. I don't want to withhold pleasure from her, and I don't want to pretend.

I want us to lose ourselves in desire, together. And when we emerge, I want that to be together, too.

You feel like a second chance at something I thought I'd lost forever. The words rise to my lips, unbidden, but I bite them back. It's not the place to say something like that or the time to give her that sort of power over me. Not until I'm certain of her—not until I know that I can trust her to stay.

I've only ever been that vulnerable with one other woman. It won't come easily to me a second time.

"I know the truth," Caterina says, breaking through my train of thought. "You didn't want me. You wanted Sofia because she was half-

Russian, because of her mother's pedigree. You would never have looked at me again if you could have had her."

There's no jealousy in her tone, only a flat sort of acceptance. But she couldn't be more wrong.

"I did, at first," I admit. "But Caterina—" I reach out, tipping her chin up gently so that she's looking into my eyes. I put all the sincerity that I can into my voice, my expression. "it didn't take long for me to see how wrong that was. Now that I have you—"

Caterina's eyes widen, just a fraction, and I know that I shouldn't say what comes to my lips next. It's too much, for now. But I can't help myself. The music is swelling, vivid and intense in the colorful room. My wife is beautiful, in my arms and dancing with me, and for a moment, I'm transported to another place, where the words I have to say can't ever be the wrong ones.

"I know, Caterina, that in choosing you, I made the perfect choice."

CATERINA

I know I shouldn't allow myself to be taken in by it. Viktor is a good talker—he always has been. He's had to be to rise so high. Even a man like him can't rule through violence alone, no matter how much the Bratva might like to. He wants my compliance, and perhaps he's decided to change tactics, to romance me instead.

Seduce me into trusting him, wanting him, maybe even loving him.

It won't work, I tell myself. But even as I think it, I know that to an extent, it is. As much as I resent my lifelong designation as a man's trophy, I'm good at the things I was raised to do. I'm good at talking, at entertaining, at making guests feel good, at small talk. I'm good at dancing, at being the most charming person in a room, at all the social graces that were instilled in me from a young age. Maybe it's not the most progressive thing, but we all like to be good at something. Sofia has her violin…I have making small talk with overstuffed members of crime families.

Everyone needs a purpose in life.

I've tried my best to stifle my desire for Viktor. But it was only just last night that he had me spread open on the bed, making me come again and again as he fucked me in every possible way. Just last night that he'd taken what remained of my innocence and made me scream out in pleasure while he did it.

He's good in bed. *Too* good, because he could become addictive. Intoxicating. I already crave more, and the touch of his hand on my waist and the closeness of his body, the scent of his skin and the warmth of him so near, makes me want to beg him to take me back to the loft and strip the velvet dress off of me, run his tongue down my body, to plead with him to lick me until I come and then fill me with every inch of his cock.

I want my husband. It shouldn't feel so wrong to want that. And yet, in every fiber of my body, it feels as if my desire for Viktor is committing a sin.

When he takes me back to the table, I finish my glass of red wine and then another. The gala feels endless, "business associates" to talk to, their wives and their mistresses, and it's easy to tell which is which. The wives are always a bit more subdued, a little pinched around the edges, worn down by their husbands' lives. The mistresses are brighter, shinier, newer, like new pennies, wearing more jewels, talking more animatedly. They have no idea how expendable they are, or maybe they just don't care. As long as, in the end, they get to keep the jewelry, why would they care?

They're less interested in me too, looking at me with thinly veiled jealousy, as if I might have designs on the men they've caught. The wives are interested in how I've settled into the house, how different things are for me, how Anika and Yelena are, if I think I might already be pregnant. The last sends a ripple of something between fear and excitement through me—despite everything, I still want a child of my own. Even knowing what my son will grow up to inherit, a small part of me wants to believe that it will be okay no matter what. That I can have my baby and none of the guilt.

There's very little jealousy from the wives, though. If anything, they're jealous of my youth, but none of them fear me stepping in and taking their husbands. If anything, I'd guess they'd be glad for the reprieve. There's not a single one of them that appears to be happy in their marriage or in love, and I think back to what I was told about

Viktor's first wife, that it was a love match. How unusual that must have been! It makes me wonder even more how she died. But no matter how often the house or his daughters are brought up, everyone carefully skirts around the topic of the first Mrs. Andreyva.

It makes me more than a little afraid, bringing up all those old dark thoughts about what Viktor might have done, how he might have been connected to it. But as the night wears on, and the wine warms my blood, and Viktor's hand creeps to my thigh, those dark thoughts slip away, replaced by something else.

It's not until we're in the car that I find myself unable to hold back any longer. And it immediately becomes clear that Viktor feels the same.

The moment the doors close, I turn towards him, and I see him moving towards me in the same instant, closing the space between us as he reaches for me.

It feels like a dream, his hand on my waist, in my hair, pulling my mouth towards his. He tastes sharp like vodka, and I know I taste sweet like wine, and I tell myself *just for tonight, just in this place, you can go back to the way things were before when you're back home.* For one night, I want to lose myself in pleasure, to imagine that I'm married to a man who can be mine in every way, who I can be a wife to and never feel conflicted about it, never feel that I'm committing a sin simply by wanting the man I made lifelong vows to.

Til death do us part. It's such a long time, so many days, so many hours, so many nights between now and when that's fulfilled. *It's not supposed to be a goal,* I've heard joked before, and I don't want it to be. As Viktor's mouth comes crashing down on mine, his hand fisting in the soft velvet at my waist, I want more than anything to love my husband. To be devoted to him.

To not fear and mistrust him.

Why is that so hard to find?

"Caterina." He rasps my name against my lips, his hand sliding down, finding the slit in my skirt, slipping beneath it. I feel his callused fingers against my thigh and make a note to ask him about them later, the roughness of his skin, so unlike any man I've ever known. When I raise my hand to his face, I feel the hint of stubble scraping over my palm the way his fingertips scrape over my inner thigh. I pull his mouth back to mine for another kiss, just as his fingers slide up to find the edge of my silk panties.

"Are you wet for me, princess?" he asks, all in English now, and I should lie to him, tell him no, but tonight I don't want to. I want to give myself everything I've been desiring and hold nothing back.

Just for now. Just here. Just tonight.

"Yes," I whisper, my hips arching against his fingers, wanting his touch, wanting more. "I am."

He groans when his fingers slide beneath my panties, feeling that I'm telling the truth, how wet I really am. I bite back a moan when they circle my entrance, sliding up through my folds to my aching clit, not wanting the driver to hear what we're doing back here. When he kisses me, I let myself make the sound I've wanted to, the moan that rises to a whimper swallowed up as his fingers press against my clit. I reach out, my hand rubbing over the hard ridge of his cock, straining against his trousers.

"Tell me you want me, Caterina," Viktor groans, his voice rough. "Say it out loud."

After everything he's done, it feels depraved, unholy, like the words are coming from the darkest part of my soul. But here, wrapped in darkness in the back of the car, I whisper them aloud.

"I want you."

He makes a noise deep in his throat that's something like a growl, his fingers thrusting up inside of me as he pulls my mouth back to his. "Good," he murmurs, and then his lips are on mine again as my hands go feverishly to his fly, tugging at the buckle and button and zipper, wanting to feel his hot, hard flesh in my hands. "I want you, too."

Something about that admission in his rough, thickly accented voice drives me wild. I reach for the back of his head with my free hand, pulling him to me, his mouth to mine. My hand finds its way inside of his trousers, fingers wrapping around the hot, pulsing shaft, and Viktor groans against my mouth as my tongue tangles with his.

"My little spitfire princess." His fingers thrust into me, curling, pressing against a spot that I never even knew was there. I know that he's going to make me come, I can feel it tensing every muscle in my body, and I want it. I want it so badly.

My hand tightens around his cock, not so much stroking it as holding it, squeezing it. I feel Viktor's thumb against my clit, rubbing, his fingers thrusting into me and pressing against that unknown spot, and I know I can't hang on a second longer.

"I'm—I'm going to—" I gasp out, my head tilting back, and I feel myself convulse in the instant before it crashes over me, a cry of pleasure coming from my mouth that I can't stifle no matter how hard I try.

"That's right, little princess, come for me," Viktor croons, his fingers still moving, coaxing me through the orgasm, giving me more pleasure than I'd thought was possible. "Come on my fingers, that's right. Take it. *Fuck*, yes."

It seems to go on forever, rippling through my body, my pussy clenching around his fingers as he thrusts, and I can still feel the hot hardness of him against my hand. I still feel as if I'm floating in a dream when the orgasm starts to fade, when Viktor slides his hand out from underneath my skirt, licking me off of his fingers as I sink down to my knees in front of his seat, my hands sliding up his thighs as I reach for his cock.

"Oh fuck," Viktor groans, his eyes widening as I encircle him with my hand, bringing the head to my lips. "Christ, yes, Caterina, suck it. Oh *fuck*."

It's not the first time I've given head in a limo, I think wryly, but I don't say it aloud. Instead, I focus on him, how thick he is, the glistening tip already slick with his arousal, the way he throbs in my fist when my lips slide over the head, my tongue swirling around it until Viktor makes a guttural noise that's hardly even human.

It's easier to take all of him tonight, with a few glasses of wine in me, more relaxed, wanting it unashamedly this time. I suck and lick every inch of him, sinking all the way to the base, my throat muscles clenching around him as I swallow around his cock, and Viktor's hand threads through my hair, his moans coming out from gritted teeth as his hips thrust up shallowly, wanting more.

I'm gasping by the time I come up for air, sucking and licking at the head as I give my throat a break, and then I go down again, taking every inch of him. He's harder than I've ever felt, his cock swollen and taut, straining against my lips as I take him again and again, my hand finally wrapping around the base to give myself a few inches of grace, stroking him as I suck at his rock-hard shaft. Every groan sends a dart of lust through me, every curse under his breath makes me wetter still, until his hand finally tightens in my hair and I hear him mutter, "Fuck, I'm about to come, oh god—"

I thought I was prepared, but nothing could have prepared me for the hot rush of him, his cum filling my mouth faster than I can swallow, coating my tongue and throat as he thrusts into my mouth, taking up every inch of space as he groans above me. "*Fuck*, that's good," he grunts, and I keep sucking, wanting more of it, wanting it all.

He tastes good, thick and salty on the back of my tongue, and I swallow every drop, looking up at his face and the way it goes tight with pleasure as he comes, his hand hard on the back of my head.

When the last drops of cum are on my tongue, and I can feel his erection starting to wilt, he strokes my hair, his head falling back against the seat. "Fuck, your mouth is incredible," he groans. When I slide up to sit next to him again, he pulls me closer, running his fingers through my hair and kissing me lazily, seemingly not caring that only a moment ago I was swallowing his cum.

"I can't wait to fuck you," he whispers, his hand caressing my cheek. "When we get back to the apartment, I'm going to rip that dress off of you and make you come again before we even make it to the bed."

When the driver pulls up, we barely make it out, up the steps and into the loft before Viktor's hands are on me again, pushing me back against the door, his mouth hard and hot on mine as he combs his fingers through my hair, the pearl-tipped pins flying everywhere as he pulls my thick curls loose, sending my hair tumbling around my shoulders as his mouth devours mine. He bites at my lower lip, his tongue laving away the sting, sucking it into his mouth before his lips find their way to my jaw, my throat, all the way down to my collarbone, where he bites and sucks again, his hand wrapped in my hair all the while.

"You have too much clothing on," he groans, his other hand sliding up my thigh, pushing my skirt up. And then, to my absolute shock, Viktor Andreyev drops to his knees in front of me, his hand fisting in my skirt as he yanks the velvet up to my waist, grabbing my silk panties and dragging them down my thighs. I gasp as he pushes my legs apart a little wider. Then for the first time, I feel a man's mouth between my thighs, pressed against my pussy as his tongue flicks out, caressing my folds in one long lick that sends my head falling back as I gasp.

He grips my skirt, holding it above my waist as he parts me with his other hand, spreading my folds so that his tongue can delve inside more easily. I gasp again as his tongue slides up to my clit, circling it with a warm, wet heat that makes me feel almost dizzy with pleasure, my knees weak.

I don't know how I'm going to stand up, teetering on my heels as I shiver with the sensation, his tongue making circles around my clit, flicking and then circling again, stopping to run over every inch of my pussy with long slow licks that feel as if they might drive me insane with pleasure. It feels so fucking good, better than I had ever even imagined. I run my fingers through his hair, pulling his mouth closer to me the way he does when I suck him, my hips tilting forward against his face.

"God, yes, that feels so fucking good," I moan, and Viktor makes a sound against my heated flesh, a noise that's almost surprise. I've never said anything like that before, never talked dirty, and it surprises me too, a new flush of arousal washing over me at the boldness of it.

He reaches for my leg then, hooking it over his shoulder as he tosses my skirt over his head, using his hand to grip my thigh instead, steadying me as he begins to lick me with a new fervor. He seems to be trying to find every spot, memorizing what makes me twitch and what makes me moan, his fingers sliding up my inner thigh on the other side and teasing my entrance, delving just a little inside and pulling back out as he licks in tight circles around my clit, bringing me higher and higher until I know I've got to be close.

I want to come, and I never want it to end. His tongue is soft and wet and hot, the best thing I've ever felt, the pleasure so intense that I can't imagine what the orgasm will feel like when it comes. My hips arch forward, grinding against his face, wanting more, and Viktor gives it to me. He eats my pussy the way he kissed my mouth earlier, devouring, hungry, his tongue everywhere. Nothing has ever felt so good, and when his fingers thrust into me as he circles my clit again, I let out a sound of pleasure that's almost as guttural as the one he made earlier, my whole body convulsing on the edge of orgasm.

And then, as his fingers curl inside of me, he sucks my clit into his mouth, his tongue pressed against that sensitive flesh.

That's all it takes. I make a sound that's almost a scream, my hand tightening in his hair as I throw my head back, clinging to him as he grips my thigh, still fingering me and sucking at my clit as the orgasm washes over me in wave after wave of indescribable bliss. I can feel myself shaking, trembling, and somewhere in the middle of it, I hear myself crying out his name, my hips still bucking against his face as I chase every last bit of the pleasure, wanting more of it as it starts to fade.

When Viktor stands up slowly, the ridge of his erection pressing against the front of his trousers once again, there's a victorious smile on his face.

"I told you I'd make you come before we got to the bed," he says, his lips curling in a satisfied grin.

And then he scoops me up into his arms and carries me straight there.

CATERINA

When I wake up the next morning to the sun streaming through the window, it takes me a moment to remember where I am.

I'm in my husband's loft apartment in Moscow. In *Russia*. I'm naked next to him in bed because I let him take me there last night after I'd had too much wine at the gala.

I should regret it. But I don't.

What I remember are all good things. I remember Viktor tossing me onto the bed and following me down, stretching his lean, muscled body the length of mine as he pinned my wrists over my head, devouring my mouth. I remember that I could taste myself on his lips as he kissed me, but it didn't disgust me. Instead, all it did was remind me how he'd made me come with those lips only moments before, grinding shamelessly down onto his mouth as he'd introduced me to the pleasure I'd never even known existed.

I remember him feverishly undoing the front of his trousers, the hot press of his erection against my thigh, the way he'd whispered *I can't wait any longer, printsessa*, before pushing the thick head of his cock between my folds and thrusting into me, hard and deep.

He'd fucked me roughly, desperately, as if he were afraid it might be the last time. I'd wondered, as he'd sank into me and held himself there, hips arched against mine, if he were savoring the fact that I'd gone willingly? Or did he assume, like I did, that once he got me pregnant, there'd be no more excuse to fuck me?

I'd felt a pang of something, almost like loss, at that thought. I'd known that I shouldn't want him, shouldn't be a willing party to any of this. Instead of pulling away, I'd wrapped my arms around his neck, my legs around his hips, and pressed myself against his body.

It had felt so fucking good—my nipples brushing against his hard chest, the slide of his thick cock inside of me, stretching me, filling me until I couldn't have taken an inch more, his lips against my mouth and his hands in my hair. He'd whispered things in Russian I couldn't understand, but it didn't matter, because the rasp of his voice and the thick heat of his words told me everything I needed to know about what they meant.

For the first time in my life, I'd felt real, raw passion. I'd found out what it was like to want someone physically so much that I tossed aside my own ideals and stubbornness, and I'd gotten the same in return. What I'd felt with Viktor last night was unlike anything I'd experienced before.

It can't happen again, my mind whispers as I roll over to look at him, and I feel myself instantly rebel.

Why? Why not?

Because he's Russian. He's Bratva. He sells women—how could you ever love a man like that?

I close my eyes, fighting off the whisper in my head. *He's also my husband,* I think to myself. *I'm bound to him forever. Am I also bound to be miserable for the rest of my life? Shouldn't I just sneak out of this room right now, find the nearest bridge and leap off of it, if that's all I have to hope for?*

I think about what he'd told me on the plane last night, about how things are different here, about what might have happened to those women otherwise. About how he said that he's giving them a chance for a better life than they might have had.

I'm not entirely sure I believe him or that any part of it is as altruistic as he tries to make it sound. Surely he could just rescue them or give them jobs, something other than turning them into concubines for wealthy men. It isn't as if his family hasn't gotten rich off of it over the years. It makes it hard to believe that it has anything to do with what's best for them.

But at the same time, if that explanation is true—

It doesn't make it okay, but does it make it so much worse than anything my family has done, or Luca, or the Macgregors? The Irish and Italians deal in arms that kill innocents and rip apart families, and foster wars. My father ran strip clubs as a front for addictive party drugs. My entire life has been built on top of things that are illegal and criminal.

Viktor is still asleep, and I reach out to touch him, trailing my fingers through the soft dark hair on his chest. I can see a soft sprinkling of grey here and there through the dark hair, and I brush my fingertips over it until he groans softly and his eyes slowly open.

"Morning, *printsessa*," he says, turning his head to look at me. The sunlight angles off of his face, making him look softer than usual, his face less sharp and commanding.

"I don't like it when you call me that."

Viktor rolls onto his side, smirking. "What should I call you, then? What do your friends call you?"

"My friends call me Cat," I say softly. "But I don't think we're friends yet, you and I."

"No?" He cocks his head. "Do friends not do this?"

He reaches out, his finger running down the valley between my breasts. He curves his fingertip around the small swell of one, tracing it up to my nipple, which he pinches lightly.

"None of my friends have ever done that."

"What about this?" He rolls the nipple between his two fingers until I gasp, and as he leans closer to me, I feel his naked cock hardening against my leg.

"No." I shake my head, licking my dry lips.

He squeezes my breast, bending to run his tongue over my other nipple, making a slow circle. "This?"

I can't speak. I can feel the growing ache between my legs, my clit throbbing with every swirl of his tongue and pinch of his fingers, as if there were a line directly from my nipples to the apex of my thighs. I just shake my head, and Viktor tightens his lips around my nipple, sucking at the tender flesh as his hand leaves my breast to skim down my stomach, down to where I'm wet and aching for him.

I gasp when his fingers brush over my clit, rubbing gently, teasing me into an even more heightened state of arousal. He nips at my breast, sucking at it as his teeth scrape over my nipple while his fingers press against my clit, and then suddenly, he's shifting over me, nudging my legs apart with his knee as his mouth comes down hard on mine.

"I need to be inside of you again," Viktor groans, his lips brushing over mine. "I can't wait—*bladya*, I need to feel you."

A thrill runs through me at that, to see my terse, disciplined husband losing that control, his cock swollen and hot between my thighs as he guides himself between my legs, his cockhead parting me roughly as he thrusts inside.

He groans with relief as the first inches of his cock slip into me, and my body tightens around him, eager for more, for how good it feels. Viktor sinks all the way to the hilt, his tight, heavy balls pressed against me as he rocks his hips, and I gasp with pleasure as he cups my face in his hand and kisses me again before he starts to move.

"I love fucking you like this," he groans, sliding out to the tip and then thrusting into me again. "I love fucking you knowing that you're still full of my cum from last night. That I'm going to fill you up again, fuck you until you take every last drop—ah!" Viktor lets out a deep grunt of pleasure as I feel myself clench around him, my body reacting to his voice murmuring those filthy things to me.

He leans back, spreading my thighs apart so that he can watch himself thrust into me, every long, hard inch disappearing into me again and again. "You feel that?" he groans, reaching down to spread my folds so that he can get a better view, my swollen clit visible to him and aching for him to touch it. "Feel your tight little pussy getting fucked by that thick cock—"

Viktor never talks like that in his day-to-day life. It makes it filthier somehow, even more arousing, and I moan as he slides into me again, my clit pulsing with need.

"Please," I whisper, my hips arching as he fucks me slowly, making me feel every inch as he thrusts his cock into me. "Please make me come, Viktor—"

"That's right, princess. Beg for it." He flicks his finger over my clit, and I cry out, my back arching. "You come when I tell you to."

I nod breathlessly, swept away on a tide of desire. "Please, please—"

"You get off when I do." He pants, fucking me harder as the pleasure builds. "I want to feel you tighten around me while I fill you with my cum—*bladya!* Fuck!"

I feel him shudder, and I know he's close. It feels dirtier somehow, this morning in broad daylight than it did last night. "Play with yourself, princess," he murmurs. "Play with that little clit until I come."

He grips my hips with both hands then, surging into me in long hard thrusts, and I hesitate. I've never touched myself in front of a man before, but Viktor's pale blue eyes burn into mine, full of heated need.

"Touch yourself, or you don't come, princess," Viktor groans hoarsely, and I tentatively reach down, sliding my fingers between my folds so that I can touch my needy, aching clit.

The moment my fingers brush over it, it's nearly impossible to keep myself from coming. The sight of my handsome husband leaning over me, his muscles flexing in the morning light as he thrusts into me, the feeling of that thick length stretching me, the scent of his skin, and the sound of his groans all push my arousal higher and higher until I feel as if I'm going to shatter at any moment.

"Don't come," he repeats, breathless. "I'll punish you if you come before I start to."

It's almost a promise rather than a threat. I can feel my face flushing at the memory of his belt coming down across my ass, the sting and burn of it, the way I'd gotten wet for him anyway. Part of me wants it again, to feel that hot flash of pain followed by a strange pleasure that I'd never expected to experience.

But I hold back anyway, my fingertips gingerly teasing my clit as he speeds up. His movements are more erratic with every thrust.

"That's right, touch yourself just like that. Oh *fuck—*" Viktor groans aloud, and I feel him surge inside of me, thrusting himself in hard as he shudders. "I'm going to fucking come, yes, rub that little clit, fuck I'm coming, *fuck—*"

He groans the last word, and I press my fingers down, rubbing frantically as I feel the first hot rush of his cum inside of me, his cock swollen and throbbing as my orgasm crashes over me instantly, the moment I stop holding back. I feel myself clench down hard around him, my back arching and my other hand clawing at the blanket as I cry out, my entire body convulsing with the sheer pleasure of it.

Viktor thrusts again, and I can feel some of his cum sliding out, dripping down as he pushes himself deeper into me, his cock still pulsing as I shudder around him. "Oh god," I moan as he squeezes my hips, grinding against me as I keep touching myself, wanting every bit of pleasure that he can give me as he arches forward, his face taut with the last shudders of his climax.

He falls forward on his hands, panting before rolling to one side. I feel almost hollow without him, and I start to get up, thinking I'll go and shower, but Viktor puts out a hand to stop me.

"Wait a moment," he says, reaching to pull me back down against him. "I want to lay like this with you for a minute."

This wasn't part of the deal, I think stiffly. *Cuddling wasn't part of it.* But his arms feel warm and strong, pulling me back down to lie next to him as the sunlight streams over the crisp white sheets. I force myself to relax a little, but it's hard. His cum is dripping down my thighs, and it still doesn't feel as intimate as this, as Viktor's muscled arm holding me against his chest, the faintly sweaty musk of his skin, and the hint of his cologne from last night filling my nostrils.

This is more dangerous than good sex. The feeling that I could be safely wrapped up in this man's arms, that I could find love. I remember last night on his arm, charming the crowd, making small talk, floating through the gala like I was always born to do, and I know that we could make a good pair if I would let us.

If I would stop fighting him, stop being angry that I was given to the enemy, and try to make a life with him. Not a fairytale, maybe, but something else. A partnership.

That almost terrifies me more than the alternative.

Viktor said that wasn't what he wanted. But the way he's holding me now tells me a different story.

And I know that at some point, if I'm going to stay, this war between us has to end.

VIKTOR

I'd wondered if what I had planned for today was the right choice. But after the gala last night and what happened between us this morning, I don't falter.

Caterina was the picture of the perfect Bratva wife last night. She was beautiful, elegant, polite, well-spoken, everything that I could have ever dreamed of. She charmed the men and was friendly with the women, and I find myself looking forward to tonight and the second gala we'll be attending.

Not least of which because I'm hoping for a repeat of what came after.

I hadn't expected my wife to come on to me, wine-drunk and eager, but I wasn't complaining. I certainly wasn't this morning, either, when I awoke to her gaze lazily drifting over me and her naked body next to mine and knew that I had to have her again.

Sex with Caterina has been alternately frustrating, infuriating, longed-for, and more passionate than I could have expected. Her body feels made for me every time I slip inside of her, hot and tight and wet for me, and her delicate beauty never fails to arouse me. I know that I don't want it to end after I've gotten her pregnant. I don't want her to stop coming to my bed once she's fulfilled my most basic demand.

I want to possess her in every way, entirely, for as long as I live.

I want my *wife*.

Is that such a sin?

Part of me is still terrified to get too close to her. To let myself feel anything, even lust, for her. The memory of what happened with Vera is still too fresh.

Which is why I've made the decision about today and what Caterina needs to see.

I need to know that she can handle it before I let this go any further.

We shower together, taking our time. My meeting isn't until the afternoon, and I enjoy the time with Caterina now that things have thawed between us somewhat. I'm not entirely sure what changed, but I'm not eager to examine it too closely. Instead, I enjoy the peace and the simple pleasure of doing something like showering in the morning with my wife.

I've fucked her twice in the last several hours, and yet I can't stop myself from reaching for the soap and washcloth, turning her back to me as I run it over her smooth body. She stiffens momentarily and then relaxes into my arms, and I bring my hand lower, washing away the traces of my cum from her thighs.

But I don't stop there. I bring the washcloth higher, letting the textured cloth drag between her folds, over her clit. When I feel her shudder of pleasure, I let the cloth fall, rubbing her clit in quick, tight circles before thrusting my fingers into her, feeling the heat of her arousal and her pussy still full of my cum from last night and this morning.

Her head falls back against my shoulder, and my cock hardens against her ass as I finger her, intent on making her come again. "Come on my fingers, princess," I whisper in her ear, and she whimpers, shuddering against me as her thighs start to tremble.

God, I love the feeling of her pussy tightening around my fingers or cock when she comes. She always clamps down like a vise, squeezing as if she doesn't ever want to let me go, as if she wants to milk every last drop of cum out of my cock. I feel her shudder against me as she cries out, her ass arching back and grinding against me, and I slide my other arm around her waist, pushing her up against the wall as I grab my cock and thrust it into her hard.

It's been years since I've fucked a woman this many times in this short a span, but it's as if every time I get close to Caterina, my cock is instantly rock-hard. I can't remember the last time I was this turned on by a woman, but I'm not about to fight it. I'd rather give in to it, feel every inch of my cock being enveloped by her wet heat as I fuck her to another orgasm.

It doesn't take long. I'd thrust myself into her just as she was coming down from her first, replacing my fingers with my cock. I feel her start to tremble with another climax only moments later, her head thrown back as she arches against me, her gorgeous, pert ass grinding against me as I fuck her like it's the last time I'll ever be inside a woman.

In my line of work, you can never be sure.

"Fuck!" I curse aloud as I feel myself start to come again, my cock almost painfully hard as I spill myself inside of her, the hot rush of my cum mingled pain and pleasure after coming so many times since last night. She feels so fucking good, hot and tight. I pump myself into her again and again, the feeling of her wet pussy dragging along my oversensitive shaft and tip, sending waves of ecstasy all the way down to my toes.

Caterina's head drops forward as I slip out of her, and I can see her panting softly. There's a moment of tension as she straightens, not looking for me, and then she bends down, scooping the washcloth off of the shower floor. Just the sight of her bent over like that is almost enough to make me hard again—I feel a throb in my wilting cock—but four times is asking a bit too much.

"Well, I was clean," she says with a laugh, "but I guess I'm going to need this again."

I let her have the bathroom while I dress, and I can hear her going through the motions of getting ready. When she emerges, her hair is curled and shiny around her face. She's dressed in a cranberry-red sheath dress made out of what looks like a light, almost summer-weight wool that clings to her, outlining the shape of her slender body. She steps into her heels, not quite looking at me, and then when she does look up, the smile on her face is cool and collected. "I'm ready when you are," she says.

I can feel her starting to get spooked, to withdraw, after what's happened since last night. That's the last thing I want, and it once again makes me question if I've made the right decision today. But all I can do is push forward, so I grab a light coat, nodding towards the door. "Let's go."

Caterina is quiet on the drive, but she doesn't look angry. I can only guess what she's thinking, and that feels like a losing game, so I focus instead on the meeting ahead and how Caterina will react.

She looks slightly confused as we pull up to the private airport, and the car stops on the tarmac. I take her hand as she steps out, and she glances at me, frowning.

"What's going on?"

I nod towards the plane as the door opens and the ramp is lowered. "I wanted you to see. What I told you yesterday—that the women are treated well, that I'm kind to them, that I'm giving them a chance for something better than they might otherwise have had—I wanted you to see that for yourself. So that we can move forward, together."

Caterina is absolutely silent. I see two of my brigadiers getting off the plane, and then the girls start to come down the ramp, shivering and quiet. Not one of them speaks, hustled towards the waiting vans by the brigadiers and lower-level men waiting by the van for them, and I reach for Caterina's elbow, steering her around so that she can see the inside of the vans.

"They're comfortable. See? No cages, no cuffs, no cruelty. These girls—all ten of them—are going to be sold from here rather than back in New York. They have buyers lined up already, rich men who are paying hundreds of thousands, if not millions, for them. They're going to be cleaned up and dressed, and then they'll meet their new—"

"—owners." Caterina cuts me off, turning to face me. Her expression is horrified, her face pale, and I know in that instant that this hasn't helped anything.

It's most likely made it much worse.

"I wanted you to see that this is better for them—"

"Being *sold* isn't better for anyone!" Caterina shakes her head, backing away. "I should have known better. After all, I was all but sold to *you*. Why should you think any differently about anyone else?"

She takes several steps back towards the car. "Caterina—" I start to say her name, but she shakes her head vehemently.

"I'll do what I need to until we get home," she says tightly. "And I'll do what I have to, to keep the peace at home that you bargained for. But I won't do any of it willingly. And I won't ever fucking want *you*, Viktor Andreyev, ever again."

She whirls, nearly stumbling, and rushes back to the car, slamming the door. I want to follow her, but mixed with that urge is a hot, angry sense of frustration at her inability to understand, her insistence that this is so much worse than what her own family has done.

And I have a meeting to go to and sales to handle.

My father taught me that business must always come first, and that lesson is one I've learned well. I'll deal with what I have to, here.

And then I'll deal with my stubborn Italian bride later.

CATERINA

Viktor ended up sending the car back to the loft, with only me in it. I don't know how he's getting back, but I can't bring myself to care. I'm shaking the entire drive back to the apartment, my hands knotted together in my lap until my knuckles turn white.

I know what he's going to say later. That this is a necessary evil. That it's what his family has always done. That he's doing something "better" for these girls. I wonder what Sasha would say about that if she thought her life was better or worse before she was kidnapped to be sold as a concubine for some rich man. If she's happier now, working in our home, or if she wishes she'd never been taken at all.

I can't reconcile any of it.

The last thing I want is to go to another gala with him tonight—to dance, make small talk, pretend to care about anything anyone there says. Part of me almost misses Franco—at least with him, by the time I really got to know him, there was no question that he was selfish and arrogant, an asshole in every respect. With Viktor, it's confusing. He's a good father at home, generous in bed, and respectful to me in most ways. He could be a good husband—if not for the fact that he buys and sells women, traffics in sex slavery.

I can't come to terms with it, no matter how I try. I simply can't.

I lean back against the door of the apartment, closing my eyes and trying to breathe. I feel disgusted with myself for ever thinking that things could be different, for wanting him, for imagining a real marriage. I feel horrified at what I just saw, the faces of those girls imprinted on my mind, and I want nothing more than to go home.

But I don't even really have a home anymore.

I rip my dress for the gala tonight off of the hanger, striding into the bathroom. As I strip down to put the dark blue silk gown on, I press my hand against my stomach, still so flat that it's nearly concave. I think of how many times Viktor and I fucked since last night, how many times I encouraged it, and I feel sick.

What if I'm already pregnant?

The thought is terrifying. Imagining my son standing where Viktor was today, watching kidnapped women walk off of a plane, is terrifying. I don't know how I'm going to do it. How I'm ever going to give him a son knowing that this life is what he'll be brought up in, made to think is okay. Desirable, even.

I ball the dress up in my fist, trying to think. To think of a way out —but there's nothing. No way for me to escape without breaking what Luca so carefully tried to arrange.

And besides that, the thought of leaving Anika and Yelena hurts. They're not mine, but I'm coming to love them anyway and want to be there for them. To keep caring for Yelena, to be a good mother to Anika until she comes around one day, hopefully. To be a light in the dark world that they've been born into.

I want to stay for them, if nothing else, but I can't stand the thought of bringing another innocent child into this life. I'm horrified by how easily I was taken in by Viktor again, even after seeing the truth in his office the other day. It makes me wonder if his first wife found out, too, if she couldn't handle it. If Viktor removed her from the picture because she couldn't come to terms with the man she married.

I decide, then and there as I slip into the dress and press my hand against the flat of my stomach again, that I won't give Viktor the son he so desperately wants. I'll find a way to get my hands on some sort of emergency contraceptive as soon as we're home tomorrow, and I'll find a way to get on the pill. Anything to keep him from bringing up a son to inherit this ghastly empire of his.

Lying to my husband and preventing us from having children together might be a sin. Still, I think bringing another child into this family would be a much greater one.

I'm almost finished pinning up my hair when a knock comes at the front door, firmly and then more insistent.

Why is Viktor knocking? He has a key to his own home. I wonder if it's one of his brigadiers, come to tell me that he'll be home late.

Maybe they've come to tell me he won't be going to the gala tonight at all.

I could only be so lucky.

"Just a moment!" I slide the last pearl-tipped pin into my hair, trying desperately not to think of the way they scattered across the floor last night when Viktor buried his hands in my hair, pulling it down around my face as he's kissed me wildly. I stride out of the bathroom and towards the heavy front door, pulling it open only to see a tall, pale man with bright blue eyes and two heavily muscled men behind him.

They're no one I recognize, but I don't know anyone here. I stare at them for a beat before raising my eyebrow as authoritatively as I know how, looking directly at the man in front. "Well? What did Viktor send you to tell me?"

"Nothing," the man says with a smirk.

My heart skips a beat. "Well, he's not here, but if you give me your name, I can tell him—"

"We're not here for him." Before I can slam the door in his face, the pale man strides forward, shoving the door open as the two bigger men push their way around him. "Grab her."

"What? No! My husband will—" I shriek as one of the men clamps his hand over my mouth, and I try to bite it without much effect. The other is grabbing at my wrists, my clawed hands, binding them behind my back with plastic cuffs as the pale man advances towards me, his hand raised.

I see with absolute, bone-chilling terror that there's a syringe in his hand, liquid beading at the tip of the needle. I try to scream again, but the hand over my mouth is too heavy, and all I see is it descending towards me as I kick and squirm.

The last thing I hear as the needle slides into my neck and the world starts to spin is the pale man's accented voice, ringing in my ears.

"We're here for you, Caterina."

Buy the next chapter in this Saga. Stolen Bride here. Want to get an exclusive scorching bonus chapter? Sign up here.

Printed in Great Britain
by Amazon